He Knew How To Pleasure A Woman.

Perhaps the largest part of his appeal was that Caine wanted to give pleasure as much as receive it. He knew all the tricks, the slow subtle moves of seduction.

But now, with her pliant in his arms, her mouth growing hungrier on his, he forgot them. Her scent was clouding his mind until he was crushing her against him with too much need for finesse. She was luring him, and it was he who was seduced before he knew the rules had changed.

He heard a moan, low with longing, and realized, dimly, that the sound had been pulled from him. And she met him fire for fire, touch for touch.

NORA ROBERTS
lives with her two sons in the Blue Ridge Mountains of western Maryland. To be a published author was her lifetime dream, which she has seen fulfilled in the many books that she has written for Silhouette. Renowned for her warm characters and wit, Nora Roberts is a favorite with readers of romance.

Dear Reader:

Romance readers have been enthusiastic about Silhouette Special Editions for years. And that's not by accident: Special Editions were the first of their kind and continue to feature realistic stories with heightened romantic tension.

The longer stories, sophisticated style, greater sensual detail and variety that made Special Editions popular are the same elements that will make you want to read book after book.

We hope that you enjoy this Special Edition today, and will enjoy many more.

The Editors at Silhouette Books

NORA ROBERTS
Tempting Fate

Silhouette Special Edition

Published by Silhouette Books New York

America's Publisher of Contemporary Romance

For all my brothers

SILHOUETTE BOOKS
300 E. 42nd St., New York, N.Y. 10017

Copyright © 1985 by Nora Roberts

Distributed by Pocket Books

ISBN: 0-373-09235-0

First Silhouette Books printing May, 1985

10 9 8 7 6 5 4 3 2

Map by Ray Lundgren

SILHOUETTE, SILHOUETTE SPECIAL EDITION and
colophon are registered trademarks of the publisher.

America's Publisher of Contemporary Romance

Printed in the U.S.A.

Books by Nora Roberts

Silhouette Romance

Silhouette Special Edition

Silhouette Intimate Moments

Pocket Books

MACGREGOR CLAN: Book II

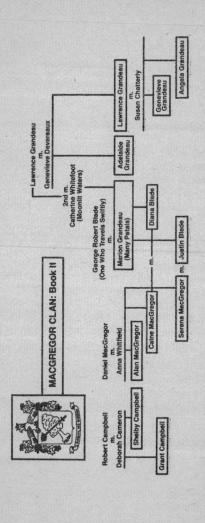

Chapter One

She wasn't sure why she was doing it. Diana studied the cloud formations spreading beneath her and tried to reason out if the trip she was making had been impulse on her part or calculated. Though she was scheduled to land in less than thirty minutes, she still wasn't certain.

It had been nearly twenty years since she'd last seen her brother. When Diana thought of him, she thought of him as a remote, exciting, casually affectionate teenager. Diana had loved him with all the single-minded intensity that a six-year-old girl can have for a sixteen-year-old boy.

Her image of him was frozen in the past—a dark, rangy youth with sharp good looks and cool green eyes. She remembered an arrogant sort of pride and self-sufficiency. He'd been a loner. Even at six, Diana had understood that Justin Blade had gone his own way.

With a mild, humorless smile, she leaned back in the soft comfort of her first-class seat. Justin had certainly gone his own way twenty years before. When their parents had died, he had comforted her, Diana supposed. But she'd been too bewildered to understand. She had thought her parents had left because she'd made a fuss about going to school. If she behaved and was quiet and attentive in class, her parents would come back. Then Aunt Adelaide had come, and Justin had gone. For months she had thought he'd gone to heaven, too, tired of her tears and questions. Her aunt had taken her east, to a different world, a different life. Not once in the span of two decades had Justin contacted her.

So now he's married, Diana mused. Perhaps because she still saw him as an intense, rather brooding teenager, she couldn't picture Justin as a husband. Serena MacGregor. Diana ran the name over in her mind. Odd that she should find herself with a sister-in-law when she barely felt that she had a brother.

Oh, she knew of the Hyannis Port MacGregors. Aunt Adelaide wouldn't have considered Diana's education complete if she hadn't been made aware of the background of one of the country's leading families—particularly when they lived close enough to Boston to be considered neighbors. After all, monied dynasties were the only royalty America claimed.

Daniel MacGregor was the patriarch, a full-blooded Scot and financial wizard. Anna MacGregor, his wife, was a highly respected surgeon. Alan, the oldest son, was a United States senator earmarked for bigger things.

Caine MacGregor. Here, Diana stopped her mental list. Though he was barely thirty, she'd heard his name bandied about the hallowed halls of Harvard Law School. Both she and Caine had chosen law and she'd slaved over the same books, studied under the same professors and walked the same corridors. At length, she'd passed the same bar. He'd graduated the year before she'd entered and had already begun what looked to be a brilliant career.

Once when Diana had been a freshman, she'd overheard two female upperclassmen talking about Caine MacGregor. And, she remembered with a smirk, they hadn't been discussing his mind. Obviously, the inestimable MacGregor hadn't spent all of his time sweating over his books.

Then there was Serena. From all accounts, she was brilliant—it seemed to be in the MacGregor genes. She'd graduated from Smith with honors, Diana recalled, then had spent the next few years collecting degrees. She seemed an odd match for the Justin Blade Diana remembered.

For a moment, Diana considered whether she would have attended their wedding if she'd been in the country. Yes, she decided. She would have been too curious not to. After all, it was primarily curiosity that had her traveling to Atlantic City now. Then again, she thought ruefully, it would have been difficult to refuse the invitation Serena had sent her without being childishly rude. If there were two things Aunt Adelaide had taught her, they were never to be childish or rude—at least not to those considered your peers. Diana pushed her aunt's quaint double standards to the back of her mind and unfolded Serena's letter.

Dear Diana,
   I was terribly disappointed that you were in Paris

last fall and unable to attend the wedding. I'd often requested a sister, but my parents wouldn't oblige me. Now that I have one, it's frustrating not to be able to enjoy her. Justin speaks of you, but it's not the same as meeting you face to face—especially since his memories are of a little girl. After all these years, I can think of nothing he'd like better than to meet the woman you've become.

Taking a page out of his book, I'm sending you an airline ticket. Please use it and be our guest at the Comanche for as long as you like. You and Justin have a lifetime to catch up on, and I have a sister to meet.

                                                Rena

Diana arched a brow as she refolded the letter. Warm, open, friendly, she mused. Not the sort of woman she would have paired up with Justin. With a quiet laugh, Diana leaned back. She didn't even know a man named Justin Blade.

If there was a part of her that longed to know him, she'd buried it long ago. She'd had to, in order to survive in her aunt's world. Even now, if her aunt were to discover she was planning on spending time with Justin at a gambling hotel, the woman would be horrified. And, Diana added, the lecture on where and with whom a lady is seen would begin.

She gave her attention to the clouds again. It hardly mattered, she mused. She would meet her brother and his wife, satisfy her curiosity, then leave. The little girl who had idolized unquestioningly didn't exist any longer. She had her own life, her own career. They'd both been stagnant for too long. It was a new year,

Diana reminded herself. The perfect time for beginnings.

She probably won't show, Caine thought as he walked toward the terminal. Since Diana Blade hadn't responded to Serena's letter, he didn't understand why his sister was so certain she'd be on the plane. He was less certain why he had allowed himself to be drafted as chauffeur.

Rena would have come if things hadn't gotten so busy at the hotel, he reminded himself. And since the hell they'd been through only a few months before, Caine found himself willing to indulge his sister's whims. Otherwise, he mused, he'd be spending his week off skiing in Colorado instead of walking a northern beach in January.

A gust of wind blew down the collar of his coat as he reached for the door at the terminal entrance. A blonde, wrapped in red fox, passed through, pausing long enough to run her gaze up Caine's body and over his face before her eyes met his. Caine took the brief, speculative look with a half-amused smile and waited for her to move by.

He had a lean, somewhat pale face with sharp, strong bones offset by eyes that edged toward violet. At a casual glance, he might be deemed a scholar—a longer one might reveal the recklessness that was far removed from academia. Because he was hatless, the wind tossed his burnished gold hair around his face. The smile added charm to what were intense, almost wolfish features. He was a man aware of his looks and comfortable with them.

Caine moved through the terminal in a quick, rangy

stride, looking neither right nor left. He'd spent enough time in airports to ignore the sounds and crowds. With a brief glance at the monitor, he checked the gate for the incoming flight from Boston, then settled down to wait for a woman he didn't expect.

When the arrival was announced, Caine sat back in the black plastic chair and lit a cigarette. He'd wait until the last passenger had deplaned, then go back to the hotel. Serena would be satisfied, and he'd have an afternoon workout in the gym. Since completing his term as state's attorney and resuming his private practice, Caine hadn't had time for an hour's relaxation, much less a week's. When he relaxed, he believed in doing it as thoroughly as he worked.

The next seven days, he told himself, were going to be dedicated to doing nothing. He wouldn't think of the chaos of his office, the cases he was going to have to turn down because there simply weren't enough hours in the day, or the reams of paperwork.

Caine knew her the minute he saw her. The high, slashing cheekbones were so much like Justin's, as was the smooth, almost copper complexion. The Indian heritage they shared was perhaps even more apparent in the sister. Her eyes weren't the light, unexpected green of her brother, but a rich, dark brown. Camel eyes, Caine thought as he rose. Luxuriously lashed and heavy lidded so that they appeared sleepy. The nose was straight and aristocratic, the mouth passionate. Or stubborn, he mused. It wasn't a face a man could easily categorize—beautiful, appealing, sexy—but it wasn't one he'd easily forget. Caine knew he'd already memorized it, feature by feature.

As she shifted her flight bag to her other arm, Diana's thick raven hair swung, not quite brushing her shoulders. She wore it loose and nearly straight, so that the tips just curved under, with a fringe of bangs over her forehead. The style suited her, easy but cleverly and meticulously cut, as was the deceptively simple burgundy suit.

Unnoticed, Caine let his eyes trail up, taking in the slender, well-disciplined body, narrow-hipped, slim waist, strong, swimmer's shoulders. She walked like a dancer, confident, smoothly rhythmic, so that when he stepped in front of her, Diana paused in midstride without any show of awkwardness. Unlike the woman in the red fox, she scanned his face briefly and with no show of interest.

"Excuse me." The words were perfectly polite and left the unmistakable impression that he was in her way.

Interesting, Caine mused, and didn't bother to smile. "Diana Blade?"

Diana's left brow disappeared under the fringe of bangs. "Yes?"

"I'm Caine MacGregor, Rena's brother." Keeping his eyes on her face, Caine held out a hand.

So this is the deadly MacGregor, Diana mused, accepting the hand he offered. "How do you do?" She'd expected a smooth palm and was surprised to find her hand clasped against hard, callused skin. A faint prickling of pleasure crept up her arm. Diana acknowledged it, broke contact, then forgot it.

"Rena would have come herself," Caine went on, still studying her face minutely, "but there were a few minor emergencies at the hotel." Because he was a man who could be diplomatic or blunt depending on his mood, Caine spoke as he started to take the flight bag from her shoulder. "I didn't expect you to come."

"No?" Diana kept her hand on the strap of the bag, refusing to relinquish possession. "And your sister?"

Caine considered engaging in a brief tug-of-war over the bag. Something about those large sleepy eyes made him want to annoy her. With a shrug, he dropped his hand. "She was certain you'd come. Rena believes everyone has strong family feelings because she does." The fleeting smile softened his features before he took her arm. "Let's go get your bags."

Diana allowed him to lead her down the wide crowded corridor, while behind the deceptively lazy eyes her mind was active and sharply alert. "You don't like me, do you, Mr. MacGregor?"

Caine's brows lifted and fell, but he didn't even glance at her. "I don't know you. But since we're in the position of being family, so to speak, why don't we bypass the formalities?"

During the short speech, she had another clue why he was so successful in his field. His voice was gold— rich, mellow gold with a hint of steel beneath. "All right," she agreed. "Tell me, Caine, if you weren't expecting me, how did you know who I was?"

"Your bone structure and coloring are very much like Justin's."

"Are they?" she murmured as they stopped in front of the conveyor belt.

Caine studied her again with the same thorough, unapologetic intensity as before. Her scent was something he couldn't quite identify, wild rather than floral, and very French. He wondered if it suited her as well as the smartly cut wool suit. "The family resemblance is there," he commented. "But I think it would be less apparent if you stood side by side."

"That's something I've had little opportunity to do,"

Diana returned dryly and indicated her bags with a gesture of her hand.

Used to servants, Caine concluded as he hefted the two leather cases. But self-reliant, he added, remembering their silent battle over the flight bag. "I'm sure Justin will be pleased to see you after so many years."

"Possibly. You seem very fond of him."

"I've known him for ten years. He was my friend before he became my brother-in-law."

She wanted to ask what Justin was like but swallowed the question. Diana had her own opinion. If she were to change it, it wouldn't be through Caine's influence or anyone else's. "You're staying at the Comanche?"

"For a week."

As they stepped out into the frigid January air, Diana automatically stuck her ungloved hands in her coat pockets. The sky was a cold, hard blue, the street slick and grimy with melted snow. "Isn't it an odd time of year to be vacationing at the beach?"

"For some." The wind whipped his hair into his eyes, but he didn't seem to notice. "Then again, a great many people come for the gambling. Weather doesn't matter when you're inside a casino."

Because the top of her head was level with his shoulder, Diana tilted her face back to see his. "Is that what you come for?"

"Not particularly." He looked down and discovered the sun brought out the faintest hint of gold in her eyes. "I enjoy an occasional game, but Rena's the gambler in the family."

"Then she and Justin must be well suited."

Caine set down her bags and slowly drew the keys out of his pocket. "I'll let you decide that for yourself." Without speaking, he loaded her cases in the trunk, then unlocked the car. "Diana . . ." Caine put his hand on her arm before she could slide in.

She'd never known her name could sound like that—soft and smooth and vaguely exotic. When she turned large, puzzled eyes to his, he brushed at her bangs in a gesture that was completely natural to him. Because his touch surprised her as much as it disconcerted, Diana said nothing.

"Things aren't always as they seem," Caine said quietly.

"I don't understand you."

For a moment, they merely stood in the windy parking lot with the thunder of planes and smell of fumes. Diana thought she could almost feel the texture of his hard palm through the thickness of her coat. His eyes, she thought, were oddly gentle in such a strongly featured face. Briefly, she forgot his reputation as a demon in the courtroom—and the bedroom. She found herself wanting to reach out to him, for help, advice, comfort, before she was fully aware she needed any.

"You have a beautiful face," Caine murmured. "Do you have any compassion?"

Diana drew her brows together. "I'd like to think so."

"Then give him a chance."

The puzzled, vulnerable look dropped away to be replaced by something cool and guarded. It was a look, though she didn't know it, that her brother could adopt at a moment's notice. "Some might consider my coming a sign of good faith."

"Some might," Caine agreed, then walked around to slide into the driver's seat.

"But you don't." Diana let the door shut with a peevish snap.

"If I had to guess, I'd say you came primarily out of curiosity."

"It must be gratifying to be right so often."

He flashed her a grin, powerful and quickly gone. She almost wondered if she'd imagined it. "Yeah." The Jaguar roared to life when he twisted the key. "For the sake of our kin, why don't we try to be friends. How was Paris?"

Idle conversation, she decided. Turn off the brain and give all the standard, meaningless answers. Diana leaned back. She'd enjoy the ride. One of her secret weaknesses was for fast, well-constructed cars. "It was chilly," she began.

"There's a little café off the rue du Four," Caine remembered as he maneuvered the Jag through airport traffic. "The best soufflés on either side of the Atlantic."

"Henri's?"

He sent her a curious look. "Yes, you know it?"

"Yes." With a hint of a smile, Diana turned her attention back to the window. Henri's was a noisy little hole in the wall. Aunt Adelaide would have starved before she stepped over the threshold. Diana loved it and always made a point of slipping away for an hour or two when she was in Paris to enjoy a meal and the company. Strange that it would also be a favorite of Caine MacGregor's. "Do you get to Paris often?"

"No, not anymore."

"My aunt will be living there now. I've been helping her settle into her apartment."

"You're living in Boston. What part?"

"I've just moved into a house on Charles Street."

"The inevitable small world," Caine murmured. "It seems we're neighbors. What do you do in Boston?"

Flicking back the hair that fell across her cheek, Diana turned to study him. "The same thing you do." Caine lifted a brow as he twisted his head to look back at her. "You remember Professor Whiteman, I'm sure," she continued. "He speaks very highly of you."

Caine's grin was quick and off center. "Do the students still call him Bones behind his back?"

"Of course."

With a laugh, Caine shook his head. "So, Harvard Law. It appears we have more in common than we bargained for. Family, alma mater, career. Are you practicing?"

"I'm with Barclay, Stevens and Fitz."

"Mmm, very prestigious." He shot her a look. "And staid."

For the first time, Diana's features relaxed into a smile. It was both wry and stunning. "I get all the fascinating cases. Just last week I represented a council-man's son who has a habit of ignoring the posted speed limit."

"You can work your way up in fifteen or twenty years."

"I've other plans," Diana murmured. By the time she was thirty, she calculated, she'd be ready for the break. After four years with a respected, conservative firm, she'd have the experience and the backing neces-sary to start her own practice. A small, elegant office, a competent secretary and then . . .

"Which are?"

She brought herself back to the present. She wasn't a woman to lay all her cards on the table. "I want to specialize in criminal law," she said simply.

"Why?"

"A thirst for justice, human rights." Laughing, she swung her face back to his. "And I love a good fight."

Caine acknowledged this with a thoughtful nod. Perhaps she wasn't as polished and proper as the trim suit indicated. He should have gotten a hint of who she was from her choice of scent. "Are you any good?"

"A second-year law student could handle what I'm doing at the moment." Her chin angled as she rested her elbow on the back of the seat. "I'm much better than that . . . and I intend to be the best."

"An admirable ambition," Caine commented as he swung off the Strip toward the Comanche. "I've already earmarked that spot for myself."

Diana gave him a long, cool look. "We'll have to see who gets there first, won't we?"

For an answer, Caine only smiled. Diana thought she could see something of the demon in him now, a hint of that volatile, dangerous energy that had already propelled him far up the ladder. Without speaking, she stepped out of her side of the car. She wasn't intimidated by wolfish grins or challenging eyes. If there was one area where Diana was completely confident, it was law. Caine MacGregor would be hearing her name over the years, she was certain. He'd remember what she'd said.

"Ms. Blade's bags are in the trunk," Caine told the doorman as he handed over a folded bill and his keys. "I'm sure Rena'd like to see you right away," he went on as he took Diana's arm again. "Unless you'd rather go to your own rooms first."

"No." Rena, not Justin, she noticed. She felt the quick jumpiness in her stomach again and struggled to ignore it.

"Good. Then we'll go right up."

"So . . ." Diana glanced around, taking in the understated elegance of the lobby. "This is Justin's."

"He only owns half of this Comanche," Caine corrected as they stepped into the elevator. "Rena bought in as a full partner late last summer."

"I see. Is that how they met?"

"No." When he laughed, she turned her head to eye him curiously. "It's a complicated family joke. I'm sure Rena will tell you about it—though perhaps you'd have to meet my father to completely understand." He gave her a long look, then twisted the ends of her hair around his fingers. "On second thought, I'd better see that you don't meet him, or I'm likely to find myself in a similar situation." He kept his eyes on hers, stirred by the wildly seductive scent she wore. Was that mouth as passionate as it looked? he wondered. "You really are very beautiful, Diana," he murmured.

It was the way he said her name, Diana told herself, that caused that odd, almost uncomfortable prickling along her skin. He was an expert at making women uncomfortable, she remembered. And making them enjoy it. She gave him a steady look from half-closed eyes. "You left quite a reputation behind you at Harvard, Caine," she said mildly. "Not all of it in the lecture halls."

"Is that so?" Apparently amused, he gave her hair a quick tug before he released it. "You'll have to tell me about it sometime."

"Some things are best left unsaid." When the doors opened, Diana stepped out, then glanced over her shoulder. "Though I've often wondered if the . . . incident in the law library was based on fact."

"Hmm." Rubbing a hand over his chin, he joined her. "Suppose I plead the Fifth on that, counselor."

"Coward."

"Oh, yeah." He started to stick the key Serena had given him into the lock of the penthouse door, then stopped. "Are they still talking about that?"

Diana struggled with a smile as she studied his face. He wasn't particularly embarrassed, she mused, more curious. "It's become the stuff legends are made of," she told him. "Champagne and passion between Massachusetts Criminal Law and Divorce Proceedings."

Caine gave a shrug as he turned the lock. "It was beer, actually. These things get blown out of proportion with time." He gave her a very charming smile. "You don't believe everything you hear, do you?"

Diana paused long enough to return the smile. "Yes." With this, she pushed open the unlocked door and stepped inside.

Diana didn't know what she'd been expecting. Whatever it had been, it had little to do with the warm elegance of her brother's suite. Muted tones accented with bold slashes of color, large expanses of glass with a panoramic view of the Atlantic, small, exquisite carvings, pastel sketches, low inviting furniture snuggled into plush carpeting.

Was this her brother's taste? she wondered, suddenly feeling more remote from him than ever. Or was it Serena's? Who was this man who shared parents and a heritage with her? Why was she here, looking, opening herself to emotions she'd locked out most of her life? They needed to stay locked out, she told herself frantically. That was survival. In a moment's panic, Diana turned toward the door but found herself face to face with Caine.

"Whom are you going to run from?" he asked as he lifted his hands to her arms. "Justin, or yourself?"

Diana stiffened. "This isn't any of your concern."

"No," he agreed, but his eyes dropped, of their own accord, to her mouth. She was tense, muscles tight. What would it be like, he wondered, to loosen her, to get beyond that finely drawn wall of control and elegance? He'd always preferred more flamboyant women—women who knew how to laugh and to love without undercurrents. But this, after all, would just be a test. It wasn't as if there were a chance of involvement.

There was a moment's temptation to satisfy his curiosity—bring her those few inches closer and taste. The fact that her response could fall anywhere between fury and passion only made it the more difficult to resist.

Diana felt the need come unexpectedly, and uninvited—to be held, driven, possessed. Somehow she knew he could bring her to that. There'd be no unanswered questions, no uncertainties, only floods of pleasure and passion. Mindless, no thought, no reason, no justifications—she could find that heady, forbidden world if only she reached for it. And for him.

For a moment, she swayed between temptation and rationality—that thin razor's edge understood by all lovers. It would be so easy. . . .

A faint mechanical rumble snapped her back. Diana turned her head toward the doors of an elevator she hadn't even noticed. Without speaking, Caine slid his hands up to her shoulders and slipped her coat off as they opened.

Diana watched a woman walk through, small and blond and striking in a simple violet sheath that matched her eyes. "Diana." Serena walked to her, enveloping her in a hard, unselfconscious hug. "I'm so glad you came!" Serena slid her hands down until they gripped her sister-in-law's. "Oh, you're lovely," she said with a wide, welcoming smile. "And so like Justin, isn't she, Caine?"

"Mmm." Standing back, he watched the meeting as he lit a cigarette.

A bit overawed by the greeting, Diana retreated a step. "Serena, I want to thank you for the invitation."

"It's the last formal one you'll get," Serena told her. "We're family now. Caine, how about a drink? Diana, what would you like?"

Diana glanced from brother to sister and lifted her shoulders. "A little vermouth." Nervous and unwilling to settle, she wandered to the window. "The hotel's beautiful, Serena. Caine tells me you and Justin are partners."

"In this one, and the one we're rebuilding in Malta. I haven't wormed my way into the others as yet. I will." Accepting the glass Caine handed her, Serena took a seat on the sofa.

"It turns out Diana and I are neighbors." Caine crossed the room with another glass and offered it to Diana.

"Really?"

That strange moment had passed, Diana told herself. And it had been nerves, not needs, she thought as she took the drink from Caine. Then their eyes met, their fingers brushed. She wasn't as certain as she wanted to be. "Yes." Deliberately she turned away from Caine to face his sister. "It's quite a coincidence."

Caine smiled slowly as he let his gaze sweep up Diana's back. "Even more of a coincidence," he drawled as he walked back to the bar. "We have the same profession."

"You're a lawyer?" Serena watched Diana's eyes follow Caine. It appears my brother doesn't waste any time, she mused, then sipped thoughtfully at her drink.

"Yes, I was at Harvard a few years behind Caine." Diana switched her drink to her other hand and wished she hadn't asked for it. "But his presence was still felt," she added.

Serena threw back her head and laughed. "Oh, I don't doubt it. In most cases you should take stories with a grain of salt. In Caine's . . ." She trailed off, sending him a provocative smile. "I always wonder just how much was left out."

"Your faith in me is touching," Caine murmured.

They're close, Diana mused. They've shared years and know dozens of foolish things about each other. She stared down into her drink. What am I doing here? "Serena," she began. "I want you to know I appreciate the invitation. But I wonder . . ." Diana stopped and fortified herself with a sip of vermouth. "I wonder if Justin's any more comfortable about this than I am."

"He doesn't know you're coming." When Diana's eyes shot up, Serena went on quickly. "I wasn't certain you would, Diana. I didn't want him to be hurt if you refused."

"Would he be?" Diana murmured, then lifted her glass again.

"You don't know him," Serena returned. "I do." The cool, quiet look Diana sent her was so like Justin's that Serena's heart twisted. "Diana, I think I have some idea how you must feel." Setting her drink on the table, she rose. "Please don't shut him out. He's—"

At the sound of the elevator, Serena broke off.

Damn it, I need a few more minutes! She glanced at Diana to see her sister-in-law standing stiff and silent. Serena cast one helpless look at Caine and got a shrug for an answer. Diana watched the doors slide open.

"There you are." Justin strode directly to his wife. "You disappeared."

"Justin—" Serena found her words muffled against his mouth.

He's so tall, Diana thought numbly. Confident, successful, her mind went on as she could do nothing more than stare at him. How much was left of the moody, intense boy she'd known? Was this her brother? He'd lifted her on his shoulders once so that she could see over the crowd when a circus had come to town. Dear God, why should she remember that now?

"Justin," Serena began breathlessly when her mouth was free. "We have company."

He spared Caine a brief glance, then gathered Serena closer. "Go away, Caine, I want to make love to your sister."

"Justin." With a half laugh, Serena pressed her hands against his chest. When she glanced toward the window, Justin followed her eyes.

"Oh." Smiling, he ran his hand down his wife's hair but didn't release her. "I didn't realize Caine had brought a friend."

He doesn't even know me, Diana thought as her hands tightened on the glass. We're strangers, we'd pass each other on the street. At a loss, she stared back at him, struggling for words that wouldn't come.

Slowly, Justin's eyes narrowed. Serena felt his hand tighten on her hair, then release gradually until he was no longer holding her. "Diana?" In her name was recognition and incredulity.

Dry-eyed, she stood perfectly still. Her knuckles were white against the glass. "Justin."

He crossed to her, searching her face. The clock was spinning backward and forward so quickly it left him shaken and disoriented. He wanted to reach out, touch her, but didn't know how. She'd been so small when he'd left her, and pudgy with baby fat. Now she was a tall, slender woman with his father's eyes. His face was as expressionless as hers as they studied each other.

"You cut your pigtails," he murmured, and felt foolish.

"Several years ago." Diana called on every lesson in deportment Aunt Adelaide had ever drummed into her. "You look well, Justin," she said with a polite smile.

Whatever overture he might have made was smothered by that one, impersonal sentence. "And you," he said with a nod. "How's your aunt?"

"Aunt Adelaide's fine. She's living in Paris now. Your hotel's very impressive."

"Thank you." He gave her a wry smile as he slipped his hands into his pockets. "I hope you'll stay with us for a while."

"For a week." The ache in her hand told her to loosen her grip on the glass. Diana concentrated on doing so while his eyes stayed steady on hers. "I haven't congratulated you on your marriage, Justin. I hope you're happy."

"Yes, I am."

Finding the stilted conversation unbearable, Serena stepped forward. "Please, sit down, Diana."

"If you don't mind, I'd like to unpack, settle in a bit."

"Of course." Justin spoke before Serena could protest. "You'll join us for dinner tonight?"

"I'd be glad to."

"I'll show you to your rooms." Caine drained the rest of his drink, then set it down.

"Thank you." Diana crossed toward the door, pausing long enough to give Serena a brief smile. "I'll see you tonight, then."

There was faint, but unmistakable disapproval in the violet eyes. "Yes. Please let us know if there's anything you need. Does eight o'clock suit you?"

"I'll be ready." Without looking back, Diana walked through the door Caine already held open. Neither spoke as they moved down the hallway. In a few minutes, Diana thought frantically, she could untense her muscles, unstrap her emotions.

Silently, Caine drew the door key out of his pocket and slipped it into the lock. Diana walked through, then turned, intending to give him a brief thank-you. He closed the door behind him. "Sit down."

"If you don't mind, I'd really like to—"

"Why don't you finish that drink?"

Glancing down, Diana saw that she still held the glass. With a shrug, she turned away as if studying the room. "Very nice," she said without having the vaguest idea what she was looking at. "I appreciate you showing me my room, Caine. Now I really have to unpack."

"Sit down, Diana. I'm not leaving while you're churned up this way."

"I'm not churned up!" Her voice was too sharp. In defense, she took another swallow of vermouth. "I am tired, though, so if you don't mind . . ."

"I was watching you." Firmly, Caine took her by the

shoulders and pushed her into a chair. "If you'd stood in there another five minutes, you'd have keeled over."

"That's ridiculous." Diana set the glass on the table beside her with a click.

"Is it?" He took her hand between both of his, rubbing absently as he watched her face. "Your hands are like ice. You can lie with your eyes, Diana, not with your hands. Couldn't you have given him something?"

"No." The word wavered and she sucked in her breath to steady it. "I don't have anything to give him." Snatching her hand away, she rose. "Please leave me alone."

They were close now, so close she could see the fractional lift of his brow. "Stubborn," Caine murmured and absently traced the shape of her mouth with his thumb. "I thought as much when I saw you get off the plane. Diana . . ." With a sigh, Caine brushed the hair away from her cheeks. She felt everything slip out of focus. "You're hurting yourself by binding your feelings up this way."

"You don't know anything about my feelings." Her voice was low and unsteady as she fought to keep tears from misting her vision. She wasn't going to cry—not in front of him or anyone. There was nothing, absolutely nothing to cry about. "This is none of your business. My feelings are none of your business." She choked on a sob and pressed her hand to her mouth. "Leave me alone," she demanded, but found herself cradled against his chest.

"When you've finished," he murmured, and held her.

The wordless, unquestioning comfort was more than she could resist. Clinging, Diana let her emotions break loose in a storm of weeping.

Chapter Two

The water was slate gray with jagged crests of white-caps. It was angry, noisy and fascinating. Diana could smell the sea and the promise of snow. As she walked across it, the sand was brittle with cold, crunching quietly underfoot. She had her coat buttoned high against the wind but lifted her face to it, enjoying its slapping fingers. And the solitude. She reveled in the solitude that could be found on a winter's beach just past dawn.

So much of her life had been crowded with people. She'd never been alone in her aunt's house on Beacon Hill. Diana tossed back her hair and smiled ruefully. She'd never been *allowed* to be alone. Beneath Adelaide's fussing and lectures on deportment had been the fear that Blade blood, Comanche blood, would prove too strong and too wild to be controlled.

Diana had controlled it, because there was nowhere

else for her to go. At first, Diana had done everything she was told, allowed herself to be molded into the quiet little lady her aunt had wanted. Everyone else had left her, and Diana had lived with the daily fear that she would be left again.

She'd learned to control the fear, but she'd never been able to alleviate it. It was the ability to control her emotions that had become her most successful defense against Adelaide's criticisms and her own insecurity. Even as a child Diana had understood that her aunt had taken her in because of a sense of duty. There was no love between them, despite the fact that the young girl had thirsted desperately for love.

Diana had been the offspring of Adelaide's half sister, a dark-haired, golden-skinned girl born of their father's second marriage to a woman of mixed blood. Comanche blood. And the half sister whom Adelaide had accepted out of duty had compounded their father's lack of judgment by marrying a Blade. Blood had called to blood, Adelaide had often said when she spoke of what she considered her half sister's betrayal of their name and heritage. With Diana, she'd been ruthlessly determined to correct her family's previous errors.

The Comanche strain was to be ignored—more, it was to be erased. Adelaide demanded perfection. She was a Grandeau. Diana was to be a mirror of her own values, opinions and wishes. The child learned to be cautious, to be obedient and to question only in her head. The wrong question, voiced aloud, could be met with tight-lipped impatience, or worse, another lecture on deportment.

Diana had accepted, then had excelled in her studies, in music, in poise. They'd been an escape that had fulfilled her quest to learn and her need to belong. Her calmly determined will to succeed had begun as a way of surviving. Over the years the cool, elegant demeanor she'd adopted had become second nature.

If there were moments when she'd longed for something more, something . . . exciting, unfathomable, she'd suppressed the needs. She'd come to believe that if she played by the rules, if she followed the steps carefully, she'd win in the end. So her rebellions had been very discreet and her dreams meticulously subdued.

Still, Adelaide would have been appalled to know that her niece enjoyed restaurants that didn't have a four-star rating and movies that didn't have strict cultural significance. And sports cars, Diana mused with a quiet laugh. Steamed crabs and beer. Stopping, she slipped her hands into her pockets and looked out to sea. And wild winter beaches, she reflected.

Is that why Justin seems to have settled here? Diana wondered as she turned to face the back of the hotel. Does he find himself drawn to the cold passion of a winter sea? Was the heritage they shared stronger than the years of separation—the years when he had gone his own way to gamble and win, and she had submitted and quietly rebelled?

Shaking her head, Diana continued to walk. She knew nothing of the man who'd sat across from her at dinner the night before. He was smooth and sophisticated with something like thunder just beneath the surface. They'd had little to say to each other. Even when Serena's eyes had pleaded with her, Diana could find nothing more than meaningless cocktail talk.

What did a woman like Serena MacGregor know of her feelings? Diana thought with quick resentment.

She'd grown up surrounded by family, love. She'd had a place and a lineage she didn't have to ignore. Just watching how easy she was with Caine . . .

Caine, Diana thought with a sigh. It was impossible to pin down what she thought about him, what she felt about him. She hadn't been prepared for the sensitivity he'd shown her when she'd fallen apart—or more, his insight in knowing how close she'd been to the edge. Yet he, like Justin, had a certain polish that seemed like a thin glaze over something very dangerous. When her weeping had run its course, she hadn't felt safe in his arms, though he'd done no more than stroke her hair as if she'd been a child.

He threatened to ignite some spark in her, like the reluctant flame that comes from rubbing two sticks together with steady, endless patience. A forest fire can be started that way, Diana reminded herself. She wasn't about to have her life interrupted by one.

"You're up early."

Diana whirled to find Caine behind her. He was dressed more casually now in a leather bomber jacket, jeans and sneakers. It occurred to her that he should be freezing, but he seemed perfectly comfortable as he scanned her face. "I wanted to watch the sun rise over the water," she began, then glanced up at the thick, lead clouds. "I didn't have much luck this morning."

"Let's walk." His hand closed over hers before she could answer. "Do you like the beach?"

Diana relaxed. He wasn't going to badger her about Justin or the strained dinner they had shared the night before. "I've never been much of a summer beach person," she began. "But I never knew how appealing it could be this time of year. Do you come often?"

"No, not really. Luckily both Alan and I were here a few months ago when Rena was kidnapped, but—"

"What?" Diana stopped, her fingers tightening on his.

Caine's eyes came to hers, dark and curious. "Didn't you know?"

"No, I—I suppose I was in Europe. What happened?"

"Long story." Caine began to walk again and was quiet so long Diana thought he'd refuse to tell her. "There'd been a bomb threat in Justin's Vegas hotel. When he went out to handle things, there was another threat, handwritten, addressed to him. He didn't like the feel of it. When he came back, he tried to convince Rena to leave, but . . ." With a quick grin, he glanced out to sea. "She's another stubborn woman. Justin was downstairs talking to the police about a second threat when the guy got to her."

The grin was gone, as though it had never been, and a look of barely controlled fury took its place. "He held her for almost twenty-four hours, handcuffed to the bed. He wanted Justin to pay two million in ransom."

"Good God." Diana thought about the small, violet-eyed woman and shuddered.

"It's the only time in all the years I've known Justin that I've seen him so close to losing it," Caine remembered. The look of cold fury was still in his eyes, but his voice was calm. "He didn't eat, sleep—he just sat by the phone and waited. It wasn't until the boy let him talk to Rena that we finally had a clue to who he was. In some ways, that was worse."

"Why?"

This time Caine stopped and looked down at her.

She wouldn't know, he thought. Perhaps it was time she did. "When Justin was eighteen, he was in a fight in a bar. The man who started it didn't care to be drinking in the same place as an Indian."

The rich, dark eyes frosted over. "I see."

"He pulled a knife. During the struggle, Justin was ripped open—about six inches along the ribs." Caine saw her pale, but he continued in the same tone. "The man was killed with his own knife and Justin was charged with murder."

Diana felt a sudden wave of nausea and fought it off. "Justin was on trial?"

"He was acquitted once the witnesses from the bar were subpoenaed and under oath, but he spent a few grim months in a cell."

"My aunt never told me." Diana turned away to face the sea. "She never said a word."

"You would have been around eight. I don't imagine you'd have been a great deal of help to him."

She could have been, Diana said silently, thinking of her aunt's comfortable income, her influential connections. And I should have been told. *God, he was only a boy!* Squeezing her eyes shut, she struggled to clear her mind and listen. "Go on."

"It turned out that the boy who had Rena was the son of the man Justin had killed. His mother had drummed it into his head that Justin had murdered his father and had been freed because the courts had felt sorry for him. He had no intention of hurting Rena, only Justin."

The sea seemed louder somehow, more violent. "So Justin paid the ransom."

"He was prepared to, but it wasn't necessary. Rena

phoned just as he was leaving to make the final arrangements. She'd knocked the kid out with a skillet and cuffed him to the bed."

Stunned, and amused despite herself, Diana turned back. "She did?"

Caine acknowledged her smile with one of his own. "She's tougher than she looks."

Shaking her head, Diana began to walk again. "And what about the boy?"

"His trial comes up later this month. Rena's paying his legal fees."

Her eyes whipped up to his. In them was a mixture of anger and admiration. "Does Justin know that?"

"Of course."

She digested this in silence, walking again. "I'm not sure I could be so forgiving."

"Justin's more resigned than agreeable," Caine commented. "And when we had Rena back, safe, it was hard to refuse her anything. My first reaction was to get the kid locked up for the next fifty years."

Diana tilted her head to study his face. "I doubt he'd have much of a chance if you could prosecute. I've read some of your trial transcripts. You go for the jugular, counselor."

"It's cleaner," he said simply.

"Why didn't you run for state's attorney again?"

"Politics has too many walls." He sent her an off-center grin. "I imagine you've run into a few with Barclay, Stevens and Fitz."

"Barclay is the epitome of the dry, stern-eyed attorney. Dickens would have loved him. 'My dear Miss Blade,'" she began in a whispery thin voice, "'please try to remember your position. A member of our firm never raises her voice or challenges a judge in the courtroom.' Only on the golf course," Diana added in a mutter.

Still grinning, Caine swung an arm around her shoulders. "And do you challenge judges, Miss Blade?"

"Frequently. If Aunt Adelaide wasn't bosom buddies with Barclay's wife, I'd have been out on my ear by now. As it is, I'm a glorified law clerk."

"So why are you still there?"

"I have a deep supply of patience." His arm felt warm and friendly over her shoulders. Without thinking, Diana moved closer. "Aunt Adelaide wasn't thrilled about my choosing law in the first place, but she was instrumental in my securing a position at Barclay's." That rankled. Diana swallowed the light trace of bitterness. Her voice was low and even when she continued. "In her way, she was pleased that I was working for an old friend and a prestigious firm. If I hang in long enough, they might just give me something other than traffic."

"Afraid of her?"

Instead of being insulted, Diana laughed. The fear had been gone for years. Even the memory was vague. "Aunt Adelaide? I hope I've got more spine than that. No." She tossed her face up to the wind. "I owe her."

"Do you?" Caine murmured, half to himself. "My father has a saying," he mused aloud. "There's no fee for family."

"He doesn't know Aunt Adelaide," Diana remarked dryly. "Oh, look at the gulls!" She pointed skyward as a pair of them swooped overhead and out to sea. "One flew close enough to touch when I stood out on my balcony this morning. I wonder why they make such a lonely sound when they seem perfectly content." When she shivered, Caine tightened his arm around her.

"Cold?"

"Yes." But she smiled up at him. "I like it."

His breath was cool against her face, showing itself in a thin white mist that was quickly snatched by the wind. Diana was so entranced by his eyes that she hardly noticed that the arm around her shoulders had shifted, drawing her closer. Then they were face to face and her arms had slipped up his back, over the cold, smooth leather. Her heartbeat was a dull thud that might have belonged to someone else. She heard the wind echo off the water and surround them as if they were on some lonely northern island. With one hand, he cupped the back of her neck with cool, strong fingers. Diana felt the cold, wet drops land on her face before she saw the flakes.

"It's snowing."

"Yeah." Caine lowered his lips to within a whisper of hers, then hesitated. He heard her quiet shudder of breath before she banished the distance.

Softly, slowly, his mouth roamed over hers. It was a cool, lazy seduction at odds with the biting wind and racing snow. He drew her closer gradually, until her body fit tightly against his. She could feel those hard, seeking fingers run up and down the nape of her neck, teasing her mind with images of what they could do to her body. While she was distracted by them, his mouth became more greedy, pulling response from her before she was aware of the demand.

Her hands hooked around his shoulders and locked tight. Her passion seemed to rise like the wind, but it was hot, sultry, as he took his lips on a long, mesmerizing journey over her face. She heard the thick echo of crashing waves, then nothing but the whisper of her own name as he traced her ear with his tongue. Diana pressed herself against him, searching and finding his roaming mouth with her own.

There was no teasing this time, no subtle greed. Now it was all flash, all fire. Neither of them was aware of the cold any longer as they demanded everything the other possessed. Diana felt all of her small, inner secrets slipping away from her, exposed, even as she felt herself being filled again with needs that were as much Caine's as her own. And the needs were deeper and more complex than anything she'd ever known.

Not just a hunger for the taste of a mouth, not just a desire for the hard, strong feel of a man's arms—it was a longing for a match, a mate. In her stirred the oldest, most primitive need to be completed physically and the oldest, most basic need to be fulfilled emotionally.

As if she felt herself drowning, she clutched at him but was suddenly unsure if he were anchor or lifeline. The will to survive smothered the yearning for pleasure, and she pulled away. Breathing jerkily, Diana stared at him while the wind whipped her hair and snow into her eyes.

"Well." Caine's breath puffed out in a long stream. "That was unexpected." When he reached up to touch her cheek, she backed out of range. His brows lifted and fell as he stuck his hands in his pockets. "A bit late to throw up walls now, Diana. The foundation's already crumbled."

"Not walls, Caine," she said, calmer now. "Just basic common sense. I'm not your passion-in-the-bookstacks type."

Something flashed in his eyes, but she couldn't be

certain if it was annoyance or amusement. "The statute of limitations on that misdemeanor must have run out by now."

"I have my doubts that you're rehabilitated," Diana returned mildly.

"God forbid." Before she could avoid him, Caine reached out to gather her tossing hair in one hand. "Diana." With a laugh, he brushed snowflakes from her cheek. "You belong in the desert, or someplace steamy with a white sun—wearing exotic clothes that would suit that face of yours."

She held herself very still to combat the desire to feel his skin against hers again. "I'm very well suited to a New England courtroom," she retorted.

"Yes." The smile remained in his eyes. "I think you are—or part of you is. Perhaps that's why you're beginning to fascinate me."

"I'm not interested in fascinating you, Caine." She met his eyes levelly and with the quick wish that she could knock the gleam out of them. "I am interested in going back in before I freeze."

"I'll walk you back," he said with such apparently boundless amiability that Diana wanted to deck him.

"That isn't necessary," she began as her hand was clasped by his.

"I suppose I could walk ten paces behind or ten paces in front." As she let out a frustrated breath, Caine grinned down at her. "You're not angry because we exchanged a friendly kiss? After all, we're family."

"There was nothing friendly or familial about it," Diana muttered.

"No." He lifted her hand to his lips, then lightly nipped at her knuckle. "Maybe we should try again."

"No," Diana said firmly and tried to ignore the thrill racing up her arm.

"All right," he said, a bit too agreeably for her taste, "let's have some breakfast."

"I'm not hungry."

"A good thing you're not under oath," he murmured. "You must have eaten all of three bites last night. Well," he continued before she could think of a comment, "have some coffee while I eat. I'm starving. We'll talk shop." He held up a hand, anticipating her protest. "If it makes you feel any better, I'll even put it on my expense account."

With a reluctant laugh, she climbed the beach steps with him. "It sounds to me as though you didn't get out of politics soon enough."

"You haven't the eyes of a cynic," he commented.

"No?" He was climbing the steps quickly now, so she had to jog to keep up.

"They're more like a camel's. Careful, it's getting slick."

"A camel!" Not certain whether to be amused or insulted, Diana stopped near the top of the steps. "Now that's a terribly romantic statement."

"You want romance?" Before she knew what he was doing, Caine had swept her up in his arms to carry her toward the back entrance.

Laughing, Diana pushed snow-coated hair out of her eyes. "Put me down, you idiot."

"It worked for Clark Gable. Vivien Leigh didn't call him an idiot."

"They were inside at the time," Diana pointed out. "If you slip on this snow and drop me, I'm going to sue."

"Some romantic you are," Caine complained as he pushed the door open with his back. "Whatever happened to women who liked to be swept off their feet?"

"They got dropped," Diana said flatly. "Caine, will you put me down?" She tried wriggling, but he only tightened his grip and kept walking. "You're *not* carrying me into the dining room."

"No?" For him it was a direct challenge, and he accepted it with a grin. She was light and carried the scent of snow. Her eyes held an indignant laughter that appealed to him. Caine decided then and there to put that expression on her face more often. She had a mouth that was meant to smile, and he had an urge to show her just how little effort fun could be.

"Caine." Diana lowered her voice as she caught a few interested glances. "Stop this nonsense. People are staring."

"It's all right, I'm used to it." Twisting his head, he kissed her briefly. "Your mouth's very tempting in a pout." As she made a frustrated sound in her throat, Caine stopped to give the dining room hostess a smile. "Table for two?"

"Of course, Mr. MacGregor." Her eyes swept up to Diana for only a moment. "Right this way."

Diana clicked her teeth shut as he carried her around tables scattered with breakfast customers. She watched a middle-aged woman tug on her husband's sleeve and point.

"Your waitress will be right with you," the hostess told Caine as she stopped by a corner table. "Enjoy your breakfast."

"Thanks." With a great deal of style, he deposited Diana in a chair, then sat opposite her.

"You," Diana began in a low voice, "are going to pay for that."

"It was worth it." Caine unzipped his coat and shrugged out of it. He'd already decided she needed to be hit with the unexpected from time to time. In his opinion, she'd been pampered, sheltered and restricted. As a MacGregor, he thought they were all one and the same. Absently, he combed his fingers through his hair, scattering already melting snow. "Are you sure you won't have something more than coffee, love?"

"Quite sure." Watching him, she began unbuttoning her coat. "Do you always get away with the outrageous?"

"Mostly. Are you always so beautiful in the morning?"

"Don't waste your charm." Diana slipped out of her coat to reveal a pumpkin-colored angora sweater.

"It's all right, I have more." While Diana gave a disgusted sigh, he smiled at their waitress, who returned his smile and offered them menus. "I'll have the pancakes," he told her immediately. "With a side order of bacon, crisp, and eggs over easy. The lady only wants coffee."

"Is that a normal breakfast for you?" Diana asked when the waitress bustled off.

Caine leaned back, observing she'd already forgotten to pretend she was angry. "I enjoy eating when I get the chance. There are days when I'm lucky to get more than a few gallons of coffee and a dried-out sandwich."

"Is your private caseload as heavy as it was when you were state's attorney?"

"Heavy enough, and I don't have a staff of assistants." He watched as she added a miserly drop of cream to her coffee. "That's one of the things I wanted to break away from."

"No law clerk?"

She had hands made for rings, he thought, but wore none. Caine had to force his attention back to her question. "Not at the moment. My secretary is disorganized, untidy and addicted to soap operas."

Diana gave him a mild smile as she lifted her cup. "She must have . . . other virtues."

Caine laid his elbows on the table and leaned toward her. "She's fifty-seven, sturdy as a rock and a hell of a typist."

"I stand chastised," Diana murmured. "Still, I'd think with your reputation and background, you'd have one of the slickest firms in Boston."

"I leave that for Barclay, Stevens and Fitz. Don't you like to get your hands dirty occasionally, Diana?"

"Yes." With a sigh, she set down her cup again. "Yes, damn it. I'd work for nothing if I could dig my teeth into something that wasn't cut straight out of a textbook. Traffic violations and property settlements," she muttered. "I'm not going to get anything else if I don't stick with the establishment for a while longer. The world of law wouldn't give me a standing ovation if I opened an office tomorrow."

"Is that what you want? Standing ovations?"

"I like to win." The sleepy eyes became suddenly intense. "I intend to make a career out of it. Why do you do it?"

"I have a talent for arguing." For a moment, he frowned down at his coffee. "The law has a lot of shades, doesn't it?" Caine lifted his eyes and locked them on hers. "Not all of them equal justice. It's a very thin rope we walk and balance is crucial. I like to win, too, and when I do, I like to know I was right."

"Haven't you ever defended someone you knew was guilty?"

"Everyone's entitled to legal counsel and representation. That's the law." This time Caine lifted his coffee, drinking it black, strong and hot. "You're obliged to give them your best and hope that justice is the winner in the final analysis. It isn't always. The system's lousy, and only works part of the time." Shrugging, he drank again. "It's better than not at all."

Interested, Diana studied him with more care. "You're not what I expected you to be."

"And what was that?"

"More hard-line, maybe a young, more fiery version of Barclay. Quoting precedents, a little Latin for effect, claiming that the law is carved in granite."

"Ah, an idiot." Diana burst into quick spontaneous laughter. He found it warm and wild, like her scent. "You don't do that enough, Diana—let yourself enjoy without thinking it through," he explained.

"My training." Even as she said it, it surprised her. Just what doors was he opening, she thought with a frown, before she had a chance to check the locks?

"Are you going to clarify that?"

"No." She shook her head quickly, then glanced up. "Here's your breakfast. I'm fascinated to see if you can really eat it all."

Secrets, Caine thought as the waitress arranged the plates. Perhaps it was her underlying mystique that had her crowding his mind. There seemed to be so many layers to her, and he couldn't resist the temptation to peel each one off to see what was underneath. Then there was the vulnerability . . . it wasn't often you found a strong woman with that soft, vulnerable edge. The combination, with those unmistakable hints of passion, was very . . . appealing.

Her manner, her speech, her style shouted Lady with a capital L, but there were those bedroom eyes and that wicked, promising scent.

He remembered her hot, unrestrained mouth on his and found he wanted her taste again . . . and to feel the skin she kept hidden beneath the discreetly sophisticated clothes. He'd always found women enjoyable puzzles to be solved. In this case, he could pick up the challenge, play the game, and do her the favor of showing her that life wasn't as full of boundaries and rules as she thought. Yes, he mused, Diana Blade was likely to keep him occupied and entertained for quite a while.

"Want a bite?" he said quietly and offered a forkful of fluffy pancakes.

"Afraid you've overdone it?" He only smiled and moved the fork closer to her mouth. With a shrug, Diana allowed him to feed her. "Oh." She closed her eyes a moment. "It's good."

"More?" Caine took a bite himself before offering her another. "Food, like other solutions to hunger, can be habit-forming."

With her eyes on his, she accepted the second bite, then leaned back. "I'm watching my intake at the moment."

"Oh, here you are." Serena swept up to the table, pressing a kiss to her brother's cheek, then Diana's.

"Isn't that disgusting?" she demanded, gesturing to Caine's plate. "And he never gains an ounce. Did you sleep well?"

"Yes." Diana found herself at a loss in the presence of such easy kinship and offered a cautious smile. "My rooms are lovely."

"Want some breakfast?" Caine asked his sister.

"Going to share yours?"

"No."

"Well, I haven't got time, anyway." Serena made a face at him as he continued to eat. "I was hoping you could stop by the office a little later, Diana. Have you made plans for the day?"

"No, not yet."

"You might want to take advantage of the health club or the casino. I'd love to show you around."

"Thank you."

"Give me an hour." Serena shot Caine a look. "Only believe half of what he tells you," she advised, then was off again.

"Your sister . . ." Diana trailed off, then with a quick, wondering laugh accepted the slice of bacon Caine offered. "She's not what I expected, either."

"Do you always have a picture in your head before you meet someone?"

"Yes, I suppose. Doesn't everyone?"

Caine merely moved his shoulders and continued to eat. "What did you expect Rena to be like?"

"Sturdier, for one thing." Diana chewed the bacon absently as she considered. "She seems so fragile, until you really look and see the strength in her face. And I guess I was looking for someone more obviously intellectual, glossier. She's not the sort of woman I would have pictured Justin married to, though I had difficulty picturing him married at all."

"It could be," Caine said quietly, "that he's not what you think, either."

Her eyes lifted at that, instantly cool and remote. "No, I don't know him, do I?"

It was difficult not to be annoyed at how easily she could slip into her armor. Caine sliced through his eggs and continued mildly. "It's never easy to know anyone unless you want to."

"It isn't wise to lecture on a subject you know nothing about," she retorted. "You had a tidy little childhood, didn't you, Caine?" The futility began to rise in her, and with it, anger. "Mother, father, sister, brother. You knew exactly who you were and where you belonged. You've no right to analyze or disapprove of my feelings when you have no way of comprehending them."

Caine leaned back and lit a cigarette. "Is that what I was doing?"

"Do you think it's easy to erase twenty years of neglect, of disinterest?" she tossed back. "I needed him once, I don't need him now."

"Then why did you come?"

"To exorcise those last, lingering ghosts." She shoved the coffee cup aside. "I wanted to see him as a man so I'd stop remembering him as a boy. When I leave, I won't think of him at all."

Caine eyed her through a thin mist of smoke. "You can't pretend you're ice and steel with me, Diana. I was with you yesterday after you saw Justin."

"That's over."

"You aren't pleased I caught you being human, are

you?" When she started to rise, he gripped her wrist, making no effort to keep his strong fingers gentle. "If you want to be a winner, Diana, you have to stop running away."

"I'm not running." Her pulse was beginning to pound. The polish had vanished and she had her first clear view of the man beneath—strong, threatening, exciting.

"You've been running since you stepped off the plane," he corrected. "And likely long before that. You're hurt and confused and too damn stubborn to admit it even to yourself."

"What I am," she said between her teeth, "is none of your business."

"The MacGregors take their family very seriously." His eyes had narrowed, their color only more dramatic when seen through slits. "When my sister married your brother, you became my business."

"I don't want your *brotherly* advice."

He smiled, and his grip gentled abruptly. "I don't feel brotherly toward you, Diana." His thumb brushed across her knuckles in a long, slow sweep. "I think we both know better than that."

He could switch his mood with more speed than she. Rising, Diana gave him a coldly furious look. "I'd rather you felt nothing toward me."

Caine took a lazy drag on his cigarette. "Too late," he murmured, then smiled at her again. "The Scots are a pragmatic race, but I'm beginning to believe in fate."

Diana picked up her coat and meticulously folded it over her arm. "In the language of the Ute, Comanche means enemies." She lifted large angry eyes to his, and for the first time, he saw the full power of her heritage in her face. "We're not easily subdued." Turning, she walked away in her controlled dancer's step.

With a smile, Caine crushed out his cigarette. He was beginning to think it would be a very interesting battle.

Chapter Three

The Comanche, Diana discovered over the next few days, was as slickly run a hotel as any her aunt would have patronized. The food, the service, the ambience, all catered to the wealthy and the successful. It became obvious that though Justin might have started his career as a penniless teenager, he had made the most of the time in between. She told herself she could respect him for that, even cautiously admire him, without involving herself. She wasn't willing to take the risk of looking closely—Diana had never considered herself a gambler.

Justin was invariably polite when they met, but if she had been more open-minded, she might have seen he was as cautious as she.

Despite herself, Diana learned more about him—the ingrained integrity she would never have associated with a gambler, the shrewd, sharp brain he had honed on the streets, the flashes of vulnerability only Serena could bring out in him. Her brother was a man, she discovered, who would have held her interest and affection if it hadn't been for the years she couldn't erase.

Of Caine she saw little, deliberately. He had, in a very short space of time, been witness to too many of her private emotions. She could almost accept that he'd been there to comfort her when she had wept because he was sensitive and kind. But those few moments on the windy beach played in her head too often.

That kind of passion, the depth and suddenness of it, held its own special danger. She could remember it too easily, feel it again too effortlessly. If he could stir her by a look, or the mere speaking of her name when they were in a room full of people, Diana was well aware of what would happen if they were alone. She made certain it wasn't an issue.

Then there was the anger. How easily he strained her temper! Diana had always been pleased with her ability to control or channel her more violent emotions. She'd had years of practice concealing fury and frustration from her aunt in order to avoid the inevitable lecture. Somehow Caine could bring her to the boiling point with a casual sentence.

It wouldn't pay to dwell on it, Diana told herself as she finished dressing. They might run into each other in Boston occasionally, but that was her turf. His, too, she reminded herself. With a shrug, she ran a hand over the hip of her gray flannel slacks. In any case, Boston would be professional ground. She knew exactly who she was and where she was going. She'd never been a woman ruled by mood, she reminded herself. She was much too disciplined for that. Once she was back in

Boston, back to work, she wouldn't be so susceptible to these wide emotional swings.

She didn't want them, she told herself almost violently. She didn't know how to deal with them. What she wanted, what she intended to have again, was the calm order she'd maintained for herself. As long as she was here, she felt like something was tearing at her, ripping at her. Threatening her.

Justin, and all those memories, all those emotions he brought back to her—she didn't want to remember or to feel what she'd once felt.

Caine was widening an opening she hadn't been aware existed. He was playing on vulnerabilities she shouldn't have, on passions she didn't want. When she was near him she needed . . . needed what she couldn't afford to need.

On a long breath she fought back the rage and the confusion. She could still control it, she told herself. She *would* control it. And when she was back in Boston, she would go on with her life just as she had before.

Absently, she adjusted the cowl collar of her dark rose sweater. She was glad she had come. Now that she had seen Justin face to face, she would stop wondering about him and that part of her life would be at rest. She'd also grown to love Serena quickly. It wasn't characteristic of her, Diana admitted. She had learned to be very careful about sharing her affections. They had always been too easily tapped and, she felt, too easily rejected. For the first time in her life, Diana knew the pleasure of having someone who could be both family and friend.

Swinging her purse over her shoulder, she left the suite. She'd stop by her sister-in-law's office before she went for a walk on the beach. Caine invariably went out early, and Diana had timed her own outings around his. There was no point, she concluded, in tempting fate.

As she made her way through the casino, Diana was again impressed by the smart, informal decor. No glitter or chunky chandeliers. From what Serena had told her, the casino, like the rest of the hotel, reflected Justin's taste. It was a far cry from the tiny house with a rickety porch they had shared in Nevada.

But then, they'd both come a long way from there, Diana mused. She thought of her aunt's house on Beacon Hill with its strict, undisturbed elegance. Polished antiques and gleaming Georgian silver. Soft-voiced servants. She gave a last glance around the casino: silver slot machines and green baize tables, croupiers in crisply cut tuxedos, the faint wisp of expensive whiskey and tobacco. Yes, they'd both come a long way from a little box house with a parched yellow lawn, Yet, perhaps she'd been happier there than at any other time in her life.

Immersed in her own thoughts, Diana entered the reception area and nearly walked headlong into her brother.

"Diana." Justin took her arm to steady her, then dropped his hand to his side. She was so lovely, he thought. And the fleeting, polite smile she gave him tied his stomach into knots. He wouldn't reach her, he'd known it in the first instant. But seeing her made it more difficult to accept the loss he'd lived with all of his adult life.

"Good morning, Justin. I thought I'd stop in to see Rena, if she's not busy." How cool his eyes are, she thought. And how odd that that one mark of their white heritage should make him seem so wholly Indian.

"She's just going over the scheduling." When she continued to stare, he lifted a brow. "Is something wrong, Diana?"

"I just remembered that story about the settler one of Mother's ancestors captured." Her brow creased as she tried to recall a story told to a child so many years before. "She ended up staying with him freely. Isn't it strange that because of her, green eyes come out at least once in every generation?"

"You have our father's eyes," Justin murmured. "Dark, secret eyes."

Because she felt herself softening, Diana straightened her spine. "I don't remember him," she said flatly. She thought she heard him sigh, but there was no change in his expression.

"Tell Serena I'll be back in a couple of hours. I have a meeting."

Aching with guilt, afraid of rejection, Diana held herself very still. "Justin." He turned back, but she noticed his hand remained on the doorknob. "I didn't know about the trial . . . about your being in prison. I'm sorry."

"It was a long time ago," he said simply. "You were only a child."

"I stopped being a child when you left me." Without waiting for his response, she turned and went into Serena's office.

"Diana." Smiling, Serena set aside the stack of papers in front of her. "Please, tell me you're dying to be entertained so I can get out from under this mountain of paperwork."

"I was afraid I'd interrupt you."

"There are days I pray for interruptions," Serena

countered, then her brows drew together. "What's wrong, Diana?"

"Nothing." Turning, Diana faced the two-way glass and looked into the casino. "I'd never be able to work with this here. I'd always feel I was in the middle of a party."

"It's just a matter of concentrating on two levels."

"Justin asked me to tell you he'd be out for a couple of hours."

So that's it, Serena thought, and rose. Crossing the room, she placed her hands on Diana's shoulders. "Diana, talk to me. Just because I love Justin doesn't mean I won't understand how you feel."

"I shouldn't have come." On a long breath, Diana shook her head. "I keep finding myself going back, remembering things I'd forgotten for years. Rena, I didn't know I'd still love him. It hurts."

"Loving someone has its disadvantages." Serena gave Diana's shoulders a squeeze. "But if you love Justin and give yourself some time—"

"I resent him every bit as much," Diana countered as she turned around. "Maybe more. I resent him for every day of all those years I did without him."

"Diana, don't you see he did without you as well?"

"His choice; I never had one." The emotions began to push at her so that she swung away to pace the room. "He turned me over to my aunt and went his own way."

"You were six, he was sixteen." Frustrated, Serena tried to balance her loyalties. "What did you expect him to do?"

"He never wrote, never phoned or visited. Not once." As the words she'd held inside for years tumbled out, Diana whirled back. "I was so sure that if I did everything I was told, he'd come for me. Those first few years I was the picture of the model child. I minded my manners and studied my lessons and waited. But he never came. While I was waiting for him, he never gave me a thought."

"That's not true!" Serena said heatedly. "You don't understand."

"No, you don't understand," Diana fired back. "You don't know what it's like to lose everything that belonged to you and have to live on someone else's charity! To know every mouthful of food you ate, every stitch of clothing on your back had a price."

"Who do you think you owe for the food and the clothes, Diana?" Serena asked evenly.

"Oh, I know whom I owe," Diana retorted. "She never let me forget it, in her own discreet way. Aunt Adelaide doesn't believe in generosity without strings."

"Generosity?" Serena crossed the room as her temper snapped. "She doesn't know any more about generosity than you do."

"Perhaps not," Diana agreed with a faint nod. "But she gave me everything I've ever had."

"Justin paid for it all." The words came out on a crest of temper she couldn't control. "He sent her a check every month from the time she took you in until you graduated from Harvard. The checks might have been small in the beginning," Serena continued coldly. "He was living on little more than his wits then and dodging social workers. But they got larger—he's always been very good at what he does. She took his money, and you, on his word that he'd stay out of your life. He paid, Diana, with a great deal more than money."

She seemed to be frozen. Diana was afraid to move

for fear that she would crack and scatter into a dozen irretrievable pieces. "He paid her?" Her voice was very quiet, very disciplined. "Justin sent Aunt Adelaide money, for me?"

"He had nothing else to give you. Damn it, Diana, you're a lawyer. What would have happened to you if he hadn't arranged for your aunt to take you in?"

Foster homes, she thought dully. An orphanage on the reservation. "She could have taken him in, too."

Serena gave her a long, steady look. "Would she?"

Diana pressed her fingers to her eyes. She didn't know when the headache had begun, but it was pounding mercilessly. "No." With a sigh, she dropped them again. "No. Later, when I was older, he could have contacted me."

"He thought you were happy, and certainly better off in Boston than you would have been trailing around the country with him. Justin chose his own life, it's true, but he did what he thought was best for you the only way he knew how."

"Why didn't he tell me?"

"What do you think he wants, your gratitude?" Serena demanded impatiently. "Can't you see what kind of a man he is?" She dragged a hand through her hair. "He won't thank me for telling you. I wouldn't have," she added in a calmer tone, "if you hadn't said you still loved him." As her temper cooled, Serena noted the wide, distressed eyes, the pale cheeks, the frozen expression. Without question, she reached out. "Diana—"

"No." Diana held up a hand to hold her off. Her voice was frigid, her body stiff. "You've told me the truth?"

Serena met her eyes levelly. "I've no reason to lie."

A brittle laugh escaped, but perhaps she wouldn't have bothered to suppress it. "How odd, when it seems everyone else has, all of my life."

"Let me take you upstairs, fix you a drink."

"No." Gathering what remained of her self-control, Diana walked to the door. "I appreciate you telling me, Rena," she said coolly as she turned the knob. "It was something I needed to know."

As the door shut quietly, Serena dropped into the chair behind her desk. Oh, God, she thought, rubbing her hand across her forehead. How could I have done that with so little compassion? Remembering the stricken look on Diana's face, she started to rise, then stopped herself. No, Diana needed some time, and Serena didn't think it would be she Diana would want to see in any case. Catching her bottom lip between her teeth, she lifted the phone.

"Page Caine MacGregor please."

Even after an hour had passed, Diana hadn't found her control. Her mind ran in circles, chased by her emotions. Everything she had believed was false. Everything she had was owed to someone she'd paid back with cold resentment. The only thing that was clear to her now was that she would have to face Justin once more, and she would have to leave. It was easier to prepare for the latter.

Taking out her suitcases, Diana began to pack, slowly, very meticulously, making the simple chore occupy her mind. If she chose, she could make it last for the better part of the afternoon. Perhaps by then the headache would be gone and the sickness deep in her stomach would have eased. Perhaps by then she wouldn't feel so utterly lost.

At first, she ignored the knocking at her door, then when it continued she reluctantly went to answer.

"Caine." Diana stood in the opening, showing clearly he wasn't welcome.

"Diana," he said in the same tone as he scanned her face. Seeing that her eyes were composed and dry, he moved forward until she was forced to give way.

"I'm busy at the moment."

"Don't let me stop you," he said agreeably as he wandered to the window. "I've always liked the view from this room."

"By all means enjoy it, then." Turning on her heel she walked back into the bedroom. While she battled annoyance, Diana continued to pack.

"Change your plans?" Caine asked as he leaned against the doorjamb.

"Obviously." Diana folded a sweater and carefully laid it in the suitcase. "Rena must have told you about our talk this morning."

"She said she'd upset you."

Diana found it more difficult to keep her hands relaxed as she folded a blouse. "You've known all along," she said dispassionately. "You knew that Justin was responsible for my room and board and education."

"Rena talked to me about it after she'd written you. Justin never mentioned it." Coming into the room, Caine idly lifted the sleeve of a silk dress she'd spread on the bed. "Why are you running, Diana?"

"I'm not running." She tossed the blouse she'd been attempting to fold into the suitcase.

"You're packing," he pointed out.

"The words are not synonymous." Diana turned away from him again to give her attention to her packing. "I'm sure Justin'll be more comfortable when I'm gone."

"Why?"

Diana threw a tangle of clothes into the first case and slammed the lid. "Back off, Caine."

Her emotions were fighting to get out, he observed, and wondered why she felt they had to be suppressed. Healthier to let them out, he thought. Perhaps it was one more thing he could teach her. "Whom are you angry with?"

"I'm not angry!" Turning to the closet, Diana dragged clothes off hangers. "It was all lies!" Incensed, she slammed the closet door shut and stood facing him with her hands full of clothes. "All those years she made me feel as though I depended on her good nature, her sense of family obligation. She tucked me into pinafores and patent-leather shoes when I wanted to be barefoot. I wore them because I was terrified of her. Because I owed her. And all the time it was Justin."

Her hands gripped at the clothes as frustration overwhelmed her. "She wouldn't speak of him. She insisted I forget the first six years of my life as if they'd never existed. I was Comanche," Diana said with sudden fierceness, "but she allowed me no reminders of it. She took my heritage, my birthright, and still I felt I owed her. I learned about my blood in books and museums and had to struggle all my life to remember who I was—to remember in secret. I paid her, and while my brother was alone in prison I was taking ballet classes and eating off Sèvres."

Caine took a step toward her, watching the tears well up and be forced back. "Doesn't it matter that it was what he wanted?"

"No!" Diana tossed the clothes aside so that some landed on the bed and others fell to the floor. "I spent most of my life resenting him and catering to a woman who could never accept me for what I was. Now, I don't even know what that is. I thought I paid her for my education by dating the kind of men she approved of, by taking the kind of job she could accept. Balance the scales first, then do what you want." With a laugh, she dragged both hands through her hair. "But it wasn't her, and I don't know who I am anymore. Is it this?" She held up a white silk blouse, tailored, trim, elegant. "I thought I knew where I belonged." Crumpling the blouse into a ball, she hurled it to the floor. "I know nothing!"

He waited a moment while she stared at it, breath heaving. "Why should where the money came from make so much difference?"

"It doesn't to someone who's always felt entitled to it."

Caine grabbed her arms and gave her an impatient shake. "You're being a fool. You found out your aunt wasn't completely honest with you and that your brother hadn't forgotten you. Why does that change who or what you are?"

"Can't you see I was reared on a lie!"

"So now you know the truth," he countered. "What are you going to do with it?"

The fingers that gripped the front of his shirt relaxed abruptly as the anger drained out of her. "Oh, God, Caine, I've been so hateful to him. So cold. The more I wanted to reach out, the more I made myself back away."

He kissed her lightly, a quick, almost brotherly gesture. "You won't next time."

"No." Backing out of his arms, she stooped to pick up the clothes that lay on the floor. As if it were a symbol, she left the crumpled blouse where she'd thrown it. "I'm going to go see him as soon as I've pulled myself together." With her back to him, Diana began to smooth out the skirts and dresses she'd wrinkled. "You seem to be making a habit of being around when I fall apart. I don't think I like it."

"I'm not certain I do, either," he murmured, then found himself turning her to face him. "Vulnerability's difficult to resist." He ran a thumb down her cheekbone, following the movement with his eyes. She was soft in the way of a woman but with an underlying toughness he thought she hadn't even begun to tap. They were only two of the layers he was determined to explore.

"Don't." Diana whispered the word as his eyes came back to hers. In them she saw both desire and decision.

"I make a habit of touching what I mean to have, Diana." He ran both hands up her cheeks, combing his fingers through her hair until her face was unframed. "You stir something in me," he told her before his mouth reached hers.

She could have stopped it. As her arms drew him closer, Diana knew she could have pulled away and ordered him from her room. She still had the strength to do it. But his lips were so clever, so tempting. They whispered at hers, nibbling kisses, promises of endless delight as his hands slid beneath her sweater, up the smooth skin of her back.

He knew how to pleasure a woman. Perhaps the largest part of his appeal was that Caine wanted to give pleasure as much as receive it. He knew all the tricks, the slow subtle moves of seduction. But now, with her pliant in his arms, her mouth growing hungrier on his, he forgot them. Her scent was clouding his mind until he was crushing her against him with too much need for finesse. She was luring him, and it was he who was seduced before he knew the rules had changed.

He heard a moan, low with longing, and dimly realized the sound had been pulled from him. His hands were in her hair again, fingers grasping, unaware of their strength as he drew in all the hot, honeyed tastes of her mouth. And she met him fire for fire, touch for touch.

Diana knew nothing beyond the tide of sensation. The taste and feel of him dominated everything and still wasn't enough. Her tongue met his again and again, deeper intimacy, hotter passion, but she only hungered for more. For the first time, she fully understood the power and allure of greed.

His hands ran down her body, lingering at the sides of her breasts before they continued on over her waist and hips. He molded her like a sculptor learning the life and feel in his clay. And somehow she knew he understood her body as clearly as if she had been naked.

Caine tore his mouth from hers to stare down at her with eyes dark and fiercely intense. It seemed this time he'd been hit with the unexpected; aching desire when he'd have chosen careless, carefree passion. "I want you." His breath came fast as he smothered her lips again. "Now, Diana. Right now."

It was his anger that excited her—and that made her break free. "I . . ." Turning away, she pushed her hands through her hair. "I'm not ready for this. Not with you."

"Damn it, Diana!" Churning with needs, he spun her around.

"No." She shoved at him, gaining a few inches of distance. "I don't know what's going on inside of me right now. Everything's happening too fast. But I do know I won't be one of Caine MacGregor's women."

His eyes narrowed, but he made no move toward her. "You don't stop putting people into slots, do you?"

"I'm going to put my life back together, Caine, I'm not going to let you complicate it."

"Complicate it," he repeated with soft, deadly control. "All right, Diana, you do what you have to do." He stepped toward her then but still didn't touch her. "But Boston isn't such a big town and this case is a long way from closed."

Though her throat was dry, she spoke evenly. "Is that a threat, counselor?"

He smiled then, slowly. "It's a promise." Cupping her chin, he gave her a hard, brief kiss, then turned and left the room. Diana didn't let out her breath until she heard the door close behind him.

This was all she needed, she thought as she looked at her tangle of half-packed clothes. He'd only gotten to her because her emotions were so confused and close to the surface. If there was one thing she'd learned to do over the years, it was to hold her own with men—in the courtroom and the bedroom. Caine MacGregor would have been no different if he hadn't been there when she'd already been vulnerable.

She wouldn't think of it now. Diana closed her eyes and waited for her system to calm. If they were to meet again in Boston, she'd be more steady on her feet. Now she had to face herself and her brother, and twenty years of deceit. Before she could weaken, Diana hurried out of the suite and down the hall toward the penthouse.

He might not be back yet, she thought as she lifted her hand to knock. If he's not, she told herself, I'll go down to his office and wait. It has to be now. Her hand hesitated and nearly dropped. I have to do it now. Straightening her shoulders, Diana knocked, then held her breath.

Justin opened it, bare-chested, a shirt slung over his shoulder and his hair still damp from a shower. "Diana? Were you looking for Serena?"

"No, I—" Her eyes were drawn to the jagged white scar along his ribs. Painfully, she swallowed. "May I come in?"

"Of course." After closing the door, he watched her fingers lace and unlace as she walked to the center of the room. "Would you like some coffee? A drink?"

"No, no, nothing." She gripped her fingers together again and let them fall in front of her. "You go ahead."

"Sit down, Diana."

"No, I . . ." Her voice trailed off and she shook her head helplessly. "No."

"What is it?"

It would be easier if she didn't have to look at him, she thought. Easier if she could be a coward and turn away as she said the words. Diana kept her eyes on his. "I want to apologize."

Justin lifted a brow as he started to slip on his shirt. "What for?"

"For everything I haven't done or said since I came here."

He watched her as he buttoned his shirt, but his eyes told her nothing. He knew how to keep his thoughts to himself, she realized. That was why he was a gambler, and a success at it. "You have nothing to apologize for, Diana."

"Justin." His name came out in a plea as she stepped toward him. Stopping herself, Diana turned away a moment. "I'm not doing this well. Strange, I make my living stringing the right words together, but I just can't find them."

"Diana, you don't have to do this." He wanted to touch her, but thinking she'd only stiffen, he slipped his hands into his pockets. "I don't expect you to feel anything."

Gathering her courage again, she faced him. "I owe you," she said quietly.

Instantly, his eyes were remote and unfathomable. "You owe me nothing."

"Everything," she corrected. "Justin, you should have told me!" she said with sudden passion. "I had a right to know."

"To know what?" he countered coolly.

"Stop it!" she demanded and grabbed his shirtfront with both hands.

He thought as he looked down at her that there was more of the girl he remembered than he'd realized. Here was the verve and the fire. Lifting a brow, he studied her stubborn, furious face. "You always were a brat," he murmured. "Perhaps if you calm down, you might tell me what's on your mind."

"Stop treating me as though I were still six years old!" she demanded as her fingers tightened on his shirt.

It amused him to hear her shout, and wiped away the image of the cool sophisticate who had walked back into his life a few days before. "Stop behaving as though you were," he advised. "There've been things you've wanted to say to me since I walked into this room and found you here. Say them now."

Diana took a deep breath. She'd wanted to apologize, not to shout and accuse. But the control she'd practiced so scrupulously for so many years was lost. "All those years I resented you, even tried to hate you for forgetting me."

"I think I understand that," he said steadily.

"No." Shaking her head, she dug her fingers into his shirt in frustration. Tears began to gather and spill, but she didn't wipe them away because she didn't feel them. "How could you when I could never tell you? I lost everything so quickly, Justin. Lost everyone." Her voice trembled, but she couldn't steady it. "I thought at first all of you had left because I was too much trouble."

He made a soft sound and touched her for the first time—a hand absently passed through her hair as he had done from time to time so many years before. "I didn't know how to make you understand. You were so small."

"I understand now," Diana began. "Justin—" She broke on the word, fighting off a sob. She had to say it all, even if he turned away after she was done. "Everything you did for me—"

"Was necessary." He cut her off and was no longer touching her. "No more, no less."

"Justin, please . . ." She didn't know how to ask for love. If she had one lingering fear, it was to try and to fail. While he watched, she struggled for words. "I want to thank you," she managed. "You've every right to be angry, but—"

"There's nothing I've done you have to thank me for."

She bit down on her lip to stop the trembling. "You felt obligated," she murmured.

"No." He touched her again, just the tips of her hair. "I loved you."

Her lips parted, but there was no sound. He was offering her love. . . . He wouldn't accept gratitude. She wouldn't give him tears. Instead, Diana reached for his hand. "Be my friend."

Justin felt something unknot in his stomach. Slowly, he brought her hand to his lips, then spreading her fingers, he placed her palm to his. "We're blood, little sister. I've always loved you. From today, we're friends."

"From today," she agreed, and curled her fingers around his.

Chapter Four

It was bitterly cold. In defense, Diana had the car heater turned up full as she fought her way through sluggish Boston traffic. Oncoming headlights glared off her windshield so that she kept her eyes narrowed and tried not to remember that her ankles were freezing. By the time her car warmed up, she thought fatalistically, she'd already be inside the restaurant.

She considered it a wise move on her part to meet Matt Fairman for dinner. As assistant district attorney, he had his ear to the ground. In her current professional position, she didn't think it prudent to refuse the offer of a casual dinner date, even when she'd rather be home huddled in a warm robe drinking tea and watching an old movie. Diana didn't feel she could afford to offend anyone with Matt's kind of connections or to pass up the opportunity to make a few points on her own behalf. In any case, she was confident she could handle him on a personal level. She always had. And he was nice enough, she mused, shivering inside her coat, if you overlooked the fact that his mind worked on two levels. The law and women.

Matt was a good lawyer, she reminded herself. She thought, but couldn't be sure, that her feet were beginning to thaw. Pushing this aside, she concentrated on Matt. Besides being a good lawyer, and a shrewd politician, Matt had the inside story on every important case being tried or pending in the Boston area. He was also a gossip. If Diana wanted it known that she was now out on her own, she'd do better with a few words in Matt's ear than a full-page ad in the *Boston Globe*.

She'd resigned from Barclay, Stevens and Fitz the week she had returned from Atlantic City. It had been her way of making a stand against her aunt's manipulating. Diana knew she was taking a chance, both financially and professionally, and in the two weeks following the break she'd had her share of small panic attacks. Barclay was security, not only a steady paycheck, but a steady stream—well, at least a trickle—of cases. But Barclay had been her aunt's choice. She considered the abrupt termination her first real step toward independence. She didn't regret the decision or the twinges of doubt about the future.

On a bad day, she pictured herself sharing office space with another struggling lawyer, waiting for the phone to ring, hoping to defend someone over a speeding ticket. On a good one, Diana told herself that she was going to fight her way up the ladder, rung by rung.

If Diana had a regret, it was that she'd had so little time with Justin once they'd made peace—but she had felt it was essential that she get back to Boston and sort out her professional life. Resigning from Barclay had to be done while the heat of anger, the sting of betrayal, was still fresh—before, Diana had thought, she'd reasoned it out too well. It was too easy to be nervous, to think of all the consequences. Instead, she convinced herself that she was in a hurry to start carving out a place and a name for herself. And, she discovered, she was in a hurry to start exploring Diana Blade—all the parts of herself she had tucked away for so many years.

There'd been another reason for her leaving Atlantic City a few days ahead of schedule: Caine MacGregor. Diana acknowledged the fact that she had wanted to put some distance between them—particularly after that last emotional interlude before she had spoken to Justin. Caine was getting to her.

A man like Caine made an art out of getting to women, she mused. Smooth one minute, rough-edged and arrogant the next. It was a hard combination to resist, and she was certain he knew it. His reputation with women had been well circulated since his college days. Circumstances, or perhaps fate, had dictated that she had heard of his exploits through her years at Harvard, and then through their mutual associates in Boston. Diana had already known too much of Caine MacGregor before they'd ever come face to face—but it'd been then that the problem had jelled.

If it had been simply a physical attraction, Diana felt she could have handled it well enough. She was used to practicing self-denial, and an affair with Caine was out of the question. They had too many ties, both in business and now in family. He was, by choice and reputation, a womanizer. She was, by choice and reputation, cautious.

But it was more than desire. He kept reaching inside her and stirring emotions she couldn't define. She wasn't ready to define them. So Diana approached the problem logically—first by admitting there was one, then by removing herself from it. Now, she considered it solved because it was past.

Launching her own practice would take all her time and energy for months to come. The prospect unnerved her, excited her, though she'd yet to find suitable office space and her list of clients was still pitifully short. She'd been alone before, she reminded herself—alone and without resources. This time, there wouldn't be an Aunt Adelaide to trade security for obedience. This time, she'd make her own decisions, her own mistakes, her own triumphs. She knew exactly what she wanted: work, challenge, success. All she needed was the chance to find it.

When Diana found a parking space quickly in the crowded lot, she considered it an omen. Things were going to work out according to plan because she refused to allow it to happen any other way.

The cold bit through her coat as she hurried across the lot. A hard, icy rain had begun to fall, making the asphalt treacherous and oddly beautiful in the glow of streetlamps. She ignored her freezing legs by imagining herself already sitting near the fire in the lounge—a glass of white wine, the soothing notes from the piano, the scent of burning wood.

The rush of warm air as she opened the door brought out a sigh of pure appreciation. After checking her coat, Diana approached the maître d'.

"Diana Blade; has Mr. Fairman arrived yet?"

The maître d' glanced quickly at the list on his podium. "Not as yet, Ms. Blade."

"When he does, would you tell him I'm waiting in the lounge?"

Diana moved toward the large, comfortable room where sofas and armchairs were scattered around a huge stone fireplace. The flames were high, fed by thick oak logs that burned with a sweet forest smell. The lighting was soft, just flickering into the shadowy corners, while the hum of conversation and laughter lent an atmosphere of a large family party. Diana spotted an empty chair, and though it was farther from the fire than she might have liked, she settled down to wait.

I'd like to take off my shoes, she mused, and curl up right here for the next hour, just watching the fire. One day I'll have a house of my own, she decided, and a room something like this. No tidy little parlor like the one on Beacon Hill, with its sedate, well-behaved fire. I'd lie on the floor and listen to it roaring, watch the shadows and lights dance on the ceiling.

With a sigh, she snuggled deeper into the chair. I'm getting sentimental, she decided with a glance at her watch. Considering the weather and traffic, there was plenty of time for a drink before Matt joined her. Even as Diana scanned the room for a waiter, one wheeled a small table beside her chair. Diana glanced at the bottle of champagne as he drew the cork. An excellent year, she thought with a twinge of regret.

"I'm sorry, you've made a mistake. I didn't order that."

"The gentleman would like to buy you a drink, Ms. Blade."

"Really?" Diana turned her head as the waiter filled a glass. When she saw him, she felt a flare of excitement she couldn't quite convince herself was annoyance. He had, after all, told her Boston wasn't such a big town. "Hello, Caine."

"Diana." Taking her hand, he lifted it to his lips, watching her eyes over it. "May I join you?"

"It seems only fair." She gestured toward the champagne and two glasses.

It occurred to her that he looked every bit the smooth, sophisticated attorney in the slate-gray suit. Then she remembered how natural he had looked in the short leather jacket and jeans. It wouldn't be wise to forget the less genteel side of him. "How are you?" she asked, lifting one of the glasses.

"I'm fine." He sat back, studying her over the rim of his glass. He remembered her dress as one she had thrown onto the bed in a rage. It was thin turquoise silk and glowed against her skin. Her choice of colors, he mused, was very much like her choice of scent. Vibrant and daring.

Diana lifted a brow as he continued to stare at her in silence. "Are you here alone?"

"Mm-hmm."

Sipping, she allowed the champagne to linger on her tongue for a moment, cold and dry. The icy rain outside was already forgotten. "I'm meeting Matt Fairman. I suppose you know him."

"Yes," Caine returned with a hint of a smile. "I know him. Thinking about working for the D.A. now that you've resigned from Barclay?"

"No, I . . ." Trailing off, she narrowed her eyes. "How did you know I resigned?"

"I asked," he answered simply. "What are your plans?"

Diana frowned at him a moment, then deliberately relaxed. "I plan to open my own firm."

"When?"

"As soon as I take care of a few details."

"Have you located an office yet?"

"That's one of the details." With a frown, she ran a finger around the rim of her glass. She didn't want to discuss her problems with Caine, certainly not her doubts. Diana shrugged as though it were indeed only a detail rather than her entire life teetering in the balance. "It isn't quite as easy as I anticipated—if I want a good location and reasonable rent." Absently, she touched her damp finger to her tongue. "I have three possibilities to check out tomorrow."

Her unconsciously provocative gesture was arousing; Caine felt something warm moving through him but checked it. There'd be other times, he promised himself. Other places. "I might know of some office space you'd be interested in."

"Really?" As she shifted toward him, her hair swung to her cheek to be quickly tossed back.

"It's on the other side of the river, within a couple of T stops from the courthouse." He drank, noting that the silk clung nicely, draping down from snug shoulders. He'd been wondering for weeks what those strong shoulders would feel like under his hands. The trouble was, he'd also been wondering how she was doing on her own back in Boston, now that she'd learned about her aunt and Justin. He'd wondered particularly after he'd heard she'd resigned her position. The concern he felt worried Caine a great deal more than the desire. "A two-story brownstone," he continued. "It's been remodeled to accommodate a reception area, conference rooms, offices."

"It sounds wonderful. I can't think why the agent I'm going through hasn't mentioned it." Unless, Diana thought as she lifted her champagne again, it was a matter of the rent being as wonderful as his description. She wasn't going to touch the trust fund her aunt had set up for her. Her aunt, she corrected silently, or Justin? In any case, she wasn't going to touch a penny she hadn't earned on her own. "How did you happen to hear of it?" she asked him.

"I know the landlord," Caine remarked as he poured more champagne for both of them.

Diana caught something in the tone and studied him thoughtfully. "You *are* the landlord."

"Very quick." He toasted her.

Ignoring the humor in his eyes, she sat back, crossing her legs. "If you own such a marvelous building, why aren't you using it yourself?"

"I am. That color suits you very well, Diana."

She drummed her fingers lightly on the arm of her chair. "Why should I be interested in *your* office?"

"My caseload's packed," he told her, so briskly businesslike it took her a moment to make the transition. "I'm going to have to turn away some clients for the simple reason that I won't be able to give them my best in terms of time and energy."

She lifted a hand, palm up. "So?"

"Interested?"

Her brows drew together as she took a deep breath. "In your clients?"

"In making them *your* clients," he countered.

Interested? she thought. She'd stand on her head in a snowdrift for the chance at a few choice cases. Diana resisted the urge to kiss his feet. She had to be practical. "I appreciate it, Caine, but I'm not interested in forming a partnership at this time."

"Neither am I."

Confused, she shook her head. "Then what are you—"

"I happen to have some space in my building you could rent. I have some cases I'm going to have to refuse or refer. I prefer to refer them." As yet, he hadn't completely worked out why he wanted to refer them to her. She was family—that's what he told himself. He let the stem of the glass twist between his fingers. "It's a simple matter of supply and demand."

Diana was silent for a long moment. Caine knew that though her eyes had that heavy-lidded, sleepy look, she was thinking carefully. He almost smiled. He rather liked the way she plotted her way from point A to point B. By God, she was even more beautiful than he'd remembered, and it had barely been two weeks.

He'd resisted the urge to call her, until tonight when he'd finally accepted he wasn't going to get her out of his head. Still, he'd told himself he was just checking on her, one family member to another. Her answering service had told him where to find her. He'd come on impulse, with the offer he'd just made her already forming in his brain. If she accepted, he'd have the advantage—and the disadvantage—of being around her every day. That was business, he reminded himself. Once they'd settled that, he'd begin on the nights. If she was indeed going to begin a discovering of Diana Blade, he wanted to be around for it.

"Caine," she began, bringing her eyes back to his. "It's very tempting, but I'd like to ask you a question."

"Sure."

"Why?"

Settling back, he lit a cigarette. "I've given you the professional one. We might add that you and I are in-laws in a manner of speaking."

"Your family obligations again," she said flatly.

"I prefer the word loyalty," he countered.

Her face cleared with a look of surprised consideration before she smiled at him. "So do I."

"Think about it." Reaching in his jacket pocket, he drew out a business card. "Here's the address; come by tomorrow and take a look."

She couldn't afford to turn her nose up at a ready-made solution. "Thank you. I will." Diana reached for the card and found her hand caught in his. Their eyes met, his confident, hers wary.

"I like the way you look in silk," he murmured, "drinking champagne with just a touch of firelight in your eyes." His thumb skimmed over her knuckles and the buzz of conversation around them vanished. "I've thought about you, Diana." As his voice deepened, intimately, she felt a thick, enervating flow of desire. Her hand went limp in his. "I've thought about the way you look," he said quietly. "The way you smell, taste. The way you feel, pressed against me."

"Don't." The word was a whisper, the whisper desire itself. "Don't do this."

"I want to make love to you for hours, until your body's weak and your mind's full of me. Only me."

"Don't," she said again and pulled her hand free. Diana sat back quickly, her breathing unsteady. How could he make her feel as though she'd been ravaged with just words? Her body was throbbing as though his hands already knew it. He knew it, she reminded herself. It was a skill he had, one he'd honed to perfection. "This won't work," she managed at length.

"No?" Seeing her struggle against need gave him a small thrill of power—and of pleasure. "On the contrary, Diana, it's going to work very well."

Diana picked up her champagne again and drank. Steadier, she brought her eyes back to his. "I need office space, and I need clients." She took a deep breath, wondering if her pulse would ever slow to a normal rate again. "I also need an atmosphere of professionalism."

"The offer was and is strictly professional, counselor," he told her with a fresh gleam of humor in his eyes. "Whether you take it or not has nothing to do with other . . . aspects of our relationship, nor will it change what's going to happen between us."

"Can't you get it through your head I don't *want* any relationship with you?" she tossed back. "I don't intend for *anything* to happen between us."

"Then it shouldn't matter if we work in the same building, should it?" With another smile, Caine set his card on the table beside her. "I find it difficult to believe you're afraid of me, Diana. You strike me as a very strong-willed woman."

Her eyes chilled. "I'm not afraid of you, Caine."

"Good," he said amiably. "Then I'll see you tomorrow. Fairman's just walked in, so I'll get out of your way." Rising, he brushed her cheek with a friendly kiss. "Enjoy your evening, love."

Annoyed, Diana watched him walk off. Damn the man for stirring her up! Snatching his card from the table, she ripped it in two. The hell with him, she told herself. He could take his office and his clients and jump in the Boston Harbor. *Afraid?* a tiny voice asked her. With a sound of frustration, Diana opened her purse and dropped the pieces of his card inside.

No, she wasn't afraid. And she wasn't going to cut off her professional nose because Caine MacGregor could drain a woman with a few soft words. She'd go to his office, Diana vowed, and drank the rest of her champagne in one impulsive swallow. And if the accommodations suited her, she'd grab them. No one was going to stop her from getting where she was going. Not even herself.

In the morning, Diana checked out two of the addresses given to her by the rental agent. The first was a positive no, the second a definite maybe. Instead of going to the third on her list, she found herself steering toward the address on Caine's business card.

She'd treat it exactly as she had treated the other potential offices, Diana reminded herself. She would be objective, consider the space and location, the rent and the condition of the building. She couldn't afford to let the fact that it was Caine's building influence her one way or the other.

With any luck, Caine would be out of the office and his secretary could show her around. The decision, Diana thought, would come more easily without him there.

She loved it the moment she saw it. The building was rather narrow, old and beautifully preserved. It had the quiet elegance found in Boston, snuggled in the midst of steel-and-glass skyscrapers. There were patches of snow on the lawn, but the tiny parking area beside it was scraped clean. Pale gray smoke puffed out of the chimney.

As she started up the flagstone walk, Diana glanced around. There was a naked oak standing sentinel in the yard, a long, trim hedge separating yard from sidewalk. The courthouse was less than a mile away. So far, Diana reflected, it's too good to be true.

The door was thick and carved. Beside it was a

discreet brass plaque: *Caine MacGregor, Attorney at Law*. It wasn't difficult for her to imagine a similar plaque below it with her name scrolled. Back up, Diana, she warned herself. You haven't even seen the inside yet. Still, as she opened the door, she remembered Caine's comment a few weeks before about fate.

The reception area was done in rose and ivory. Duncan Phyfe tables flanked a carved arm settee. Diana caught the scent of fresh flowers from the mix of blooms in a thin cut-glass vase. The floor was hardwood, gleaming and bare except for a faded Aubusson carpet. The mantelpiece was pink grained marble topped by a long oval mirror. Below it a fire crackled eagerly.

Style, Diana thought instantly. Caine MacGregor had style.

Behind a satinwood desk, a round-faced, middle-aged woman had a phone tucked between her shoulder and ear as she pounded the keys of a typewriter. The surface of the desk was buried under stacks of files, scraps of paper and legal pads. She gave Diana a wide smile, then, hardly breaking rhythm, gestured toward the settee.

"Mr. MacGregor's schedule is filled through next Wednesday," she said into the phone in a surprisingly girlish voice. "I can give you an appointment Thursday afternoon." She stopped typing long enough to dig a thick date book out from under the wreckage on her desk. "One-fifteen," she continued, shuffling more papers until she found the stub of a pencil. "Yes, Mrs. Patterson, that's his first free slot. One-fifteen on Thursday, then. . . . Yes, I'll get back to you if he has a cancellation." She scribbled in the book, pushed it aside, then began typing again. With a faint lift of brow at the procedure, Diana slipped out of her coat and laid it on the arm of the settee. "Yes, I'll be sure to tell him. Good-bye, Mrs. Patterson." The secretary paused in her typing long enough to replace the receiver and smile at Diana. "Good afternoon, may I help you?"

"I'm Diana Blade—"

"Oh, yes." The woman cut into Diana's explanation and rose, revealing that the rest of her body was as round as her face. "Mr. MacGregor said you might be dropping by today. I'm Lucy Robinson."

"How do you do?" Diana found her hand taken for a firm, brisk shake. "You seem to be very busy," Diana began. "Perhaps it would be better if I made an appointment—"

"Nonsense." Lucy gave her a maternal pat on the arm. "Mr. MacGregor's with a client, but he gave me orders to show you around. I'll take you upstairs, you'll want to see your office first."

Before Diana could explain that it wasn't *her* office yet, Lucy was moving into the hall toward a staircase. She'd left her typewriter on, Diana noticed, and wondered if she should mention it. "Mrs. Robinson—"

"Now, you just call me Lucy. We're not formal here, it's more like family."

Family, Diana thought with something like a sigh. There seemed to be no getting away from it.

The staircase rose, uncarpeted and without a curve. The mahogany rail gleamed like satin. Thinking of the desk in the reception room, Diana decided the housekeeping wasn't Lucy's province. The woman glided up the stairs like a ship in full sail. A hairpin was dangling from the knot at the back of her neck.

"There's a conference room downstairs and a small kitchen," Lucy was saying. "There're plenty of times we don't get out of here for lunch, so it's handy. Can you cook?"

"Ah . . . not very well."

"Too bad." Lucy paused at the top of the stairs. "Neither Caine nor I are anything to rave about in the kitchen." She gave Diana a long look that was as friendly as it was assessing. "He didn't tell me you were so pretty. You're a connection of his, aren't you?"

Diana took a moment to work out the conversation. "I suppose you could say so. My brother married his sister."

"Knew it was something like that," Lucy said with a nod. "Caine's office is through there, used to be the master bedroom. Yours is just down the hall here."

With a glance at the door they passed, Diana continued down the hall. "It's a lovely house," she commented. "Caine doesn't seem to have made too many changes in the structure to turn it into offices."

"Only took a couple walls out," Lucy agreed. "He said he'd had enough of working in four dull walls and brown carpeting. I say when a body spends most of their day in a place, it ought to be comfortable."

"Mmmm." Diana thought about her cubbyhole at Barclay, Stevens and Fitz. The carpet had been brown there, too, she remembered. "Have you worked for Caine long?"

"I worked for him when he was state's attorney," Lucy told her. "When he asked me if I wanted to work for him in his private practice, I packed up my desk and went. Here you are." Lucy pushed open a door, then stepped back to let Diana enter.

It was too perfect, Diana thought as she walked into the empty room. Small, but not cramped, with two sashed windows that faced east. Her heels echoed on the wood floor, bouncing to the high ceiling as she crossed to a neat, white marble hearth.

The wallpaper was silk, faded a bit but still beautiful. She could easily see the room furnished with a trim, Federal desk, a few comfortable chairs, perhaps a small Victorian love seat with a low table. She could have a shelf on the north wall for her law books. If she wanted to begin her practice with style, she would never find anything more appropriate.

"I'm surprised Caine hasn't found a use for this room," Diana thought aloud.

"Oh, he had it furnished for a while. He'd stay here instead of going home when he was working late." Lucy discovered the pin trailing onto her neck and shoved it back into place. "Then he decided it was getting too easy to spend his life here. Caine's dedicated but he's not obsessed."

"I see."

"The law library's up here," Lucy went on. "That's where he had the walls taken out. There's a powder room downstairs and a full bath on this floor. It has the original porcelain taps. Oops, there's my phone. You just prowl around." Before Diana could say a word, she was bustling back down the hall.

Lucy, Diana decided, was nothing like the sharp young secretary she had shared with two other attorneys at Barclay. There everything had been done with quiet, unshakable efficiency. And the building had had all the charm of a tomb. An aristocratic tomb, Diana reflected, but a crypt was a crypt. This, she thought as she glanced at the faded wallpaper again, was much more to her taste.

Clients could relax here, assured of a personal touch.

What few clients she could claim, she added with a rueful smile. Still, the location and the atmosphere would add to her caseload as much as her skill would. When you were selling something, it paid to sell it with flair.

Mulling over the angles, Diana went back into the hall and wandered. Surely the mahogany wainscoting was the original, she reflected. No one paneled in mahogany any longer. Opening a door at random, she found Caine's law library.

Barclay's was no more extensive, she thought with a quick flash of professional interest. A long table dominated the center of the room on which a few books were stacked. Going to one that was left open, Diana saw it was marked *State v. Sylvan.* Murder one, Diana mused, recalling the case from her studies at Harvard. It had been a volatile, splashy affair in the late seventies. National publicity, packed courtrooms and a long, emotional trial. Just what, she wondered, was Caine working on that he was digging for precedents here? Intrigued, she bent over the book and began to read. When Caine came to the doorway ten minutes later, she was engrossed.

He didn't speak for a moment, realizing that it was the first time he had seen her completely self-absorbed. There was the faintest line of concentration between her brows, and her lips were slightly parted. She'd rested both palms on the table as she'd leaned over so that the jacket of her suit—a deep, vivid red this time—fit snugly over her back. Her hair was tucked behind her ear, revealing round, fluted-edged earrings of etched gold. He could picture her in court in that outfit—or at an elegant formal tea. He knew when he stepped closer that her scent would be there, making hundreds of dark promises. Cautious, he dipped his hands into his pockets and remained where he was.

"Interesting reading?"

Diana's head jerked up at his voice, but she straightened slowly. *"State versus Sylvan."* She tapped the open book with a finger. "A fascinating case. The defense pulled everything but a rabbit out of its hat over the three-month trial."

"O'Leary's a hell of a defense attorney, if a bit flashy for some tastes." Leaning against the jamb, he studied her. The light coming in the window at her back slanted across the hands that still rested on the table.

"Still, after two appeals, he lost," she pointed out.

"His client was guilty—the prosecution put together a very carefully structured case."

Diana ran a fingertip down the opened book. "Do you have a similar one, or is this just casual reading?"

He smiled for the first time. "Virginia Day," he said, then waited for her reaction.

The sleepy look in her eyes was replaced by quick interest. "You're defending her?"

"That's right."

Diana knew the story, from scraps in the news and speculation from other attorneys. A society murder. Unfaithful husband, jealous wife, a small, deadly revolver. "You don't pick easy ones, do you?"

He only gave her a shrug for an answer. "Lucy tells me she showed you the office."

"Yes. I saw evidence of her untidiness and disorganization," Diana began with a faint smile. "As well as an almost terrifying efficiency. The only thing I didn't catch was her addiction to soaps."

"She has a tape machine at home with a timer."

Diana laughed, turning toward him fully. "You're joking."

"No. Unless you've got the better part of an hour, I wouldn't ask her about any plots."

With a chuckle, she crossed toward him. "Your building is very impressive, Caine. I'm forced to admit it's better than anything else I've looked at."

"Forced to?" he countered, discovering he'd been right about her scent.

"I'd half hoped that it would be totally unsuitable so that I wouldn't have to make a decision. Did you buy the furniture yourself?"

"Yes. I've a weakness for auctions and antique shops. And then, I don't trust anyone else's judgment when it comes to something I have to live with."

"Very sensible. My aunt had her home redecorated professionally every three years. It never reflected anything. Tell me . . ." Diana steepled her fingers, pressing them against her bottom lip a moment. "If I don't take the office space, will you lease it out anyway?"

"Not necessarily." Again he found it almost sinful that such hands should be unadorned. "I'm not willing to spend so much time in the same place with someone I'm not sure is compatible."

Her brow lifted in amusement. "And you think you and I are compatible?"

"I think you and I will deal with each other well enough, Diana. Why don't we go into the office and sit down?" As they started up the hall, Caine glanced at her. "I can have Lucy bring up some coffee if you'd like."

"No, I'm fine . . . and she has more than enough to do."

His office was large, but craftily dominated by an antique oak desk. Like Lucy's, it was loaded with files and pads, but it reflected a scrupulous organization that hers lacked. Obviously, he hadn't been exaggerating about his workload.

The fire was lit here, too, burning greedily as though he'd just added fresh logs from the woodbox beside it. Rather than black framed degrees, Caine had hung a pair of vivid watercolors that picked up the faded tints in the wallpaper. Diana took one long look around before she chose a Sheridan chair.

"Very nice," she commented as he took the chair next to her. "I won't keep you, Caine; according to Lucy your schedule's full through next week."

"I think I can squeeze in a few minutes." Drawing out a cigarette, he allowed his shoulders to relax against the back of the chair. He'd just spent an hour with a hysterical client who was too close to jumping bail for comfort. It had taken Caine three-quarters of that time to calm him down. "Since you don't find the accommodations unsuitable, it seems you have that decision to make after all."

"Yes." Diana felt the warmth from the fire reach out to her and sighed. "I'd like to take it, Caine. Of course, there's the matter of terms."

Blowing out a stream of smoke, he named an amount that was within her budget but stiff enough to absolve her feelings of accepting charity. "Lucy's agreeable to taking on your work until you're settled. Then it'll be between you and her if you want to continue that way or hire your own secretary."

Diana digested this with a nod, then took the next steps. "All right, I think we can come to an agreement.

As to the matter of your referring clients to me, I'm not sure I'm comfortable with that."

"Why not?" he countered. "Weren't you hoping for a little quick advertisement by having dinner with Fairman last night?"

Diana glared at him a moment, smoldered, then settled back. "I don't particularly like the way you put it, but yes. That's a bit different from what you're talking about."

"If you don't want them, I'll send them to someone else," he said simply. "At the moment, there are two I'd like to take, but simply can't. The Day case alone is going to require hundreds of hours."

She itched to ask for details but made herself wait. "Why would you refer them to me? You don't know if I'm any good or not."

"On the contrary. I checked you out."

"You what?"

He smiled briefly at her indignation. "You wouldn't expect me to recommend clients to an attorney unless I knew they were competent, would you? You can't have it both ways, Diana."

She let out a frustrated breath. She'd certainly backed herself into that corner. "No. All right, what two cases am I considering?"

"The first is a rape charge. The kid's nineteen. Hot head, bad reputation. He claims the girl was willing— several times, in fact—then they'd had a blowup. The next thing he knew, he was being booked. The second is a divorce case. The wife's the plaintiff. When she came in here, her left eye was swollen closed and she was going to require extensive dental surgery."

"Wife-beating," Diana said with a surge of disgust.

"Apparently. According to her, it's been going on for some time, but she's reached her threshold. He's countersuing her on desertion charges. He has the power because he has the money and as yet she's reluctant to charge him formally with battery. It's going to be a mess."

"Never let it be said you're tossing me anything simple," she murmured. "I'd like to talk to them both next week."

"Good."

"You'll draw up the contract for the lease then?"

"I'll have it ready for you Monday."

"I'll let you get back to work." With a smile, she rose. "It appears I'll have to buy myself a desk." Diana saved the moment of excitement, of anticipation, for later when she was alone. "Thank you, Caine," she added, extending her hand. "I do appreciate you giving me first shot at this."

"I'll take the gratitude now. You might not feel so amenable after you've talked to these two people." Standing, he accepted her hand. "Business concluded," he stated. "Now . . ." Lifting a finger, Caine toyed with the wide bow of her blouse. "Have dinner with me tonight."

How easily his voice could take on that soft, intimate tone, she thought, feeling her blood heat in instant response. "I think it would be much wiser if we concentrated on the business, Caine."

"At the appropriate time," he murmured. She had a preference for silk, he mused as he ran a fingertip over the knot in the bow. Soft materials, flashy colors. "My mind begins to move toward other things on cold, windy Friday nights. There's a little place in the Back Bay where the fish is fresh and the cheese isn't. In a corner there's a table the light barely reaches. You can smell the candle wax and never see anyone you know."

He gently traced the line of her earlobe, idly fingering the gold she wore there. "I'd like to take you, drink wine, hear you laugh. Then later, I'd take you home and light the fire." Slowly, his eyes skimmed over her face, lingering on each feature. Yes, he'd like to do all those things and watch the changes in those features—the softening, the opening and the yielding. He was going to do those things, he vowed as something knotted in his stomach. He understood women, didn't he? And what they looked for in a lover. "I'd make love to you until the fire was only embers."

He'd stepped closer, but she hadn't noticed. Her unsteady breath feathered over his lips. He painted a picture with his words that she could see much too clearly. He'd be a terrifying lover—the kind women longed for, even knowing they might not survive the experience. And she wanted him, more than she had known she could ever want a man. Wanted him, knowing she would just be one more woman on his list. It was this that had her backing away.

"No." But the denial wasn't as strong as she would have wished. "That isn't what I want."

"It is," he corrected. Caine pulled her into his arms and kissed her with an anger his quiet words had hidden.

Deeper and deeper he drove her, ripping response from her, exploiting the panicked excitement that had her clinging even while she told herself to pull away. With one hand, he gripped her hair, drawing her head back so that he could have his fill of her.

He thought of what separated her skin from his hands—thin wool and fragile silk. The struggle built rapidly, almost painfully, to concentrate on her mouth alone and prevent his hands from pulling aside the trim, tailored suit to find her.

The days that he had gone without touching her crowded in on him, pushing him far beyond gentleness. He knew what it was to want a woman, but not to want one with a force that bordered on violence. It wasn't his way, yet he pulled her closer and ravaged.

Her mouth seemed fused to his, ignoring her mental commands to break free. Part of her, a part that seemed to be growing stronger, was driving her to submit—and more—to demand. Wild, passionate thoughts spun in her head, threatening to unleash something that might never be completely tamed again. It was tempting, so tempting to let it free, to let it sweep her wherever the current ran. Then, with a sound that was as much from fear as anger, Diana yanked out of his arms.

"No!" she said again and her voice rose with the words. "I'm telling you this is *not* what I want."

Caine's eyes lit with something closer to fury than desire, but his voice was calm enough. He wasn't used to having his desire mixed with anger and struggled to find his normal balance. "It is," he repeated, "but I can wait a bit longer for you to admit it."

"You'll have a long wait," she snapped, then snatched up her purse with a hand that wasn't steady. "You have the papers ready Monday and I'll have a check. If you can't handle things that way, then we'll forget it."

Caine said nothing as she stormed out, didn't flinch as the sound of the slamming door vibrated through the room. A log broke apart and fell with a shower of sparks. He needed a moment to get a firm grip on his temper. He hadn't meant to lose it. Indeed, he had promised himself he wouldn't. He'd been in tense courtrooms with the opposing attorney baiting him— he'd sat in grim conference rooms at the state penitentiary with clients cursing him—and he'd had perfect control. Diana could obliterate it with a word, a look.

Something unexpected was happening; he wasn't precisely certain what it was. If he were smart, Caine mused as his brain started to clear again, he'd do exactly as she demanded. They could be colleagues, discuss current cases, dissect points of law and complain about judges.

But he wasn't smart, Caine decided, waiting for the need that clawed in his stomach to ease. He was going to have her . . . and it wasn't going to be as long a wait as she thought.

Chapter Five

*W*hy would anyone be hammering in the middle of the night? Diana asked herself as she pulled the covers over her head. The sound of thudding continued to come through loud and clear. She buried her face under her pillow as she promised herself she was going to lodge a complaint with the management.

It took less than thirty seconds for her to realize she had to give up or suffocate. Surfacing, Diana gave a disgusted sigh and opened her eyes.

Seven-thirty, she thought groggily as she glanced at the clock. Not the middle of the night, but close enough on a Saturday morning. And it wasn't hammering, she realized, but someone knocking on her door. Muttering curses under her breath, she rose and tugged on a robe.

"All right!" she shouted, belting the robe as she went. "I'm coming!" Diana pulled open the door so that it hit the security chain with a thud.

"Hi." Caine grinned through the crack. "Did I wake you?"

After one fulminating glare, Diana slammed the door in his face. There was a moment's consideration, then she unlatched the chain. He'd just start pounding again. "What do you want?" she demanded as she yanked the door open.

"It's nice to see you, too." Caine brushed a brief kiss over her lips before he walked by her.

Clamping her teeth together, Diana shut the door and leaned back against it. "Do you know what time it is?"

"Sure, it's . . . seven thirty-five," he announced after checking his watch. "Got any coffee?"

"No." Diana tightened the belt of her robe with a jerk. "It's seven thirty-five on Saturday morning," she added meaningfully.

"*Mm-hmm,*" he agreed in an absent murmur as he poked around the room.

It was far from finished. Diana was being very particular in furnishing what she considered her first real home—the first, at least, that no one could take away from her. There was an Oriental rug she'd bargained for in a secondhand store, an elegant rococo sofa that had taken a huge bite out of her savings and a French Provincial coffee table she had refinished herself in the basement of the apartment building. Her one good painting had been bought only that fall in Paris.

Caine slipped his hands into the pockets of his jeans as he studied these and the few other pieces she'd chosen. They were, like her, classy, individual and carefully placed. "I like it," he said at length. "You're putting a lot of yourself into this place."

"Shall I tell you just what your approval means to me?" Diana asked, not bothering to smother a yawn.

"Hmm. Touchy this morning," he murmured, giving her a brief glance. Three times on the brief trip from his place to hers he'd asked himself what the hell he was doing. He'd gotten three different answers, so he'd stopped asking. "Why don't I make that coffee?"

"You're not staying," Diana began as he headed for the kitchen.

"I'll be glad to. No problem."

"Caine." Be patient, she ordered herself. Don't lose your temper. "I was sleeping. Some people *like* to sleep late on Saturdays."

"Throws your whole system off," he told her as he began to root through cupboards. "That's why so many people have to drag themselves out of bed on Mondays." He found a can of coffee and began to measure it out. "Then just as they're getting the hang of it again, around comes Saturday and they blow it."

"That's very profound, I'm sure," she said as sarcastically as her groggy brain would allow. "I don't mind dragging myself out of bed on Mondays. Maybe I even *like* dragging myself out of bed on Mondays." She ran a frustrated hand through her sleep-tumbled hair. Seven-thirty in the morning was a perfect time to lose your temper, Diana concluded. "What the hell are you doing here!"

"Making coffee—unless you're hungry." Caine sent her an easy, amiable grin. "I'd fix breakfast, but about the best I can do is scramble eggs."

"No, I don't want any breakfast," Diana retorted rudely, then rubbed her fingers over her eyes. "I can't believe I'm standing here having this ridiculous conversation."

"It'll make more sense after you've had your coffee."
After switching the pot on, Caine turned back to her.
She was even lovelier now, he thought, with her hair
mussed and the faint flush of sleep still in her cheeks.
Her mouth would be warm and soft. "I think I've
already told you once that you're beautiful in the
mornings."

"Oh, sure," she muttered on a frustrated breath.

"Really." He cupped her chin in his hand as
she continued to glare at him. "It probably has something to do with your skin." With his thumb he traced
just under her jawline. There was sweetness there,
and strength. He couldn't resist trying to draw out
both. "Tell me, do you use some mystical Indian
potion?"

"I don't know any mystical Indian potions," she
managed as his thumb swept slowly back and forth.
"And your coffee's ready."

"Is it?" Caine turned and poured a cup. "Are you
having any?"

"I might as well, since it's obvious I'm not getting any
more sleep." Gracelessly, she pulled open the refrigerator and found the milk.

Smiling at her back, Caine took his cup into the living
room. He'd have to remember Saturday mornings the
next time he wanted to have her at a disadvantage. "We
have nearly the same view," he told her. "My apartment's only about a block away."

"Isn't that handy."

"Fate," he countered as he took a seat on the sofa
and made himself at home. "Fantastic, isn't it?"

"One day very soon, I'm going to tell you what you
can do with that fate of yours." She took the seat beside
him, resting her elbow on the arm of the sofa and her

head on her open palm. Letting her lashes lower, she yawned again.

Not bothering to conceal a grin, Caine settled back. "Lucy has the draft of the lease agreement. She should have it ready early Monday afternoon."

"Fine. I intend to do some shopping today. With luck I can have a few things delivered early in the week." The coffee was hot, and no better than she made herself. Diana resented knowing she'd be fully awake before she'd half finished it.

"Good idea. I'll go with you."

"Where?"

"Shopping."

"I appreciate the offer, but it's not necessary. I'm sure you have other things to do."

"Not really." Then he laughed, leaning over to tug on her hair. "Why is it I find it irresistible when you tell me to go to hell so politely?"

She gave him a long, cool stare. "I have absolutely no idea."

"I like spending time with you, Diana." At ease, Caine sat back again, but his eyes never left hers. "Why do you have such a difficult time accepting that?"

"I don't—that is, I do, but . . ." *He's doing it to me again,* she realized, and frowned into her coffee.

"There're three reasons," he continued, settling back. "We're family, we're associates . . ." Caine paused, watching her continue to frown in consideration. "And I'm attracted to you," he said simply. "Not just that rather fascinating face, but to all the quirks in your mind."

"I don't have a quirky mind," she objected, then rose. Stuffing her hands in her pockets, she paced to the window. She could accept the associates. She was trying to accept the family without completely understanding it, but . . .

"You confuse me." With a sudden passion that surprised them both, Diana whirled back. "I don't want to be confused! I want to know exactly what I'm doing, why I'm doing it, how I'm doing it. When I'm around you for too long, there're all these blank spots in my head." She gestured, then dropped her hand again. "Damn it, Caine, I can't afford to have you popping up and making me forget things every time I start to work them out."

Intrigued by the abrupt burst of temper, he watched her calmly, then took a slow sip of coffee. "Have you ever considered letting things work themselves out?"

"No." She shook her head. "I let my life drift for too many years. Not anymore."

"In other words . . ." He set down his coffee and rose, eyeing her thoughtfully. "Because of a set of circumstances you couldn't avoid, you're going to shut yourself off from whatever feelings or desires you have for me because they don't suit your current plans?"

"Yes, all right." Knowing nothing was coming out as she wanted it to, Diana pulled a hand through her hair. "All right," she repeated with a nod. "That's close enough."

"That's a very weak case, counselor," Caine commented as he walked to her. "I could poke all sorts of interesting holes in it."

"I'm not interested in your cross-examination," she began.

"We could settle out of court," Caine suggested, moving closer.

"Then there's your reputation," she added, deliberately stepping back. "You've hardly kept a low profile in your pursuit of women."

"You'll never get a conviction on circumstantial evidence and hearsay." He lifted his hands to her shoulders, massaging gently. "You've got to build your case on something stronger. Or . . ." Softly, he brushed one cheek, then the other with his lips. "You might try trusting me."

She felt the weakness creeping into her and forced herself to concentrate. "I might also try jumping out the window. Either way I risk a few broken bones."

Wishing he had some defense against vulnerability, Caine drew away. He'd meant what he'd said. He wanted her to trust him—even though he wasn't sure he could trust himself. "You want promises, guarantees. I can't give them to you, Diana. Then again," he added, "you can't give them to me, either."

"It's easier for you," she began, but he stopped her with a shake of his head.

"Why?"

"I don't know." She let out a long, weary breath. "It just seems it should be."

He clamped down on the need to just gather her into his arms until she'd forgotten she had doubts, forgotten to be logical. With an effort, he kept his hands gentle. He wasn't certain what his own motivations were; perhaps he'd never had to dissect them before. He knew he wanted to introduce her to new things—excitement, fun, passions. The knight beating down the walls for the captured princess, Caine thought ruefully. In any case, he could work out the reasons tomorrow.

"Look, get dressed, spend the day with me. The circumstances when we met weren't the best. Why don't we take a little time and see what else we can come up with?"

"I'm not sure I want to know what else we can come up with," she muttered.

"Did Justin really get all the gambling blood, Diana?"

His eyes were so appealing when he smiled. She felt herself weakening again. "I don't know. I used to think so."

"What's a lawyer but a gambler figuring odds on the law?" Caine countered. The tension was easing out of her shoulders, so he resisted the need to do any more than keep his hands light and friendly.

"The problem might be I'm not thinking like a lawyer at the moment." Then, relaxing fully, she smiled. "If I were, I could probably cite several precedents that would establish, beyond a reasonable doubt, that I should toss you out the door and go back to bed."

Caine considered this a moment, then gave a sober nod. "We could probably argue that particular point of law for several hours."

"Undoubtedly."

"Diana, I'll be perfectly honest." Still smiling, he twisted a lock of her hair around his finger. "If you don't get dressed soon, I'm going to satisfy my curiosity and find out just what you have on under that robe."

She lifted a brow. "Is that so?"

"Of course, we could negotiate." Caine ran the lapel through his thumb and forefinger. "But I feel obligated to warn you I'm fully prepared to move on this point—in the very near future."

"Since you put it that way . . . I'm going to take a shower."

"Fine, I'll just finish off the coffee." Caine watched

her walk away, letting his eyes roam down to where the robe swung across her hips. "Diana . . . just what *do* you have on under that robe?"

She sent him a bland look over her shoulder. "It's nothing," she said. "Nothing at all."

"I thought as much," Caine murmured as the door shut behind her.

Laughing, Diana pushed open the door of the shop. "I can't believe you did that. I just can't believe it!"

Caine followed her in, shutting out the cold. "It was a simple matter of truth," he said mildly. "I did see that identical lamp downtown twenty dollars cheaper."

"But did you have to tell that woman in *front* of the shopkeeper?"

Caine shrugged. "He'd be wiser to keep his prices competitive."

"He was about to have apoplexy," Diana remembered with another smothered chuckle. "I'd have died of embarrassment if I hadn't been concentrating so hard on not laughing. I'll never be able to go in there again."

"I wouldn't—until he lowers his prices."

Shaking back her hair, she narrowed her eyes to study him. "There's a great deal more Scot in you than shows on the surface."

"Thanks. Let's look around."

Diana began to browse through the antique shop, toying with a collection of pewter, loitering near a display of cut glass. "It's really your fault that we've been shopping for over an hour and I've bought nothing. I rather liked that corner chair," she mused.

"We can go back if you don't find anything you like

better. Look here." He'd found a set of dueling pistols in a display case. Highland pistols, Caine reflected as he crouched down for a closer look. Yes, he was sure of it, noting the brass stock. The butt was designed as a ram's horn and there was Celtic strapwork, inlaid with silver. Eighteenth century, he calculated, seeing that the locks of both pistols were on the right. His father would love them.

"Do you collect that sort of thing?" Diana asked, intrigued enough to stoop beside him.

"*Mmm.* My father."

"They're exquisite, aren't they?"

Caine twisted his head, giving Diana as concentrated a look as he'd given the pistols. "Not many women would look at a weapon in that way."

She moved her shoulders. "They're part of life, aren't they? And you'll remember my people were warriors." She met his eyes now. "As yours were." With a half smile, she gave her attention to the guns again. "Of course, you wouldn't find a Comanche with elegant pistols like these. Do you know what make they are?"

"They're Scottish," he murmured, finding himself more fascinated by her than ever.

"That figures." Rising, Diana gave him an arch look. "And I suppose you'll buy them and I'll end up going home empty-handed." She noticed a clerk coming their way. "While you're haggling over the price, I'm going to look around."

She left him to stroll toward the other end of the shop. Who would have thought she'd enjoy spending her Saturday poking through stores? Who would have thought she'd begin to think of Caine MacGregor as both a pleasant companion and a friend? Shaking her head, Diana ran a finger over the surface of a highboy.

The more she was around him, the easier it became to be herself. There was no need to be Diana Blade of Beacon Hill. Oh, she was tired of that socially correct, polite woman! Yet twenty years of training had left its mark. How long would it be before she wasn't surprised to hear herself shouting? *A lady never raises her voice.*

Diana gave a wistful sigh. She'd worked hard to be a lady—her aunt's conception of a lady. All the strict little rules had been drummed into her head. Even when she had questioned them, Diana had obeyed them, rebelling sporadically—and, she admitted, discreetly. Those secret jaunts she had taken had been her safety valve, keeping passions and emotions under control. You can't change a way of life overnight, Diana reminded herself. But she was making progress.

Perhaps her drive to succeed in her profession was another expression of the same rebellion. She couldn't —wouldn't—be some three-piece-suited attorney who only drew up contracts and wills. She wanted more than that. In court, she could let some of her passion slip through. There it was accepted, even considered eloquent. With words, she could fight for what she believed.

The law had always fascinated her. It was broad and narrow, succinct and nebulous. Yet she had always found it solid despite its infinite angles. She needed to succeed with it—wanted the excitement, the pressure and the glory of criminal law. Her mind came full circle back to Caine.

She wanted him, too. Diana would admit it for a moment, while he was a safe distance away. He made her feel, need—whether she wanted to or not. That sharp, sweet pleasure he could bring tempted her more each time. Perhaps that was one of the reasons she fought against it. It was frightening not to have a choice—Diana knew that better than most. She'd known desire before, and pleasure, but she'd always remained clear-headed. Not with Caine. And that's why she promised herself she'd be careful. Very careful.

She glanced back to see him examining one of the pistols. Strange that the old, beautiful weapon would look so right in his hands. There was something of the aristocracy about him, part scholar, part . . . wolf? Diana gave a quick shake of her head at the thought. She was becoming fanciful. Yet studying him, she thought she could see it. There was the intelligence in his eyes—and the danger. There was that lean, Celtic face with a mouth that promised to be fierce or gentle, depending on his whim.

A century ago he would have fought his duels with the pistols instead of words, she realized. And he would have won just as consistently. There was something not quite civilized under the polish his wealth and upbringing had given him. Diana recognized it because it was as true for herself as for Caine. The combination might equal something more savage than either of them bargained for.

Caine held the gun at arm's length, testing its weight. His eyes shifted and locked on hers—cool, dangerous. As the look held, Diana felt the needs building, experienced the violent, now familiar tug-of-war between intellect and emotion. The battle seemed longer this time, with the result less certain. By the time her

intellect took control again she was shaken and weak—
just as if his mouth had been on hers, with her body at
last knowing the pleasure of his hands.

Be *very* careful, Diana reminded herself, and turned
away again.

Still idly browsing, she examined a small upholstered
chair. A lady's chair, she mused, with its pale blue
brocade still in excellent shape. It had possibilities, she
thought as she turned over its discreet price tag. After
noting the amount, Diana decided it had definite
possibilities. As she straightened to look for a clerk, she
saw the desk.

That was it—perfect. With a low, pleased sigh, she
began to examine it. Trim, elegant cherry, the desk had
both the size and the lines she'd hoped to find. The
border of the top was carved with cockleshells, frivolous enough to make her smile as she ran a fingertip
over them. A far cry from the twentieth-century pine
that was Barclay's standard for his staff. On the drawers
were ornate brass pulls, and inside the scent of cherry-
wood lingered.

Mine, she thought quickly, possessively. Already,
Diana could see it facing the fireplace in her office—
hopefully laden with files.

"You found it, I see."

Beaming, Diana grabbed Caine's arm. "It's wonderful, isn't it? Exactly what I pictured." Her grip tightened as her other hand came to his. "I've got to have
it."

He found it rather sweet that the practical Diana
Blade would lose her head over a piece of furniture.
Lacing his fingers with hers, Caine glanced down at the
price tag on the corner of the desk, then back into her

excited eyes. "Try not to look so eager," he told her dryly. "Here comes a clerk."

"But I—"

"Trust me." Bending his head, he gave her a quick kiss. "Sure it's pretty, love," he began in a different tone. "But you have to be practical."

"Caine—"

"May I be of some assistance?"

Caine turned a friendly smile on the clerk who had shown him the pistols. "The lady likes the desk." He gave a fractional shake of his head. "But . . ."

"An exquisite piece," the clerk began, turning to Diana. He hadn't been selling for over ten years without knowing whom to play to. "Just look at this carving. No one does work like this anymore."

"It's exactly what I've been looking for." She beamed at him, all goodwill. He could already see her writing out the check.

"Diana." Caine slipped his arm around her shoulder, squeezing a bit harder than necessary. Before she could protest, he brushed a kiss over her temple. "We're going to need several other pieces, remember? The desk is very nice, but so was the other one we looked at." She opened her mouth to tell him impatiently that they hadn't looked at any other, then caught the gleam in his eyes.

"Well, yes. But I do like this one. . . ." Diana trailed off, struck with inspiration. "And that chair there," she went on, pointing at the little blue brocade.

"Another excellent choice, madam." The clerk began to think it would be a wonderful morning after all. "So right for a lady, as the desk is."

Diana sighed, letting her finger run lovingly over the

desk surface. He better know what he's doing, she thought grimly, and shot a look at Caine.

With a smile, he patted her shoulder. "But you'll need a chair for the desk as well, and the right lamp. You'd almost be able to buy both of these with the difference in price between this desk and the other."

"You're right." It took effort, but Diana gave the clerk an apologetic smile. "I'm furnishing my office, you see. And there are so many things I need."

"I understand perfectly." He began to wonder if he would lose the sale of the pistols as well. The pistols, the desk, two chairs and a lamp. . . . "We like to place the right furniture with the right people," he told her rather pompously. "Why don't you let me speak to the manager? I'm sure we could come to an agreement in terms."

"Well . . ." Caine pinched her arm to prevent her from agreeing too quickly.

Diana barely restrained herself from jabbing him with her elbow. "It won't hurt to listen, darling," she said in sweet tones that weren't reflected in her eyes.

"I suppose you're right." Caine gave her a smile as he met the killing look. "We'll just look at those lamps over there while you're talking to your supervisor," he told the clerk.

"If you lose that desk for me," Diana said under her breath as the clerk hurried toward the rear of the store, "I'll murder you."

"I'm going to save you ten percent," he said easily. "And you're going to buy me lunch." Caine stopped in front of a slim brass lamp with a fluted frosted shade. "They'll be more inclined to negotiate if they think they have to sell both of us. What do you think of this?" he asked, running a hand down the base of the lamp. "It goes nicely with the desk."

"Yes, it's lovely." She toyed with the delicate shade, then looked up at him. "You enjoy haggling, don't you?"

"It's in the blood. My father makes his living at it."

"And very well, too," Diana murmured. "I warn you," she added, "I'm going to have that desk whether he bargains or not."

"Did you want the chair, too, or were you making it up?"

"Yes, I want it." Diana laughed despite herself. "I'm not as devious as you."

"Stick around, you'll learn."

"Well." The clerk came up behind them, glowing with triumph. "I think we can come to very amicable terms."

Fifteen minutes later, Diana was outside, flushed with cold and pleasure. "How did you know he'd take off ten percent?"

"Experience," Caine claimed simply as he took her hand.

"I can see I'm going to shop with an entirely different outlook from now on." She tossed her hair back and grinned at him. "Thank you for the lamp, it was sweet of you to buy it for me. And I suppose the pistols will go to your father?"

"Mmm. He has a birthday coming up."

"You haven't bought a thing for yourself," she pointed out. "Isn't there anything you want?"

"Yes." Turning, he gathered her into his arms, pressing his mouth to hers.

The sidewalk was busy with shoppers who made their

way around them with raised brows or muffled laughter. Diana noticed nothing. The air was sharp with winter, stinging her cheeks and ruffling her hair. She never felt it. Two women stopped to stare a moment. One of them sighed and said, "Isn't that lovely?" Diana didn't hear.

Her hands had gone to his face, and through the thin leather of her gloves she could feel the line of bone, the shape of jaw. A wolf, she thought again. You never know when they'll spring.

"Priceless," Caine murmured, drawing her away.

On a long, audible breath, Diana glanced around. "You enjoy having people stare, don't you?"

Laughing, he clasped her hand again and began to walk. "It really wasn't an issue. How about lunch?"

She searched for annoyance but couldn't find it. "I suppose I owe you that."

"You certainly do. There's a place around the corner."

"Charley's!" Diana exclaimed, surprised as Caine pulled her toward the door.

"Great chili."

"Yes, I know. I didn't discover it until I was in college." They shared too many tastes, Diana thought uncomfortably as they went inside to join the warmth and the noise.

Seeing her frown, Caine ran a hand through her windblown hair. "Don't you like it here?"

"Yes, I've always liked it here." She shook her head quickly, pushing away the discomfort. "I was thinking of something else." With the mood dispelled, she gave him a smile. "How do you like your chili?"

"Hot."

Laughing, Diana shrugged out of her coat. "So do

I—so it stops just short of cauterizing my vocal chords."

The atmosphere was pure Victoriana with its gilt-edged portraits and long brass-railed bar. She'd stopped in from time to time during her college years, knowing she wouldn't run into her aunt or any of Adelaide's closer friends. They preferred the subdued elegance of the Ritz Cafe. As she took her seat across from Caine, a group at the bar began to sing lustily.

"How about some wine?" Reaching across the table, he took her hands. "It'll warm you up."

"Mmm. Something red and heavy." She allowed her hands to stay in his as he ordered. She'd enjoy his company, the closeness for the afternoon. Monday morning was soon enough to get back to business. "Tell me about your family," she asked abruptly. "The MacGregors have an almost mythical reputation in Boston."

Caine chuckled as he traced a finger over the back of her hand. "I suppose you'll have to meet the rest of them yourself to be certain how much was fact and how much was fiction. My father's a huge, redheaded Scot who'd probably still fight a Campbell to the death. He can drink a fifth of whiskey without blinking an eye, but he hides his cigars from my mother. He calls each one of us regularly to nag—for our mother's sake, he claims—about our not increasing the MacGregor line. 'Your mother longs to bounce a grandchild on her knee,'" Caine quoted with a perfect Scottish burr.

Diana laughed as the wine was brought to the table. "And what does your mother think about it?"

"My mother is a very relaxed kind of person, almost a negative of my father. He blusters, she comments. And in their own ways, they're both amazingly efficient." Unconsciously, he began to toy with the thin gold bracelet she wore on her wrist. Diana acknowledged, then tried to ignore as she had once before, the pleasure of having his hard fingers brush against her skin.

"I've only seen her lose that inherent serenity of hers a couple of times," Caine continued, half to himself. "Once, I happened to be in the hospital when she lost a patient. I'd always thought she was strictly professional, almost cold about her work. After that, I realized she simply never brought it home with her. Then when Rena was kidnapped . . ."

Seeing the change in his eyes, Diana tightened her fingers on his. "That must have been hell for all of you. Those hours of waiting, not knowing if she was all right."

"Yeah." Caine shook off the lingering anger and lifted his glass. "Then there's Alan. He's more like my mother—very calm, patient. Even after growing up with him, I'm always surprised when he loses his temper. You forget he has one until it rips out and knocks you down."

Diana let the wine run warm through her system as she watched him. "Did you fight with him often?"

"Enough," he said with a nod. "More with Rena, I suppose. We're closer in temperament. And," he murmured reminiscently, "she has a hell of a right cross."

Diana caught the hint of pride in his voice and stared. "You didn't *box* with her, did you?"

Caine grinned at the astonishment in her tone as he poured more wine. "There were times I wanted to do more than just defend myself. And by God, there were times she deserved to be knocked cold." His grin widened as Diana continued to stare at him with a mixture of horror and fascination. "No, I never slugged her, but that was mostly because she was nearly four years younger and quite a bit smaller. I really didn't consider Rena as a girl until she was about fourteen. And that," he murmured, "was quite a surprise."

He loves them all, Diana mused, and it seems so easy for him. "You had a happy childhood," she commented, then looked down at her wine. "I was jealous about that before. You know, it was strange when I went to talk to Justin. The angrier I got, the less distance there seemed to be between us." With a wondering laugh, she shook her head. "Then when I wasn't angry any longer, the distance was gone. I was furious with you, too," she added, looking up again. "For interfering—and for being right. I really detested you for being right."

"It's a bad habit of mine," he said as their chili was served. "I can't seem to break it."

She gave an unladylike snort and lifted her fork. "I'm beginning to think I'd like to come up against you in court."

"Odd, I've had that thought myself. It would be," he decided after his first bite, "an interesting match." He sent her a slow, wolfish smile. "How's your chili?"

"Excellent." Diana kept her eyes level with his as she ate. "Tell me, counselor, are you so sure you'd win?"

"I rarely lose."

"Ah, the Perry Mason syndrome." When he laughed, Diana found herself more pleased with the sound than she should have been. It was too easy to forget her own rules when she was around him. Thoughtfully, she lifted her wine and studied its warm red hue. "Perhaps it's too bad I didn't go for a position with the D.A. after all," she continued. "If I were working for the state, we'd be bound to cross swords sooner or later."

"We will anyway," he murmured. "Though perhaps not in court."

"Perhaps," she agreed as she felt the little tingles of excitement begin. She fought them down, honest enough to admit them, too wary to allow them freedom. "But I wouldn't be too sure about winning."

"It could be," Caine said slowly, "that when the verdict comes in, we'll both have won."

"A hung jury?"

He smiled again, then brought her hand to his lips. The kiss was light and confident. "Justice."

Chapter Six

After spending an evening going over the police report and all the background notes Caine had given her on Chad Rutledge, Diana was no longer sure Caine was doing her a favor with the referral. It was a messy case, with several strikes against her potential client.

He'd been anything but a model of cooperation when he'd been picked up. In fact, Diana remembered as she glanced through the file again, he'd taken a swing at one of the arresting officers. Chad had denied the rape charges, then had claimed he'd been intimate with Beth Howard, the alleged victim, repeatedly over a six-month period. She denied anything but the most passing acquaintance.

Even before the medical reports had confirmed it, he had admitted to having sex with her the night of the alleged rape. When Beth's mother had brought her to the hospital for the examination, the girl had been bruised and hysterical. Chad's knuckles had been raw. Yet Caine seemed to believe his story.

With a sigh, Diana closed the file, then rubbed the bridge of her nose. She'd form her own opinion. They'd be bringing Chad to the conference room any minute. Glancing around at the dingy green walls, Diana thought that the frivolous Saturday morning she'd had with Caine only a few days before was light-years away. This part of her job had little to do with choosing the right desk.

The heavy door with its tiny thick window opened. Diana had her first look at Chad Rutledge. "I'll be right outside, Miss Blade," the guard told her as Chad dropped down in a chair at the side of the table.

"Thank you." She dismissed him without a look, giving her attention to her client. He looked younger than in his mug shots, but he had the same toughly handsome face and thick black hair. She glanced at his eyes. They stared straight ahead—sulky, disinterested. Then she looked at his hands. They clenched and unclenched slowly, as though he were working out a pain.

You can lie with your eyes, but not with your hands. Remembering Caine's words, Diana sat back. The boy was scared to death.

"I'm Diana Blade," she said briskly. Her own nerves, she discovered, weren't as steady as she might have liked. "I'll be taking over your case, if that's agreeable with you." Chad shrugged and said nothing. "Mr. MacGregor spoke with you, and with your mother before, but his workload doesn't permit him to give your case the proper time and attention it requires to insure you of the best possible defense."

"What kind of job's a woman going to do defending a guy for rape?" Chad asked the wall he faced.

"You'll get the best defense I can give you, regardless of your sex or mine," Diana returned evenly. "You told Mr. MacGregor your story, now I'd like you to tell me."

Chad hooked an elbow carelessly over the back of the wooden chair. "Got a cigarette, babe?"

"No."

He swore halfheartedly and pulled one bent, unfiltered cigarette out of his shirt pocket. "At least he passed me to a looker." For the first time, Chad turned and faced her fully. There was challenge in his eyes as he skimmed them over her, lingering deliberately on the swell of her breast. Diana waited until his gaze came back to hers.

"Why don't we cut the crap and get down to business?"

The leer turned into a look of surprise, then annoyance. "Look, you've got the police report in that file there, what else do you want?" With a quick, nervous jerk, he lit a match, then drew greedily on his cigarette.

"Tell me what happened on January tenth." Diana drew a pad and pen out of her briefcase, then waited. "You're wasting my time, Chad," she said at length. "And your mother's money."

He shot her a furious look, then blew out a stream of smoke. "On January tenth, I got up, had a shower, got dressed, had breakfast and went to work."

Ignoring his belligerence, Diana began to take notes. "You're a mechanic at Mayne's Garage?"

"That's right." He sent her a lewd grin. "Want a tune-up?"

She could read the expression on his face by his tone

and didn't bother to look up. "Were you at the garage all day?"

"Yeah." He gave another shrug at her lack of reaction. "We had a Mercedes in for an overhaul. I do the foreign jobs."

"I see. What time did you get off?"

"Six." Chad shifted in his chair as he pulled in more smoke.

"Where'd you go?"

"I went home and had some dinner."

"Then?"

"Then I went out—cruising, you know." He smiled at her again, showing a slightly crooked front tooth. "Checking out the ladies."

"How long did you . . . cruise?"

"Couple hours." Chad drew hard on the cigarette so that the tip glowed red. "Then I raped Beth Howard."

Diana continued to write without breaking rhythm, though she felt the jolt down to the soles of her feet. "You've decided to change your plea?"

He slumped back in the chair, but his left hand was balled into a fist. "I figure I'm not going to get by with the bull I was passing before."

"All right, tell me about it." She glanced up when he remained silent. "Tell me about the rape, Chad."

"You get off hearing about things like that?"

"Did you pick her up in your car?"

"Yeah." The cigarette was no more than a fingertip in width when he finally snuffed it out. "She was walking home from the movies and I offered her a lift. We'd gone to high school together. She recognized me, so she got in. We talked for a while—just a lot of bull about what we'd been doing since graduation—drove around. I liked the way she looked, you know, so I gave her some story about needing to pick something up at the garage."

"She went with you to the garage without protest?"

His tongue flicked out quickly to moisten his lips. There was already a sheen of sweat above them. "I told her I had to pick up some tools, you know? When we got there, I jumped on her."

"And she resisted?"

"Yeah, I had to knock her around a little." He put his hand to his pocket and found another mashed cigarette. Diana saw that his fingers were trembling.

"And then?"

"Then I ripped off her clothes and raped her!" he exploded. "What the hell do you want? All the graphic details?"

"What was she wearing?"

He dragged a hand through his hair. "A pink sweater," he muttered. "Gray cords."

"You're quite sure of that?"

"Yeah, yeah, I'm sure of it. A pink sweater with this little white collar and gray cords."

"And you ripped them off of her," Diana persisted, still writing. "Tore them?"

"Yeah, I said I did."

Setting down her pen, Diana met his eyes directly. "Her clothes weren't torn, Chad."

"I said I tore them! I oughta know what the hell I did." He wiped at the dampness on his lips with the back of his hand, then moistened them again. "I was there, lady, you weren't."

"Beth Howard's clothes weren't damaged when she arrived at the hospital."

His hand was shaking visibly now. "She changed them, that's all."

"No, she didn't," Diana said quietly, "because you never ripped them. Just as you never raped her. Why are you trying to convince me that you did?"

Chad put his elbows on the table, pressing the heels of his hands against his eyes. "God, I can't do anything right."

Diana studied the top of his head and listened to the sound of his labored breathing as it filled the tiny room. "You didn't put the bruises on her face, either, did you?"

Slowly, without uncovering his eyes, he shook his head. "I wouldn't hurt Beth."

"You're in love with her?"

"Yeah. Ain't it a hell of a mess."

"Start again," Diana ordered. "This time try the truth."

With a sigh, Chad lowered his hands and began.

He and Beth had gone through high school together each hardly aware of the other's existence. They'd run in different crowds. He'd been busy promoting his tough guy image, she'd been head cheerleader. Then one day six months before, she had brought her car into Mayne's for repairs, and everything had happened at once.

They'd started dating, her father had disapproved and ordered her to break it off. They'd continued to see each other secretly.

"It was like a game, you know?" Chad laughed shakily as he tugged his hand through his hair again. "Even my friends didn't know—hers either. She'd say she was going to the library or the movies or shopping, and we'd snatch some time together. If she could get away for a couple hours at night, we'd go to the garage, seal up inside and talk, make love. I was saving up so that we could get married."

"What happened the night you were arrested?"

"We had a fight. Beth said she didn't want to go on that way anymore. She didn't care if we didn't have enough money or anywhere to live, she wanted to get married right away. She wouldn't listen. She started crying and I started yelling. Slammed my fist into the damn wall." He looked down at it as if he still expected to see the bruise. "Then she got in her car and drove off. I went out and had a few beers before I went home. Then the cops came. God, I was so scared at first, everything came pouring out."

"Why do you think she's accusing you of rape?"

"I know why." His eyes weren't challenging now, but helpless. "She smuggled a note to me through my mother. When Beth got home that night, she was still upset. Her father got on her and while they were arguing, she told him everything. He went nuts. Slapped her around, called her names. Scared the hell out of her. She says he threatened to kill both of us unless she did exactly as he said. Beth's scared enough to believe he means it." Chad let out a long breath as his hands began to work again. "Anyway, by the time her mother got home, Beth was hysterical. Her old man told the story and called the cops while her mother took her to the hospital."

"Where's the letter?"

"I got rid of it." Chad shook his head at Diana's expression. "My mom doesn't know what was in it, either, 'cause it was sealed. I don't think she'd have done it if she hadn't thought maybe something'd been going on between me and Beth for a while."

"If she writes you again, I want you to keep the letter."

"Look, I don't want her hurt anymore. When they first picked me up I was scared, you know. But I was mad, too. I thought she'd done it to punish me." He shook his head again, straightening his shoulders. "I'll take my chances on a few years in prison."

"You like your cell, Chad?" Diana demanded, pushing aside her notes to lean forward. "This is a picnic compared to the state penitentiary."

His mouth trembled as he swallowed. "I'll make out all right."

"They've got real rapists in there," she said coldly. "Murderers. Men who'd snap you in two without giving it a second thought. And how do you think Beth's going to feel knowing you're locked up in there, and why?"

"She'll be okay." A new trickle of sweat ran down the side of his face. "It won't be for that long."

"You want to risk twenty years of your life? You want her father to get away with setting you up? Grow up," she ordered impatiently. "This isn't a game anymore. You're going to go on trial for rape. The maximum sentence is life." Chad blanched and said nothing, but Diana could see the jerky workings of his throat. "You're going to have to sit in that witness chair and so is Beth. And you're both going to have to tell the court exactly what happened that night. If you lie, the two of you face perjury charges."

"If I plead guilty . . ."

Diana swooped the pad into her briefcase. "If you want to play hero because your girlfriend's afraid of her father, get yourself another lawyer. I don't defend idiots."

She started to rise, but Chad's hand shot out to take

her arm. "I just don't want to hurt her. She's awful scared."

"She's been hurt," Diana said flatly. "And she'll keep right on being scared until she tells the truth. Or maybe you don't believe she really loves you."

His fingers tightened on her arm, but Diana didn't flinch. After a moment they relaxed. "Tell me what I have to do."

A portion of the tension in her shoulders eased. "All right."

When Diana walked into the office an hour later, she was drained. Lucy glanced up, took one long look, then stopped typing. "You look like you could use some coffee."

Diana gave her a weary smile. "It shows?"

"Yep. Why don't I put some on and—" Before she could finish the sentence, the phone rang.

"That's all right, Lucy, take care of the phone. I'll go fix some." As she walked back toward the kitchen, Diana slipped out of her coat. She could still see Chad's pale, frightened face, see his hand reach to his pocket for a cigarette after he had no more left.

And what was Beth Howard feeling? Diana wondered, tossing her coat aside as she turned to the stove. If I could get to her, she began, then let out a frustrated breath. That was the last thing the D.A. or her father would permit. Chad was going to have to wait for his day in court.

Rubbing at the ache at the back of her neck, Diana stared out the window over the sink, the coffee forgotten. With any luck, she could get the truth out of Beth Howard during the preliminaries. But if the girl was that frightened of her father . . . if she wasn't in love with Chad but merely playing games . . . With a sigh,

Diana watched a bird peck at the lawn in search of food. So many ifs when a boy's life was at stake.

"Rough morning?" Caine asked from the doorway.

Diana turned. "Yeah." God, she was glad to see him, she realized. Glad to know here was someone she could talk to who would understand some of what she was feeling. "Busy?"

Caine thought of the brief upstairs on his desk but shook his head. "I could use some coffee." He slipped two mugs from their hooks and poured. "You saw Chad Rutledge this morning."

"Oh, Caine, that poor kid." Diana dropped into a chair at the small table while he added milk to one of the mugs. "He walked in doing an imitation of early Brando—some tough street hood—with fingers that trembled," she added in a murmur.

"Give you a hard time?" Caine set her coffee down as he sat across from her.

"He tried at first." With a sigh, she dragged her hair back from her face, holding it there a moment before she let her hand fall again. "Then he told me he'd raped Beth Howard."

Caine's mug paused on its way to his lips. "What?"

"He gave me a full confession," she began, warming both her hands on the sides of the mug. "Very casual, like it was something he'd decided to do because he was a little bored. The more he talked, the more his hands trembled."

Sipping slowly, Caine shook his head. "It doesn't follow."

"I didn't think so, either." Diana tried to drink but found her stomach was still tied in knots. "I pressed him for details, and that's where he fell apart. He tried to convince me he'd lured her to the garage where he works, then knocked her around and raped her."

Caine's frown deepened. "That jives with the girl's story."

"Chad said he'd ripped her clothes off . . . torn them."

"Her clothes weren't torn."

Diana gave him a thin smile. "Exactly. It was all some smoke screen he'd dreamed up so that he could protect her."

Caine leaned back and drew out a cigarette. "Tell me."

Diana began, relaying the conversation exactly, point by point. As she spoke, Caine said nothing, but watched the play of emotion on her face. She was fighting not to get personally involved, he concluded, but it was already too late.

"If everything Chad says is true," he mused when she'd finished, "the girl'll fall apart on the stand."

"I believe him. He wanted to plead guilty and keep her out of it."

Caine's look sharpened. "What did you do?"

"I bullied him out of it." Diana allowed her eyes to close for a moment. "I don't know how the trial will affect him or the girl—if it gets that far. I've got a list of their close friends. Chad seems to think he and Beth kept their relationship secret, but the chances are something slipped to someone over the last six months. They're so young." Pushing back her chair, Diana rose to pace to the window again. "Oh, God, Caine, I was so hard on him."

The princess had stepped beyond the castle walls, he thought. He'd wanted her to—even pushed her to. Yet now, seeing the raw emotion in her eyes, he had conflicting needs to draw her further out and to urge her back to safety. When the shell cracked and opened, there was always pain. He spoke carefully, trying to fit back into the role of colleague.

"Diana, you know we can't always treat clients with kid gloves. It's no less than his life at stake."

"I know." She laid her forehead on the glass a moment. "It isn't easy to realize all at once that you can be cruel, that you can calmly sit there and whip somebody down with words. He was pale, sweating, shaking—I didn't give him a dram of sympathy."

"You gave him exactly what he needed." Caine had risen without her hearing, but he didn't approach her. This time, he wasn't completely sure how. "Now you're tearing yourself apart because you did what you had to do. His mother'll give him sympathy. You have to give him the best defense, whatever it takes."

"I know." The bird was still there, bobbing along the grass determined to find what it was looking for. "Even if it means ripping up that girl on the stand. It's her father I'd like to get a hold of," she muttered. "Even when it all comes out—falsifying a police report—he's not likely to get much more than a slap on the wrist and a suspended sentence. And that nineteen-year-old boy's sitting in a cell, terrified."

Firmly, Caine suppressed the need to soothe and comfort. "He's not Justin, Diana."

She let out a long, shaky breath. "I'm that transparent?"

"At the moment."

"It was hard not to make the comparison." Lifting her hands, she hugged her arms as if seeking something solid. "He had that same tough, oddly attractive insolence that I remember in Justin as a teenager. And when I thought about him waiting in that cell, it was too easy to see how it had been for Justin. And I wondered . . ." She gave a small laugh. "I wondered if this could be another quirk of that fate of yours."

"You're going to lose your objectivity, Diana." His voice was tough and unsympathetic as the struggle went on inside him to be brother, lover, friend. "You've got no business in a courtroom without it."

"I know that." The words snapped out of her. She turned away with her jaw tensed and one hand balled into a fist. Objectivity, she thought, still unable to take those deep cleansing breaths that always kept her calm. She had no objectivity at the moment, but too many comparisons and too many regrets. She wanted to be held, soothed, and didn't dare ask because she needed to stand on her own. "I have to get it out of my system before I go back and see Chad again."

The words were low and tense, but they were the words he'd wanted to hear. Automatically Caine placed a hand on her shoulder. When the muscles there only tightened more, he increased his grip. He would have dealt with his sister the same way. That's what he told himself as he turned her around.

Wordlessly, he gathered her close, and though her arms came around him, she didn't cling. He knew she was looking for support, but not for answers. The answers she would find for herself.

In that moment, he discovered he'd never wanted her more; not just a warm, soft body against his, not just a mouth for tasting. He wanted her thoughts, feelings. He wanted to share what she was and feed back to her himself, so that there were no more boundaries and barriers. No more doubts. And while the tenderness enveloped him, his hands were gentle on her hair. Sensing something, Diana lifted her head.

His eyes met hers briefly, but she couldn't read them. He'd never looked at her that way before. Was there a question in them? she wondered. What was he asking her? Then his lips touched hers.

This had nothing to do with the other kisses they had shared. It might have been the first. His mouth was so soft. And careful, she thought dimly. Careful, as though he weren't so sure of himself. It ran through her head that he was kissing her as though he'd never kissed anyone before, this man who had known so many women.

His hands didn't press her closer but rested lightly on her back as though he would release her at the least movement. Diana was very still. Whatever magic this was, whatever reasons there were for it, she wanted it to go on. Yet it wasn't desire she felt, it was nothing so simple.

When he drew her away, they stared at each other— each as perplexed, each as moved as the other.

"What was that for?" Diana managed after a moment.

Caine dropped his arms slowly and stepped away from her. "I'm not sure," he murmured. Shaken, he walked back to the table and lifted his coffee. What the hell's going on? he asked himself, then drained the mug.

"Are you all right now?" he asked her as he turned back around.

"Yes." No, she said silently, but nearly managed a

smile. "I think I'll go up and try to work out Chad's defense. Mrs. Walker's coming in tomorrow morning." When he gave her a blank look, she added, "The divorce case you referred to me."

"Oh, yeah." Caine stared into his empty mug and wondered what was happening to his mind. "They've hooked up your phone."

"Good." Diana remained at the window, not certain what she should do. "Well, I'll go on up, then," she said, but still didn't move.

"Diana . . ." Caine looked over at her, not sure what he was going to say. Feeling ridiculous, he gave a half laugh and shook his head. "Must be something in the coffee," he muttered. "Listen, do you have anything else tomorrow beside Walker?"

"Ah—no, no appointments. I have paperwork."

"I've got to drive up to Salem and see someone about the Day case. Why don't you come with me?" He continued before she'd worked out an answer. "It's a nice drive. You can clear your head and draft out your work while I'm tied up."

"Yes, I suppose I could," she considered. "All right," she agreed on impulse. "I'd like that, I might not have too many free afternoons."

"Good. We'll leave as soon as you're done with Mrs. Walker."

They stood for a moment in a silence Diana found unaccountably awkward. It was strange, she thought, that two people who had no trouble with words should suddenly have such a strained conversation. "I should be done by ten-thirty or eleven." She searched for something else to say but found her mind a blank. "Well, I'll go up, then."

Caine nodded as he walked back to the coffeepot. When he heard her footsteps drift away, he set his filled mug back down, untasted.

What the hell is all this? he wondered again, passing a frustrated hand through his hair. When he'd asked her to accompany him the following day, he'd felt like a gangly teenager asking for a date. With a half laugh, Caine went back to the table. No, he'd never felt that lack of confidence as a teenager. He'd never felt it at all—not with women.

After lighting a cigarette, he stared at the glowing tip for several minutes. He'd always been sure of his ground when it came to the opposite sex. Enjoying women was part of it, not just as bed partners but as companions. That part of his life had always run smoothly. It was his firm intention that it continue to run smoothly. He knew, without conceit, that he didn't have to spend an evening alone unless he chose to.

Then why had he been spending so many alone lately? And when, he added thoughtfully, was the last time he had thought of any other woman but Diana?

Letting out a long breath, Caine began to sift the problem around in his mind—pull it apart, dissect it. He owed part of his success in his field to a synthesis of intellect and emotion. It had been that way since he'd been a boy: the quick, unexpected bursts of temper or passion, the long, quiet contemplations. He enjoyed puzzles—or the slow, meticulous solving of them. At the moment, however, he wasn't enjoying this one.

Uncomfortable. That was the first feeling he was able to clearly define. Thinking about Diana was making him uncomfortable, but why? He found her good company, enjoyed the flavor of their sparring matches. And he wanted her.

Caine drew hard on the cigarette, thinking of the sharp, turbulent passion he felt from her when he held her, when her mouth was avid on his. Desire didn't make him uncomfortable. He'd promised himself he'd be her lover sooner or later—and he always kept his promises.

It hadn't been desire moments ago, he reflected. Caine knew all the angles of that emotion. Neither had it been the brotherly type of affection he'd swung back to from time to time. It was Diana who didn't fit into any category, he told himself. She wasn't the easy sophisticate he was normally attracted to, nor was she the younger cousin he could show a good time.

Annoyed with himself, he rose and paced to the window. The light was thin—winter white. If she was making him uncomfortable, why had he asked her to drive to Salem with him? Because he needed to be with her?

Even as the answer ran through his mind, Caine made his thoughts back up and play again. *Need?* he repeated slowly. Now that was a dangerous word. *Want* was safer, and more understandable, but that hadn't been the answer that had sprung into his mind.

Very slowly, Caine walked back to the stove and lifted his cooling coffee. He drank, forcing himself to keep his mind blank for a moment. He thought of nothing but the faintly bitter taste of the coffee, saw nothing but the aged, exposed brick along the west wall. In the distance he heard the phone ring on Lucy's desk, then the quick rattle of the wind against the window behind him.

Good God, he thought, still staring straight ahead. Was he in love with her? No, that was ridiculous. Love wasn't a word he used, because love had repercussions.

In an angry gesture, he dumped the remaining coffee down the sink. A man didn't go for over thirty years, then suddenly, without giving it a second thought, jump off a bridge. Unless . . . unless he'd woken one morning and discovered he'd lost his mind.

He'd been working too hard, Caine decided. Too many late nights poring over other people's problems searching for answers. What he needed was an evening with a compatible woman, then eight hours' sleep. Tomorrow, he promised himself, he'd be thinking clearly again.

Tomorrow, he remembered as he headed out of the kitchen, Diana would still be there. Swearing quietly, Caine walked up the stairs.

Chapter Seven

$\mathcal{D}$iana would have enjoyed the ride more if she hadn't had the feeling something wasn't quite right. Caine was friendly enough—the conversation didn't lag or fall into awkward silences—yet she would have sworn there was something just under the surface of the camaraderie. Because it wasn't something she could define, Diana told herself she was imagining it—perhaps allowing herself to assign to Caine an echo of her own feelings.

There had been a tension in her since the previous day; one she attributed, at least in part, to her meeting with Chad Rutledge. It worried Diana that she couldn't shake it. An attorney—a good one—had to find that balance between callousness and emotional entanglement. The balance was as crucial for the client as it was for the attorney. Diana knew it intellectually but realized that the scales in this case were already tilting to one side. She could only comfort herself that the more involved she became in the technical points of the case, the less tendency she would have to compare Chad with Justin. For now, she would do exactly as Caine had suggested—clear her head and enjoy the ride.

"You didn't mention whom you're going to see in Salem," Diana began.

He had to force himself to gather his thoughts, to control the tension he was feeling. Like Diana, he told himself it was the case that had him tight, nothing personal. Personal relationships never made his stomach knot. He'd been telling himself that since the previous evening.

"Great-Aunt Agatha."

Diana let out an irrepressible sound of mirth. "You don't have to make something up," she said dryly. "You could simply tell me to mind my own business."

"Virginia Day's great-aunt Agatha," Caine said specifically, tossing her a grin. Discuss the case, he told himself. It might help him shake the feeling that he'd pried open a door for Diana, then stepped into quicksand. "She's reputed to be a very formidable lady and one who knows Ginnie better than anyone else. Unfortunately, she was ice-skating a couple of weeks ago and broke her hip. I'm going to see her at the hospital."

"Great-Aunt Agatha ice-skates?"

"Apparently."

"How old is she?"

"Sixty-eight."

"*Hmmm.* What are you looking for?"

Caine pushed the Jaguar forward in a burst of speed, passing a pickup before he answered. What was he looking for? he wondered. Even a few days before he would've been able to answer that with a shrug and a glib remark. *The case,* he thought with an annoyed shake of his head. *Keep your mind on the case.*

"The prosecution's going for murder one. The first thing I want to establish is that Ginnie carried that pistol with her habitually. If I'm going to prove self-defense, I have to get it into the jury's head early that Ginnie went to Laura Simmons's apartment to confront her husband with his current mistress, but not to kill."

"His current mistress," Diana repeated. "Apparently he had quite a number."

"The detective report Ginnie paid for a few months back indicates that Dr. Francis Day was a very busy man. He didn't do all his operating at Boston General." Caine punched in the car lighter. "If I can get the report into evidence, it should make the jury more sympathetic. . . . Then again, it gives Ginnie even more of a motive."

"So you're right back to the gun."

Caine nodded as he touched the lighter to the end of his cigarette. The conversation was easing the tightness at the base of his neck. *Not quicksand,* he thought now. He might've stepped into a puddle and gotten his feet wet, but he wasn't being sucked in. "According to Ginnie, she never left the house without it. She has a fixation about being robbed—not surprising, as she also has a penchant for wearing several thousand dollars' worth of jewelry at a time."

"Yes, and Ginnie Day hasn't endeared herself to the press or the public over the last few years," Diana remembered. "She comes across as a spoiled, selfish child with more money than class."

"True enough," Caine agreed. "But I can be grateful you won't be on the jury."

"I suppose I'm feeling a bit impatient with her type at the moment," Diana mused, shifting in her seat to face him. "Irene Walker," she said flatly. "She'd be the antithesis of Virginia Day."

"How'd it go this morning?"

"The bruises on her face haven't faded yet," Diana began, frowning at his profile. "I've never met a woman with less of a conception of her own worth. It's as if she felt she *deserved* to be beaten." With an impatient sound, Diana tried to push away the frustration she felt. "At least the friend she's staying with has convinced her to press formal charges against her husband, but . . ." Trailing off, Diana gave a quick shake of her head. "I have a feeling Irene Walker is like a sponge, simply soaking up the emotions of the people she's with. She's convinced herself—or her husband's convinced her—that she's a nonentity without him. I've recommended that she go into counseling. The divorce, and her husband's trial, aren't going to be easy for her." She let out a huff of breath that was as much astonishment as bewilderment. "She still wears her wedding ring."

"Taking it off would be the final break, wouldn't it?" he countered. "For a woman like Irene Walker."

"Do you know, they've only been married four years, and she can't remember the number of times he's beaten her?" Diana's eyes were hard and sharp for a moment. "I'm going to love getting him on the stand."

"As I recall, there were two witnesses to the last beating. You'd have him cold."

"That's exactly the way I want it. I'm hoping to get on the docket quickly, while Mrs. Walker still sees the bruises when she looks in the mirror. I think she's a woman who forgets too easily."

Caine glanced down at the briefcase next to her feet. "Is that what you're going to work on today?"

"I'm going to draft out interrogatories. I want to slap them on him right away. Between the divorce and the battery trial, I'm going to see that he gets nothing but trouble."

"Going for the jugular?"

She smiled then. "Someone told me once it was cleaner. Tell me . . ." Diana ran a fingertip over the back of the leather seat. "How long have you had this car?"

"The car?" He shot her a questioning look at the abrupt change of subject.

"Yes, I'd love to buy a new one myself."

The questioning look became a grin. Oh, she was definitely opening up, he mused. Breaking out. "A Jag?"

"One day." Diana arched a brow. "Or do you think they're reserved only for former state's attorneys?"

"I suppose I pictured you in a Mercedes—stately and elegant."

Diana narrowed her eyes. "Are you trying to insult me?"

"Certainly not," Caine replied gravely. "Can you drive a stickshift?"

"You *are* trying to insult me."

Without comment, Caine pulled over to the shoulder of the road. Curiously, Diana watched him get out, round the hood and open the passenger door. "You drive awhile."

"Me?"

He struggled with a grin at the half-incredulous, half-excited look in her eyes. Perhaps this, most of all, was what he couldn't resist—when the sophistication and intelligence were replaced by pure, simple pleasure. "If you're thinking about buying a car, you should get the feel of it first. Unless," he added slowly, "you can't drive a five-speed."

"I can drive anything," Diana stated as she climbed out.

"Fine." Caine settled back in the passenger seat as Diana switched places. "I'll tell you when to turn off."

Diana gripped the wheel with one hand and put the car into first. Under her palm, she could feel the light vibration of power, the promise of speed. After glancing in the rearview mirror, she shot back onto the highway. "Oh, it's wonderful!" she cried immediately. A check on the speedometer had her easing off the gas. "And tempting," she added with a quick laugh. "I'm afraid I'd end up defending myself in traffic court if I had one of these."

"I've always found it's just a matter of knowing you can press your foot down and go faster than anything else on the road," Caine commented.

"Yes, *knowing* you can, so that you don't." Tossing back her hair, she laughed again and passed a slower stream of traffic as the speedometer hovered just above fifty-five. "It would hardly be seemly for a public servant to zip down the road at ninety miles an hour, but it feels wonderful knowing you could." Diana shifted into fifth and kept the speed steady. "Is that why you bought it?"

"I like things with style," he murmured, studying her profile. "If they have enough power to challenge underneath the gloss." The hands on the wheel were confident, capable. Caine could picture her driving down an empty stretch of road on a summer night, the windows open, her hair flying. "You fascinate me, Diana."

She sent him a quick grin. "Why? Because I can drive a Jag without running into the median strip?"

"Because you have style," Caine countered. "Take the next turnoff."

While Diana settled into a corner of a waiting room to work, Caine walked down the hospital corridor to Agatha Grant's room. He found her in solitary splendor—pink lace bed jacket, white hair perfectly coiffed, thin cheeks tinted outrageously—with a bumper crop of magazines littering the bed. They ranged from gossip glossies to *Popular Mechanics*. As Caine entered, Agatha set down the sports magazine she'd been thumbing through to eye him appreciatively.

"About time they let someone with looks in here," she said in a raspy voice. "Come in and sit down, honey."

Caine's grin was spontaneous as he walked to the bedside. "Mrs. Grant, I'm Caine MacGregor."

"Ah, Ginnie's lawyer." Agatha nodded as she gestured to a chair. "The girl always did have an eye for a good-looking face. Looks like it's got her in a hell of a mess this time."

Caine took another pile of magazines from the chair before he sat. "I'm hoping you'll be able to help me with Ginnie's defense, Mrs. Grant. I appreciate you seeing me like this, so soon after your accident."

Agatha snorted and waved the words away. "I'll be up and around long before these doctors think," she told him, then gave a rueful smile. "Maybe I won't be doing figure-eights too soon. Okay, honey, tell me what you want to know."

"You know that Ginnie has been charged with murdering Francis Day." When Agatha gave a brisk, unemotional nod, Caine continued. "It's alleged that she went to Laura Simmons's apartment, knowing her husband was there and that Ms. Simmons was his mistress."

"The last of many," Agatha added caustically.

Caine only lifted a brow at the comment and continued. "Ms. Simmons left Ginnie alone with Day, at his request. When she returned to the apartment twenty minutes later, Day was dead and Ginnie was sitting on the couch with the pistol still in her hand. He'd been shot twice at close range. Ms. Simmons became hysterical, rushed to a neighbor's and called the police."

"Ginnie killed him." Agatha pushed at the magazines with gnarled, red-tipped fingers. "There's little doubt of it."

"Yes, she admits to that. However, she claims that Day became abusive when they were alone. At first, she says, they shouted at each other—something that had been habitual in their marriage for some time. Then she threatened to drag him through a messy divorce with all the trimmings—correspondents, detective reports—something he wanted to avoid, as he was next in line as chief of surgery at Boston General."

Agatha gave a low, mirthless chuckle. "Yes, he would have hated that. Ginnie's Franny guarded his reputation as a distinguished, dedicated man of medicine. It wouldn't have done for it to come out publicly that he was a lecher."

Caine made a quiet sound that might have been agreement or speculation. She's a tough one, he concluded, noting Agatha's composed, painted face. "During the argument," Caine went on, "he lost control, slapped her. By this time they were screaming at each other. She claims he went wild, knocked her to the floor and picked up a lamp. He told her he was going to kill her. When he came toward her, Ginnie took the gun out of her purse and shot."

Agatha nodded over the explanation, then leveled a hard look at Caine. "Do you believe her?"

Caine returned the look for several seconds before he spoke. "I believe that Virginia Day shot her husband in a moment of panic, and in her own defense."

"Ginnie's a hardheaded girl," Agatha said with a sigh. "Spoiled. We all spoiled her. And she has a mean temper, explodes easily without thinking of the consequences. But she's not cold-blooded," Agatha added with another level look. "She would not, could not, systematically plan to kill."

"In order to prove that," Caine returned, "the first thing I have to establish is why she had a gun when she went to confront her husband."

"The girl wouldn't step out the door without that pistol." With a sound of disgust, Agatha shifted against the pillows. "Ugly little thing. I'd ask her what the hell she thought she was going to do with it and she'd laugh. 'Aunt Aggie,' she'd say, 'if anyone tries to mug me, they're in for a surprise.'" Agatha let out another impatient sound. "Stupid girl had to glitter—diamonds, emeralds. She'd think nothing of walking in the Back Bay or dashing around Manhattan, dripping with jewelry—as long as she had that damn pistol."

"You often saw her with the pistol in her possession?"

"I might be staying with her for a few days, stop by her room before we went out somewhere. I'd see her put the thing in her bag. Once at a party I saw it there when she went in her purse for a compact. I gave her hell about it," Agatha added. "For all the good it did."

"Then you'd swear in court, under oath, that Virginia Day habitually carried a twenty-two pistol in her possession? And that on numerous occasions you saw her with the gun and discussed it with her?"

"Honey, I'd lie in hell's face for her." Agatha gave him a thin, icy smile. "Never could stand that two-timing jerk she married."

"Mrs. Grant—"

"Relax," she told him with something like a cackle. "In this case I can swear to it without risking my mortal soul. If Ginnie *hadn't* had the pistol with her that night, I'd have wondered what was going on."

"Good." Caine allowed himself to relax. "And we might keep it just between you and me about lying in hell's face?"

"You got it." She sent him a crafty smile then, letting her eyes scan his face. "I don't suppose you and Ginnie . . ."

"I'm her defense attorney," Caine countered as he rose. Reaching out, he grasped Agatha's surprisingly strong hand. "Thank you, Mrs. Grant."

"If I were forty years younger and on trial for murder," Agatha said slowly, "you'd be a hell of a lot more than my defense attorney."

Flashing her a grin, Caine brought her hand to his lips. "Don't kill anyone, Agatha. I find you very hard to resist."

Pleased, she let out a lusty laugh that followed him down the corridor.

Caine found Diana where he had left her, a law book balanced on one knee, a legal pad on the other. She was busy writing, apparently not affected by the inconvenience. Without speaking, he took a chair and waited for her to finish. He always enjoyed watching her this way—when she was absorbed with what she was doing and cut off from her surroundings. No guards now, he thought. He'd wanted to help her accomplish that, just as much as he'd wanted to make love with her. Now that she was well on her way to the first, he realized he couldn't afford to do the second.

There were too many undercurrents in her, he decided. Undercurrents had a habit of pulling in the unwary. Perhaps it had been the sudden realization the evening before that he could conquer her, with time, with care, that made him now too cautious to attempt it. It was time to put their relationship on one balanced level and leave it there. For her sake? he wondered ruefully. Or for his own?

When Diana stopped writing ten minutes later, she closed the book and started to stretch her shoulders before she spotted Caine. "Oh, when did you get back?"

"Only a few minutes ago. You know, not everyone is able to block out their surroundings and work the way you do."

"One of my more basic skills," Diana claimed, slipping everything back into her briefcase. "I developed it out of necessity when I wanted to tune out my aunt. How did it go?"

"Perfectly." Caine rose, picking up Diana's coat to help her into it. "Just how much trouble did you have with your aunt, Diana?"

Immediately she tensed up, closed up. He saw it and wondered if his princess in the tower idea had been closer to the mark than he'd realized. "My aunt?" Her voice was cool and emotionless.

"Yes. How much trouble did you have?"

"She was fond of phrases like 'a lady never wears diamonds before five.' "

"A great deal, obviously," Caine murmured as he picked up his own jacket. "I wonder if I was a little rough on you in Atlantic City."

Surprised, Diana stared up at him as they walked toward the elevator. "There's no need to apologize." But her body was still on guard, her voice still on edge. "What brought that on?"

"I was thinking about Agatha." Caine pushed the button for the lobby. "She doesn't particularly approve of her niece, but she loves her. It shows." He released a lock of hair that was caught at Diana's collar. "I'm beginning to think it was just the opposite in your case."

"Aunt Adelaide approved of what she thought she'd made me." With a shrug, Diana stepped out of the elevator. "It was enough. As for love, she never loved me—but then again, she never pretended to, either. I can't fault her for that."

"Why the hell not?" he demanded, angry all at once with the clarity of the picture her limited words drew.

She gave him a steady look that clearly told him he was too close. "You can't blame someone for their emotions, or for the lack of them." When she turned away, it was a signal that the conversation was ended. Unable to stop himself, he grabbed her arm. Where she was cool again, he was heating.

"Yes, you can," he countered. "You damn well can."

"Leave it, Caine. I did." When he started to object, she turned again, then stopped. "Oh, my God, look!" Diana stared through the wide glass doors.

Still frowning at her words, Caine glanced over.

Snow was falling fast and thick, already blanketing the ground. "So much for the weather forecast," Caine muttered. "This was supposed to hold off until tonight."

Diana drew on her gloves. "The drive back to Boston's going to be very interesting. And very slow," she added as they stepped outside into the full force of the storm.

"With any luck we'll be heading out of it." Caine took a firm grip on her arm as they walked across the parking lot. As he finished the statement, they looked toward the sky simultaneously. At Diana's arched-brow look, he shrugged. Both of them were already covered with snow. "We could go back to the hospital and wait it out."

"Not unless you don't want to risk driving in it."

Caine looked toward the road as they stopped by the car. "We'll see how it goes."

For the first twenty minutes, they drove through the storm with relative ease. Caine was a good driver, and the car hugged the road confidently. Diana watched the snow hurtle down, building quickly on the roadside, coating naked trees. The farther south they got, the more the wind picked up, so that snow covered the windshield as quickly as the wipers cleared it. Catching her breath, Diana saw the car in front of them fishtail and skid into the center lane before the driver regained control.

"It's pretty bad," she murmured, casting Caine a look.

"It's not good." He kept the speed slow and even, with his eyes narrowed in concentration on the road ahead. With every mile, the visibility became shorter and the road slicker. He'd lived in New England long enough to know the makings of a blizzard when he saw one. It was falling too thick and too fast. Caine was aware now that rather than heading out of the storm, they were heading into it. On the other side of the median strip, two cars slid into each other and stopped. Both he and Diana remained silent for the next twenty miles.

They'd reached the halfway point between Boston and Salem in nearly twice the time it had taken them to make the entire trip earlier. The light was failing, and when he turned on the headlights, the snow danced crazily in the beams. There were drifts of over a foot of snow on the side of the road, with more coming. An abandoned car sat crookedly where it had skidded off and stalled. Diana began to wish she'd taken Caine's suggestion of staying in the hospital more seriously.

A car passed them on the right, at a dangerous speed that had it sliding toward the Jag's front fender. Diana smothered a gasp as Caine swore ripely, forced to brake, then fight a skid. He was still cursing as he brought the car under control and took the first turnoff. "It's suicide to travel that road in this."

Diana merely nodded, busy trying to swallow her heart again.

"We'll stop off at the first hotel we come to, get a couple of rooms and wait until morning." He took his eyes off the road long enough to look at her. "You all right?"

Diana let out a deep breath. "Ask me again when I'm not praying."

Caine gave a quick chuckle, then narrowed his eyes as the bluish glare of a neon light shone mistily through the snow. "I think we're in luck."

The last slash of the "M" in Motel had gone out, but

the rest of the neon was garishly visible. "Ah, a *notel*," Diana said with a grin. "What better shelter from a storm?"

Caine glanced at the single-story compound before he pulled the car to a halt. "We won't get deluxe accommodations in this section."

"Will we have a roof?"

"Probably."

"That's good enough." She had to use both hands to push open the door against the wind. Standing outside, Diana sank to her knees, took a deep dreath and burst out laughing.

"What's so funny?" Caine demanded as he began to pull her toward a tiny building marked "Office."

"Nothing, nothing!" she shouted back. "It just feels wonderful now."

"You should have told me you were frightened." He tightened his arm around her waist as the wind shoved both of them back two steps.

Diana lifted her face to the full fury of snow. "I would have when I'd run out of my repertoire of prayers."

The door jingled stridently as Caine shoved it open. The cold, clean smell of snow was immediately blocked out by the scent of cheap tobacco and stale beer. Behind a laminated counter, a grizzled man lifted his eyes from the magazine he was reading. "Yeah?"

"We need a couple of rooms for the night." One glance told Caine it was the sort of establishment that normally rented them by the hour. Amused, he reminded himself beggars couldn't be choosers.

"Only got one." The clerk lit a kitchen match with his thumbnail and eyed Diana. "Blizzard's good for business."

Diana looked at Caine, then back out the glass door behind them. He was leaving it up to her, she realized as a little nerve jumped at the base of her neck. She remembered that last long skid. "We'll take it."

The clerk dug under the counter for a key. "That'll be twenty-two fifty," he told Caine, still holding the key. "Cash, in advance."

"Any place to get some food around here?" Caine asked as he counted out bills.

"Diner next door. Open 'til two. Your room's out and to the left. Number twenty-seven. Checkout at ten, or you owe another night's rent. Room's got free TV and pay movies."

Caine lifted a brow as he exchanged money for the key. "Thank you."

"Friendly sort," Diana commented as they fought their way toward number 27. "You did mention food?"

"Hungry?" Caine checked the number on a peeling gray-painted door.

"I'm starving. I hadn't realized it until . . ." Diana's voice trailed off as her eyes widened in astonishment.

The room, what there was of it, was mostly bed. One bed, she noted, but even that didn't alarm her in her present state. The walls were a sizzling pink to match the wild-pink-and-purple sunburst pattern of the bedspread. There was one chair and an excuse for a table, both painted in glaring white. The rug, though worn and thin, picked up the purple tint all the way to the door of what Diana assumed was the bath. And on the ceiling over the bed was a round, dusty mirror.

"Well, it isn't the Ritz," Caine said dryly, struggling not to burst out laughing at her dazed expression. He set both their briefcases on top of a white plastic-topped dresser. "But it does have a roof."

"Hmm." Diana gave the mirror a last dubious look. Perhaps it was best not to think about that for the moment. "It's freezing in here." Turning, she saw that the drapes unfortunately matched the bedspread.

Catching her expression, Caine couldn't hold back the grin. "It's a room that's at its best in the dark. I'll see if I can get the heater working."

Ignoring what she considered his odd humor, Diana sat gingerly on the edge of the bed. The only bed, she reminded herself. The only room, the only hotel. "One might think you were enjoying this whole fiasco."

"Who, me?" Caine gave the heater a quick kick that sent it roaring into life. Enjoying wasn't the word he'd have picked. Even the thought of spending the night with her in this laughable room had the knot back in his stomach. For the next few hours, he'd have to concentrate on pretending he was her big brother again if he was going to remember his resolution not to touch her. "I'll go pick something up at the diner," he continued when Diana only stared at him. His voice was casual, his nerves were raw. "There's no use both of us going out in this again. Want anything special?"

"Quick and edible." Remembering the storm he had driven through, she unbent enough to smile at him. If he was going to accept the situation with a shrug, then so would she. "Thanks. I owe you eleven dollars and a quarter."

"I'll bill you," he promised, then leaned over to give her a brief kiss before he went out.

Alone, Diana glanced around the room again. It wasn't so bad, really, she told herself . . . if you kept your eyes half-closed. And the heater was certainly working great guns now. She slipped out of her coat and looked for a closet. It seemed the room didn't run to such extravagances. Draping the coat over the dresser, Diana unzipped her boots.

The idea of a hot bath was appealing, but the prospect of undressing just to dress again had her vetoing the notion. She'd compensate by stretching out on the bed until Caine came back with dinner. Maybe some television, she thought idly, then noticed a black box attached to the side of the set. On closer examination, Diana noted it was some kind of timer fed by quarters. The pay movies, she remembered, and decided to try her luck. It might be wise to have a movie marathon; that way it'd be easier to remember they were both lawyers—a word without gender—rooming together through circumstance. She glanced over her shoulder at the bed again and felt a little bead of tension work its way up her spine. Resolutely, she turned away.

A search through her wallet found her three quarters, and what would amount to forty-five minutes of whatever movie was playing. Following the instructions printed on the box, Diana turned the set to the proper channel, fed in the quarters and twisted a knob not unlike one on a parking meter. She turned and went to the bed, stretched out in the center and gave a sigh of pure appreciation.

It was while she was busy arranging the pillows behind her head that the movement on the set caught her eye. After a classic double-take, she simply stared, open-mouthed. When the initial shock wore off, Diana lay back and laughed until her sides ached.

Good God, she thought as she hauled herself off the bed again, of all the motels in Massachusetts, they had to find one with pink walls and blue movies. Diana was just hitting the off switch when Caine walked back in.

"Do you know what *kind* of movies you get for a quarter on this machine?" she demanded before he'd shut the door behind him.

He shook himself like a dog, scattering snow. "Yes. Did you need some change?"

"Very cute." Though she tried, she couldn't keep her lips from curving. "I just wasted seventy-five cents. I wouldn't be a bit surprised to have the vice squad banging on the door."

"In this weather?" Caine countered and set two white bags down on the little table.

"Is that dinner I smell?"

"So to speak. I got quick, I won't guarantee edible." He pulled out two wrapped hamburgers. "You go first."

"Young attorney poisoned in notel," Diana murmured as she unwrapped one of the sandwiches.

"There're fries, too." He peeked into the bag. "I think they're fries. Anyway, I got some wine for now and coffee for later." He took out two capped Styrofoam cups and set them aside before he drew out a bottle. "The best I can say is that it's red."

"Oh, I don't know." Diana bit into the burger, taking the bottle in her free hand. "This was a great week. Does this place run to glasses, or do we swig straight from the bottle?"

"I'll check in the bathroom. No sudden stomach pains?" he asked as he went.

"No." She decided to risk the fries. "I don't suppose the storm's letting up?"

"If anything, it's worse." Caine came back with two plastic glasses. "Word over at the diner is more than a foot before morning."

Diana sat on the edge of the bed and took the offered

glass. "I suppose we could watch the news," she mused with a glance at the set. "If you can get the news on that thing."

Laughing, Caine sat down and unwrapped his hamburger. "Poor Diana, what a shock that must have been."

"I'm not a prude," she said primly. "It was simply unexpected." She took a sip of wine, grimaced and sipped again. "It's really not too bad."

"Best in the house," Caine told her. "A buck fifty-nine a bottle."

"In that case I'll sip more slowly. Caine, there is one small detail we should discuss."

He took a swallow of wine. He'd known it was coming. While he'd trudged through the storm, he'd decided exactly how to handle it. "I'm not sleeping on the floor."

Diana made a face at his accurate reading of her mind. "There's always the bathtub."

"Be my guest."

"It's becoming painfully clear that chivalry is dead."

"Look," he began over a mouthful of hamburger. "It's a big bed. If you don't want to put it to any better use than sleeping—"

"I certainly don't."

The sharp answer was precisely what he'd been working toward. If they kept it casual, kept it up front, they both might survive the night. "Then you sleep on one side and I'll sleep on the other," he finished, telling himself it was just as simple as that.

"I'm not certain I like how quickly you agreed to that," she murmured.

"If you'd like me to convince you otherwise . . ." he began with a slow smile.

"No. That's not what I meant." Frowning, Diana finished off her hamburger. After all, she mused, he'd driven for nearly two hours in that miserable storm. She could hardly deny him a decent night's sleep. "You stay on your side and I'll stay on mine?" she repeated.

He leaned over to fill her glass again. "If you insist. I hate to repeat myself by bringing up Clark Gable again."

"Clark Gable?" Diana repeated blankly than gave a brief laugh. "Claudette Colbert—*It Happened One Night.*"

"Exactly," he said with an amused smile. "In a similar situation they imagined something along the lines of the walls of Jericho."

She gave him a long look. "How's your imagination?"

Caine shrugged and sipped his wine. "I told you once I could wait until you admitted you wanted me." Deliberately, he lifted his eyes to hers and deliberately he baited her, knowing she'd step back. He desperately needed her to step back. "I can be very patient."

Refusing to acknowledge the challenge, Diana merely nodded. "As long as you know the rules."

"I think I'll skip the coffee and have a bath before I turn in." Standing, he ran a casual hand down her hair. "You should get some sleep; it's been a long day."

She felt a quick sense of regret, which she firmly stemmed. "Yes, I think I will. Shall I leave the light on?"

"No, don't bother. It's impossible to miss the bed in this room." He wanted to kiss her, badly, and made himself walk away. "Good night, Diana."

"Good night." Diana waited until she heard the water running, then slowly rose. *You're being a fool!* a voice told her with sharp, surprising impatience. *You know there's nothing you want more than to make love with him. To lose yourself in him.*

That's just it, Diana thought with a sudden panic. I would lose myself, or a part I'm not sure I'm ready to lose. He's different, and I don't trust him. Or myself. Diana ran an agitated hand through her hair and listened to the sound of the water running in the tub—an intimate sound. It wouldn't be the same with Caine as it might with any other man. He'd already broken down so many barriers, once the physical was down, he wouldn't stop there. She couldn't—wouldn't —allow him that kind of hold over her.

Oh, but she wanted him tonight.

Like Caine, Diana let her coffee sit, growing cold. She wanted nothing that might keep her awake and restless while she shared a bed with him. After a moment's struggle, she stripped down to her chemise. She wasn't going to be a fool and sleep in her clothes. Carefully, she climbed into bed, keeping close to the edge. She found this more difficult than she had anticipated, as the mattress sagged in the center. Swearing against what Caine would have called fate, Diana switched off the light and, gripping the side of the bed to keep from rolling out of her territory, firmly shut her eyes.

When Caine came out, the room was silent. He could see Diana's vague outline at the far side of the bed. He'd spoken easily enough about sharing that soft, warm rectangle with her, but the hot bath had done nothing to ease the need. It might be wise, he thought, to use the rest of the wine in lieu of a sleeping pill. God, he was going to need something knowing she was only an arm's length away. It would have been smarter, he told himself grimly, not to have given her his word he'd stay on his side. But he had.

Caine let the towel drop and got quietly into bed. Like Diana, he found himself sliding toward the center. Cursing silently, he shifted away.

With the habit of years, Caine drifted awake slowly and early. Something soft and warm was wrapped around him. Though still more asleep than awake, he knew by the scent it was Diana. Without conscious thought, he drew her closer, then heard her sigh as she snuggled against him. With lazy pleasure, he ran a hand down her, to where the silk gave way to skin, then back again. Diana pressed against him, her fingers sliding lazily over his back.

Murmuring her name, he touched his lips to her forehead while his hand slipped beneath the silk. They gave simultaneous sounds of pleasure, languid and soft. He thought it was no more than a dream—he'd dreamed of having her—but it had never been quite like this, so slow and easy. When he shifted, his leg slid intimately between hers while his mouth began a leisurely journey over her face. With an inarticulate murmur, Diana tilted her head back so that her lips found his.

The dream lingered . . . the kiss lingered, without pressure, as he continued to stroke and caress beneath the thin silk. There was no place for doubts in soft, drowsy light, no room for reservations on a soft, sagging mattress. He touched her, seducing both of them into sleepy surrender.

Warm, so warm, he thought, feeling the first real tug of desire as he found her breast. Diana moaned a little and arched against him. He thought he heard his own name whispered against his lips, and then her hands were moving over him.

Steeped in her, and the fantasy, he took his mouth to her shoulder, nudging the strap aside. They were as strong as he had imagined, and smooth. Following the gentle slope, he slipped the chemise down farther, pressing quiet, sleepy kisses along her arm.

He could hear her breathing now, a little fast, a little unsteady, and found that his mouth had fastened onto her breast to suckle and nibble. He was unaware of passion until the need was a hard knot in his stomach and his own breathing was labored. Her heartbeat was a hammer against his lips, which were now demanding more. And she was naked, although he wasn't fully aware that he had pulled the short length of silk from her.

Her fingers were digging into his flesh, her hips moving in a faster-growing rhythm. His name sighed from between her parted lips. For a moment, he tried to clear his head—separate dream from reality, but his body was in full command.

Then he was inside her, driven past fantasies and beyond reason.

Chapter Eight

The light was a dim, dark gray. Shuddering and stunned, Diana opened her eyes to see only shadows. She was cupped in the center of the bed, nestled beneath Caine and the thin blanket they had shared through the night. Though his face was buried against her throat, she could hear his unsteady breathing, feel the racing thump of his heart against hers. His skin was hot, and like hers, faintly damp. Her fingers were curled into his hair, and the taste of him still lingered on her lips. Her mind, like her body, felt heavy, as if wrapped in some thick, sweet honey. Tiny thrills of pleasure hummed over her flesh where she could still feel the pressure of his fingers. In one flashing explosion, her brain cleared.

With a quick sound of outrage, Diana struggled from beneath him, then rolled to the far edge of the bed. "How could you?"

Dazed, Caine opened his eyes to stare at her. "What?"

"You gave your word!" She began a furious search beneath the covers for her camisole.

Still throbbing from her, and equally stunned, Caine dragged a hand through his hair. "Diana—"

"I should have known better than to trust you," she said, pulling the brief covering of the camisole over her before she jumped out of bed. Her body tingled, her limbs felt weighted. In defense, her eyes grew stormier. "God knows why I thought you'd keep a bargain."

"Bargain?" he repeated blankly.

"You stay on your side of the bed, and I stay on mine," she reminded him bitterly. "You and your damn walls of Jericho."

He rubbed a hand over his face. "Are you crazy?"

"I must have been," Diana ranted, "to have thought you'd understand common decency."

"Now wait a minute." In the dim light, Caine could make out little more than her silhouette and the faint gleam of her eyes. But he could feel his own anger growing surely enough and pushed himself out of bed. His temper only increased as he felt a wave of weakness that came from a draining of passion.

"Don't tell me to wait a minute," Diana snapped, wrapping her hands around her arms as she started to shiver. "That was despicable."

Fury, and something he didn't recognize as hurt, sped through him swiftly. "Despicable," he repeated in an ominously low tone. "Despicable." In echoing the word, he fought for control. "You didn't appear to think so a few moments ago."

Her own fingers dug into her arms as she tossed back her head. No, she hadn't thought at all a few moments ago, only felt, only wanted. Caine had been right there—warm, gentle, seductive. "You had no right. No right!"

"*I* had no right?" he retorted. "And what about you?"

"I was half-asleep."

"Damn it, Diana, so was I!" Dragging a hand through his hair again, Caine struggled against a sensation of confused, frustrated fury. As he fought for calm, he grabbed his pants and stepped into them. Guilt was overwhelming, guilt that he'd taken her beyond the point she'd been prepared for. By doing so, he'd changed things between them just when he'd resolved to keep them stable. "Look, it just happened —I didn't plan it."

"Things like that don't *just happen.*" Shivering, she whipped the garish bedspread from the tumbled bed and wrapped herself in it.

"This did," Caine said between his teeth as he pulled on his turtleneck. Even anger couldn't completely dissipate the feeling that he had woken from some hazy dream. "I don't even know how the hell it got started," he muttered. His eyes seared into hers. He might be guilty, but he wasn't alone. "I know when it ended, and before it ended, you were just as much involved as I was."

The truth stung—and frightened. "You expect me to believe you didn't know what you were doing?" she shouted at him. "That you didn't plan for this to happen?"

On an irresistible wave of fury, he swooped up his coat and marched to her. "Why the hell don't you blame me for the blizzard?" he demanded. "Or for the fact that this—this dump," he bit off with a violent gesture of his arm, "only had one room? Or that the damn mattress sags in the middle?"

"I know exactly what to blame you for," Diana said. "And what to regret."

The room fell into deadly silence, broken only by the sound of angry breathing and the rumble of the heater. She saw something violent flash into his eyes, darkening them, narrowing them. In her own confused fury, she welcomed it—and a fight.

"You don't regret it any more than I do," Caine said softly. Without another word, he pulled open the door, letting windblown snow rush in before he slammed it behind him.

Alone, Diana gripped the spread tightly but still felt the icy chill on her skin. It was outrage, she told herself. Fury. She'd trusted him and he'd betrayed her, deceived her. He'd . . . made her feel wonderful, alive, desired.

A tiny, choked sound escaped her as she dropped onto the bed and huddled under the spread. No, no! she told herself as she balled her hands into fists. It shouldn't have happened. She'd sworn she wouldn't allow it to happen. Once she had given in to him, and to herself, it would be only the beginning. Wouldn't she be right back to having her life dominated by someone who could pick up and leave at any moment? Not again, Diana swore, pounding her fist on her knee. Never again.

She'd barely begun to discover herself for herself. Everywhere, in every aspect of her life, there was Caine. He'd been there, urging her to reconcile with Justin. He'd been there, with an answer to her professional problems on her return to Boston. Now, he was here, tempting her to strip away her last defenses, expose the last of her emotions.

Would she be any different from Irene Walker if she allowed it? Diana wondered. When a woman was ruled by emotion, didn't she open herself to whatever a man chose to give her?

Closing her eyes, she bit down on her lip. No, she wouldn't—couldn't—allow it. All of her life she'd been forced to accept whatever someone chose to give her.

It had been a mistake, she told herself, and one she could have avoided if she hadn't dropped her guard. And she had every right to be furious with Caine. He'd exploited the situation, he'd aroused her when she had been drowsy and defenseless. Diana's shoulders slumped under the spread.

He'd been no more to blame than she'd been herself, she admitted. Hadn't she been half dreaming when she'd run her hands up his naked back? Couldn't she remember, if she allowed herself to, that misty, sleepy pleasure in pressing her body against his? Somewhere in the back of her mind, she'd known exactly what she was doing, and yet she'd made no attempt to stop it. Then she had blamed Caine because it was easier than admitting she'd wanted to love him.

Squeezing her eyes shut again, Diana pressed her fingers against her brow. Oh, how could she have said those things to him? How could she have acted like some outraged hypocrite when he'd been every bit as overwhelmed as she had been?

Pushing the hair away from her face, she stared around the empty room. What now? she wondered. Apologize. Though the answer had her shifting uncomfortably, Diana's conscience held firm. She'd been wrong—dead wrong—and admitting it was the only way she could live with it. Remembering her hard, accusing words, she knew she couldn't blame him if he told her to take her apology and go to hell with it.

With a sigh, Diana rose. She'd take a hot shower, dress and wait for him to come back.

Two hours later, Diana paced the cramped little room, caught somewhere between worry and annoyance. What *was* he doing out there? she asked herself for the hundredth time. A peek through the drapes showed her that the snow was falling with the same steady speed. Again she considered going out and looking for him, and again she reminded herself that Caine had the only key. Diana wasn't going to depend on the likelihood of securing another from the clerk.

He's hardly walking around out there, she told herself as she pushed the drapes apart again. Across the lot, cars were half-buried in drifts. She could see no sign of life, only the endless blowing curtain of snow. She imagined Caine sitting over in the diner, enjoying one of his enormous breakfasts and cup after cup of steaming coffee. She grew irritated at the picture, particularly as her own stomach insisted on reminding her it was empty.

He was doing it on purpose, she decided, twitching the curtains back into place. Punishing me. The flood of guilt she'd felt earlier was now completely obliterated by resentment and basic hunger.

Infuriated, and undeniably trapped between four pink walls, Diana snatched up her briefcase and flopped in the center of the unmade bed. She wasn't going to waste time worrying about Caine MacGregor. She'd catch up on the rest of her paperwork and wait out the storm. If he *never* came back, she told herself, it was perfectly all right with her. Pulling out her pad, she poured all of her anger and frustration into her work.

Nearly another hour had passed before Diana heard the key rattle in the lock. Tossing down her pad, she continued to sit cross-legged in the center of the bed as Caine walked in. Covered with snow, and in no better frame of mind than when he had walked out three hours earlier, he glanced at her, then shrugged out of his coat.

Her initial intention of greeting him with an apology was overruled, as was her second idea of ignoring him. "Where the hell have you been?" Diana demanded.

Caine tossed his wet coat over the table. "The storm's due to continue through the afternoon," he said briefly. "There still aren't any other vacancies in this place and the next hotel's ten miles down the road."

Diana felt another surge of guilt that slipped away as Caine dropped into the chair and calmly lit a cigarette. "It didn't take you three hours to find that out," she snapped. "Didn't it occur to you that I was stuck in here?"

He gave her a glance that would have been mild had his eyes not been so dark. "Couldn't you find the door?"

On a sound of fury, Diana scrambled off the bed. "You have the only key!"

With a shrug, Caine reached in his pocket, drew it out, then dropped it on the table. "It's all yours," he told her as he leaned across to pull a small bag from his coat pocket. "I picked up a couple of toothbrushes."

She caught one as he tossed it at her. "Thank you," she said icily. She wouldn't apologize, Diana thought, if they were stuck in that dreadful little room for the next month. "Since it appears we're going to be marooned here for another night, we should discuss the arrangements."

Caine fought back anger as it boiled again. If he lost it this time, he warned himself, he would very likely strangle her. "Make whatever arrangements you like," he said coolly. "I'm going to shave." Picking up the bag, he rose.

"Just a minute." Diana pressed her hand to his chest as he started to walk by her. "We're going to get this straight."

The chill in his eyes turned quickly to fire. "Don't push me, Diana."

"Push you!" she retorted. "Do you think you can calmly walk back in here, announcing you're going to shave, after what happened this morning? Do you think I'm going to shrug this off as though it were a slight error in judgment?"

"That," he returned, taking her wrist and holding it aloft, "would be very wise."

Jerking her wrist free, she stood firmly in his path. "Well, I won't. And you're not going to shave or anything else until you hear exactly what I have to say."

"I heard all I wanted to hear this morning." Giving her a none-too-gentle shove out of his way, Caine started toward the bathroom.

"Don't you dare walk away from me!" As the final hold over her temper snapped, Diana grabbed his arm.

"I've had enough." Pushed beyond endurance, Caine spun back around, grabbing her shoulders with enough force to cause her to gasp in alarm. "I don't have to take this from you!" he shouted. "I won't calmly stand here while you accuse me of resorting to some devious plan to get you into bed with me. I don't need any plan, do you understand? I could have had you last night and half a dozen times before without any need for ploys." He gave her a quick, hard shake. "We both know it. Damn it, I wanted you and you wanted me, but you haven't got the guts to admit it."

Eyes wide with fury, Diana pulled out of his hold. "Don't tell me what to admit! This morning I was asleep—"

"Are you awake now?" he demanded.

"Yes, damn it, I'm awake now, and—"

"Good." In one swift move, Caine dragged her back in his arms and took her mouth in a hard, savage kiss. He heard her muffled sound of protest, felt her frantic struggles for freedom, but only crushed her more tightly against him.

He thought of punishment, he thought of releasing the anger and tension that had been building and building inside of him since that morning. Then he thought of how much he needed her and thought of nothing else.

With his fingers still digging into her shoulders, he pulled her away. Breathing hard, eyes locked, they stared at each other. Diana felt desire pounding in her, demanding freedom. She shook her head once, as if to deny it, but like an avalanche, it was already thundering its way down the mountain. Surrendering to all the needs raging inside her, she pulled his mouth back to hers and took what she wanted.

There were no gentle, sleepy explorations now. They were both awake, both ravenous, each feeding from the other's lips as though years had passed since they had tasted this kind of pleasure. Locked together, already struggling against the barrier of clothing, they fell onto the bed. Now fury was all passion, and passion all urgency.

Impatient, Diana dragged the sweater over his head, then made a deep, pleased sound in her throat as her hands found those tight ridges of muscle. Desperate for more, she shifted until she lay half across him, her mouth hot and avid on his. All the longings she had refused, all the desires she had suppressed, burst out in one violent explosion. She couldn't get enough of him.

She'd known almost from the first that he would be the one to unlock that last door she'd had so tightly locked.

Freedom. She moaned with the heady, painful thrill of it as she nipped into his bottom lip, wanting to drive him as she was driven. As she began to tug at the hips of his slacks, Caine groaned, rolling on top of her again, pushing her deep into the mattress.

As a lover, he was no less than she had expected— terrifying, vital, exciting. The slow, dreamy loving of the morning had been only a brief sample of what he could bring her to. A wildness was growing in her— some latent savageness she had once feared and now reveled in. With it, there were no rules. Her body was liberated, pulsing everywhere at once, arching, as fluid as hot wine as he pulled clothes from her in a frenzy. She heard a low throaty laugh that she didn't recognize as her own as he swore at the last barrier of silk.

As if driven mad by the sound, Caine crushed his mouth to hers again, probing deep as his impatient hand tore the strap of the chemise in an effort to find her. And her lips answered his with equal pressure, equal turbulence.

It seemed akin to war, this desperate demanding, this frantic challenging. His hands ran bruisingly over her and she pressed him closer, daring him to take more. She heard his ragged breathing match hers as his mouth rushed down to her breast to ravage greedily until they were both past the edge of control.

Passion was a blue-white fire now, searing skin to skin. The silk ripped again as he dragged it down, mouth and hands speeding after it, pausing only to find new, surprising points of delight.

Diana cried out when he drove his tongue into her center; but it was a low, smoky sound, trailing off into a throaty moan. Her body was damp and agile, her movements instinctive. Arousal came in titanic waves, thrusting her up, tossing her back, cresting again and again and remaining strong. As the musky scent of passion whirled in her head, she was unaware of the breathless, wild demands she uttered. Reality had spiraled down to one man, one need. In a single cloudy moment, she realized they might be one and the same. His name trembled from her lips, but whatever words she would have spoken were only a gasp as he drove her to a staggering peak.

Then his mouth was fused to hers again, and even as her arms locked around him, he took her over the final verge of reason.

Lids heavy, body sated, Diana opened her eyes and found herself staring at their twin reflections in the mirror above the bed. Experimentally, she spread her fingers over his back and watched the movement in the glass. How dark her skin looked next to his, she thought hazily. And what a contrast the colors of their hair made when side by side.

It was odd to watch his body move with the breathing she could hear and feel. She ran her hands over his back again and watched the muscles ripple under them.

Strong, she thought with another tingle of pleasure. Strong and reckless. And so, Diana thought with satisfaction, was she. Sighing, she let her fingers dive into his hair.

Caine made a quick, impatient sound and started to shift away. With a murmured protest, she tightened her arms. "Diana . . ." Lifting his head, he stared down at her, then with a brief oath he rolled away. "I didn't mean for that to happen. It sounds a little weak after this morning, but—"

"Caine." Diana shifted so that she lay across his chest again. "Don't." She pressed her lips to his until she felt his resistance ease. "I'm so sorry for the things I said this morning. No." She laid her fingertips over his mouth. "I was wrong. I knew it even when I was shouting at you, but I couldn't stop. If I'd stopped, I would have admitted that I wanted you." Letting her head fall to his shoulder, she shut her eyes tight.

On a long sigh he ran a hand down her hair. "I didn't mean to touch you again when I came back here."

She gave a quiet laugh as she pressed her face into his shoulder. "And I was going to apologize when you got back."

"Somehow," he murmured, "I think this was a much better idea for both of us. Diana." He drew her away until their eyes met again. "I've never wanted anyone," he said cautiously, "exactly the way I want you. I don't want to hurt you. Will you believe that?"

She opened her mouth to speak but knew he would never understand the doubts, the lifetime of small fears. "No questions now," she said instead, touching her lips to his again. "No reasons. This is enough."

Fighting back the need to press her for more, Caine gathered her close to his side. "For now," he agreed, and found an astonishing surge of pleasure at simply having her lie beside him. "You know," he began as his eyes drifted toward the ceiling, "I'm beginning to like this room. After all, it does have a fascinating view."

Following the direction of his gaze, Diana gave a wry smile. "The next thing I know you'll ask me for a quarter for the television." In the reflection, she saw his brow lift questioningly. "No."

"Okay." He rolled on top of her. "I've always preferred doing things myself rather than spectating."

"Caine." As he nibbled at her neck she sighed, tilting her head to accommodate him. "I hate to bring up something so mundane . . . but I'm starving."

"Mm-hmm." He ran his lips along her jawline as he traced the shape of her shoulders.

"Seriously starving."

"How seriously?"

"As in willing to risk another one of those hamburgers."

"That sounds more like desperately," he murmured, and with a groan, he rolled aside. "Okay, I'll go buy you another slice of ptomaine."

"Thanks," she said dryly, but sat up as he did. The moment the contact between them had been broken she'd felt some of the tension return. Foolish, she told herself. She was a grown woman and lovemaking was part of life. Wasn't it as simple as that? "I'll go with you."

"It's nearly as bad out there as it was yesterday," he began as he reached for his pants. Why did he have the need to gather her to him again, reassure her, and himself, that nothing had changed? Everything had changed.

"I'd like to get out of this room for a while." Diana

let her eyes scan the walls. "The pink is beginning to close in on me."

Caine tugged his sweater on. "All right, we'll eat at the scene of the crime." He lifted a brow as Diana examined her torn chemise. "I suppose you're going to say I owe you one of those."

"I could take you to small claims court," she declared, slipping into her blouse without it.

Caine gave a burst of appreciative laughter and grabbed her around the waist. "It'd be worth it just to hear your opening statement." As she tipped her head back to smile up at him, he was drowned in a wave of emotion too strong to resist. Desire, he told himself almost desperately. Just desire, and desire was easy. "Oh, again," he murmured before his mouth found hers.

The fingers that had been buttoning her blouse stilled, her head tilted back in surrender, but her mouth met his aggressively. Through her parted lips came a sound of quiet, lingering pleasure that seemed to skip into the core of him and expand. Once before she had felt that strange, soft texture to his kiss. It was infinitely gentle but seemed to demand more than passion. When he released her, Diana was forced to blink to clear her vision.

"Caine?" she said wonderingly. Was he telling her or asking her? Or was it something within herself that was questioning?

He took a step back, not quite comfortable with the feeling of uncertainty she could bring out in him. "I'm in the position of telling you to get dressed again." He smiled, but his eyes remained intense. "Otherwise, I won't be responsible if you go hungry."

With fingers that weren't completely steady, she

finished buttoning her blouse. "I think you like confusing me," she muttered. "I'm not very good with moods, and yours never stays the same."

"Sometimes they keep me guessing, too," he said half to himself. When she looked at him, her eyes direct, her mouth unsmiling, he consciously fought off the tension. She was vulnerable, he was responsible. He wasn't at all sure he could handle the responsibility. Play it light, Caine warned himself. Keep it simple. "Maybe I like keeping you in the same mental state I'm in myself."

Diana gave him one of her long, deliberating looks before she smiled. "Do I confuse you, Caine?"

He met the look as he slipped into his shoes. Something vibrated in the room that both of them took great care not to notice. "I'm going to decline to answer that question at this time."

"Interesting." Diana pulled up the side zipper of her skirt. "That leads me to assume that I do." She slipped into her coat. "I think I like that."

"You'll need your gloves," was all he said as he pocketed the key again.

The minute they stepped outside, Diana sucked in her breath at the force of the wind and the cold. The flakes were smaller, she thought as she hooked her arm firmly through Caine's, but the wind was going to make the drifts treacherous even after they stopped falling. Still, as she looked around, even the battered little motel seemed rather clean and picturesque in its coating of white.

"It's not such a bad little place," she decided while they struggled against the wind.

"It looks even better after you've been out in this for a while."

There was a path of sorts through the four feet of snow, where other tenants of the motel had fought their way to the diner and back again. Struggling through this, Diana still found herself buried up to her knees. When she stumbled, she tightened her grip on Caine.

"Sure you don't want to go back in and wait?" Caine shouted close to her ear.

"Are you kidding?" She lifted her face, squinting against the flying snow. "Is that it?" With her free hand, Diana pointed to the dim outline of a building with floodlights making an eerie glow against the unrelieved white.

"Yeah. The place's been doing a thriving round-the-clock business since the blizzard. Our 'notel' has all thirty-five rooms booked."

"You're a fount of information. God," she went on before Caine could retort, "I could eat *two* hamburgers."

"We'll discuss your suicidal tendencies when we get inside. Here, watch out." He tightened his grip on her arm to guide her. "There're steps buried somewhere under here."

Breathless, Diana stumbled through the door when Caine pushed it open. The heavy scent of frying grease hung in the air, overlaid by tobacco smoke and something that might have been bacon. Several scratched, plastic-coated tables were scattered around the long room, with vinyl-cushioned chairs and paper placemats. Along the rear of the room was a counter, with many of its stools already occupied by diners, most of whom turned to stare at the newcomers.

In a covered dessert dish on the far end were a few tired-looking doughnuts, while behind the counter several signs announced the specials. It seemed the meat-loaf dinner, with gravy, was only three forty-nine.

"Back again?" The chubby waitress behind the counter sent Caine a cheery smile. "And brought your lady. Come on in and warm up, honey," she told Diana. "You could use some coffee, I bet."

"Yes." The dingy atmosphere was forgotten in the face of the friendly greeting. "I'd love some."

"Coffee's on the house as long as it lasts," the waitress proclaimed, setting two cups and saucers on the counter. "I'm Peggy. Sit yourselves down and drink up. Hungry?"

"Starving," Diana said recklessly as she slid onto a stool beside a young, nervous-looking man with fly-away hair and glasses.

"We got fresh vegetable soup today," Peggy told Diana as she handed out thin, handwritten menus. "Been simmering all morning."

"Sounds fine," Caine decided with a glance at Diana.

"Mmm, for a start," she agreed, chewing on her bottom lip as she studied the menu.

"Two soups, Hal," Peggy shouted through the opening that led to the kitchen. "The BLTs are popular today," she added.

"Yes, all right, that sounds good." Closing the menu, Diana reached for a plastic container of cream as the waitress called out the rest of the order.

Caine leaned over, nuzzling at Diana's ear as he whispered into it. "Eat all you want. We're going to stock up on candy bars and canned sodas to get us through tonight."

"You're so resourceful," she murmured, turning her head so that her lips met his.

"You folks from out of town?" Peggy asked as she refilled the coffee cup of the man beside Diana.

"Boston," Caine told her, taking out a cigarette. At the small sound of distress from beyond Diana, he glanced over.

"Charlie here was on his way to Boston, too," the waitress said, giving the young man's hand a sympathetic pat. "With his bride." She tucked a strand of tumbling blond hair behind her ear and sent Caine a quick wink.

"Supposed to be our honeymoon," Charlie muttered, staring into his coffee. "Lori took one look at the room and started to cry."

"Oh." Diana gave him an understanding smile. "I suppose it isn't exactly what she was looking forward to."

"We had reservations at the Hyatt." He lifted his head then, pushing his glasses back on his nose. "Lori's very sensitive."

"Yes, I'm sure." At a loss, Diana met the helpless stare. He looked, she thought, a bit like a little boy who hadn't found his bicycle under the Christmas tree. "Well, ah, perhaps you could make the room a little more—romantic."

"That room?" With a snort, Charlie turned back to his coffee.

"Candles," Diana suggested with sudden inspiration as the soup was set on the counter. "Maybe someone has some candles."

"Well sure, I got a few in the back room," Peggy said helpfully as she gave the counter a swipe with a rag. "Your bride like candlelight, Charlie?"

"Maybe," he mumbled, but his frown became more thoughtful.

"Of course she does." Diana stirred her soup while she watched him. "What woman doesn't like candle-light? And flowers," she added. "Now where can we get flowers?"

"Got a few plastic poinsettias in the back," the waitress cut in, getting into the spirit. "We use 'em at Christmas, you know. Really brightens up the place."

"Wonderful."

"You think she'd like that?" Charlie asked Diana.

"I think she'll be very touched."

"Well . . ."

"I'm going to go dig them up." Wiping her hands on her apron, the waitress headed toward the back.

Charlie leaned forward to look at Caine. "What do you think?"

Struggling to keep his face grave, Caine glanced up from his soup. "I bow to a lady's opinion on matters such as this."

"Go ahead, kid," someone down the counter advised. "Give it a shot."

"Yeah." Abruptly decisive, he rose as Peggy came back, arms full. "Yeah, I will."

"Here you go, honey." She passed over three candles in plastic holders and several sprays of plastic poinsettia with large, glittered red bows. "You go fix up your honeymoon suite. Your little bride's gonna feel better."

"Thanks." He grinned at Diana as he stuffed as much as he could into his pockets. "Thanks a lot."

"Good luck, Charlie," Diana called after him, then swung back to her soup. Catching Caine's look, she arched a brow. "I think it's very sweet."

"I didn't say a word."

"You didn't have to, you cynic." When he only

grinned at her, Diana turned back to her lunch. "Eat your soup. Some of us," she announced loftily, "appreciate romance."

"Should I buy another bottle of wine?" he murmured, raising her hand to his lips.

"Don't you dare." Laughing, she leaned over to kiss him.

Chapter Nine

*B*ehind her desk, with the fire noisily burning, Diana worked at a steady pace. She'd given the Walker case meticulous research, careful thought and long hours. The story, Diana felt, was almost too typical. Irene Walker had been young, fresh out of college when she had married. She had never worked—her husband hadn't permitted it. Instead, she'd kept his home and fixed his meals, dedicating her life to his comfort. Now that their marriage was breaking up, Irene had no income, no training for outside work, and a small infant to care for. Diana was going to see to it that she was compensated for the four years she had worked as housekeeper, cook, laundress and hostess. The fact that Irene had been the victim of wife-beating only made Diana more determined that her client receive justice.

And I've got him, Diana thought with a sense of

satisfaction as she closed a law book. I've got George Walker cold. Now if Irene would just stick with those counseling sessions . . .

Shaking her head, Diana reminded herself not to get in any deeper. She was already much too emotionally involved in the Chad Rutledge case; she couldn't afford to spread herself too thin.

Chad, she thought, pressing her hands to her tired eyes a moment. Things were not moving as smoothly there as they were for Irene Walker. Diana had already called over half the names on the list he had given her. So far, none of the people who knew him, or Beth, could give her any corroborating evidence. I need something, she thought, tossing down her pen in disgust. I have to go into court with something more than Chad's story and my own feelings. If I can't break Beth's story on the stand . . .

Leaning back in her chair, Diana stared up at the ceiling and thought through the case as it stood. A pretty, well-liked college student, blond, delicate—privileged family background. A tough, street-wise hood with a belligerent attitude and a quick temper. If it came down to his word against hers, Diana had little doubt what the outcome would be. Then there was the medical evidence—Beth's condition when she was admitted to the hospital emergency room, Chad's admission that he had been with her. No, she couldn't go into court with nothing more than a story about star-crossed lovers and expect it to work. Especially when she wasn't too sure of her client.

Oh, he was innocent, Diana mused, frowning. She didn't doubt that. But she was very much afraid that he'd lose his head if she started pressing Beth too hard.

Diana wouldn't put it past him to stand up in open court and make a full confession.

With a weary sigh, Diana reminded herself that she still had the last few names on Chad's list to contact. There were two Diana only had first names on, which meant a trip to the university and a bit of detective work. Who said law was all books and briefs? she thought, then managed a smile for the first time in more than an hour. This was what she wanted.

"Diana?"

Distracted, she glanced up. "Oh, yes, Lucy."

"I'm going to leave now, unless you need me for something." She found a thread hanging from the sleeve of her dress, wrapped it around two fingers and snapped it off. "Caine checked in about half an hour ago. His meeting ran over, but he said he'd be stopping in here before going home."

"Oh." Diana didn't notice Lucy's speculative look as she gazed into the fire. "No, Lucy, you go on home. I have some things I want to finish up here; I'll lock up."

"Want me to make some coffee before I leave?"

"Hmm? Oh, no." Smiling, Diana glanced back up. "No, thanks. Have a nice evening."

"You have one, too," Lucy told her with a last meaningful look before she walked back down the hall. "Tell Caine I left his messages on his desk."

"All right." Diana pondered the empty doorway for a moment. Lucy, she decided, was a great deal shrewder than that placid round face indicated. And I thought I was being so discreet, Diana thought with a rueful smile, working very calmly, very practically, day after day with Caine just next door. Keeping up the polite, friendly tone of colleagues in the same office building.

But it seemed Lucy had caught something—a look, a gesture, a tone of voice. Diana wondered just how realistic she had been in thinking she could keep her relationship with Caine strictly between them. She wondered suddenly why she had felt it necessary.

Thoughtful, Diana rose to walk to the fire. It was burning low now, the coals piled high and glowing red. Stooping, she added a log and watched it catch with violent snaps and hisses. Perhaps her emotions had been like that: low and carefully banked until Caine had come into her life. Now she knew what it was to feel wild bursts of flame, fast, crackling heat. It was impossible, always impossible, to remain calm and controlled when she was with him.

It frightened her—he frightened her—Caine and his ability to make her want him with unrestrained and uninhibited passion. Caine and his ability to make her think of him at odd moments.

Emotion seemed to come so effortlessly to him, and the demonstration of emotion. She'd been trained for so long to suppress passions, control surges of feelings. Even now that she was freer with them, more comfortable with some of them, she was poles apart from Caine. She'd never have his spontaneity or his careless self-ease. Diana envied him while not completely understanding him. She did understand, however, that Caine had the ability to dominate by force of personality alone.

Perhaps that was why she had insisted that they keep their relationship on a firmly professional level during business hours. Diana was struggling to hold on to those hours, to keep them as a time where she still had complete control over her actions, her feelings and her thoughts.

I'm going to fall in love with him if I'm not careful, Diana thought with a flutter of panic as she watched flames lap greedily around the new log. If I haven't already. Catching her bottom lip between her teeth, she tried to think clearly but found, as she found so often when she attempted to reason her feelings for Caine, that logic had no place there.

She wished there was a way to escape him. She wished he would come back so that she could be with him.

With a sound of annoyance, she turned away from the fire, then heard the phone begin to ring in his office. A glance at her watch told her it was nearly six and the offices were officially closed. Shrugging, Diana walked next door to answer.

"Caine MacGregor's office," she said as she fumbled for the switch of the lamp.

"Is he back yet?" a booming voice demanded.

"No, I'm sorry." Diana picked up a pen as she slipped into Caine's chair. "Mr. MacGregor's out of the office. May I take a message?"

"Where is that boy!" Exasperation came clearly over the wire—so clearly Diana held the receiver a few inches from her ear. "I've been trying to reach him all afternoon."

"I'm sorry, Mr. MacGregor's been in a meeting. Shall I have him return your call tomorrow?"

"Damn boy never could stay put," the voice muttered.

"I beg your pardon?"

"Hah!"

Diana's brow lifted at the exclamation. "I'd be happy to take your name and number, and any message you'd care to leave."

"This isn't Lucy," the man stated suddenly. "Where the devil's Lucy?"

Amused, and just a bit perplexed, Diana put down the pen. "Lucy's gone for the day. This is Diana Blade, I'm Mr. MacGregor's associate. Is there something—"

"Justin's sister!" the voice interrupted in a bellow. "I'll be damned. Now, I've been wanting to have a few words with you, girl. I'd heard you'd set up business there with Caine."

"Yes," she began, growing more bewildered. "Do you know my brother?"

"Know him?" There was an explosion of laughter. "Of course I know him, girl. I let him marry my daughter, didn't I?"

"Oh." As the light dawned, Diana sat back in Caine's chair. Hadn't she been warned about Daniel MacGregor? "How do you do, Mr. MacGregor. I've heard a great deal about you."

"Hah!" he snorted. "You don't listen to that son of mine, do you?"

She laughed, idly toying with the phone cord, not even aware that she was relaxing for the first time in eight hours. "Caine speaks very highly of you, Mr. MacGregor. I'm sorry you've missed him."

"Hmm, well . . ." He paused as the germ of an idea formed in his mind. "So you're a lawyer, too, are you?"

"Yes, I was at Harvard a few years behind Caine."

"Small world, small world. Rena tells me you favor Justin. Good stock."

"Ah . . . well . . ." A little nonplussed by the phrase, Diana trailed off.

"Good blood's an important thing, don't you know?"

"Yes." Brows knit, she shook her head. "I suppose."

"No supposing to it, girl, got to keep the line strong. I've a birthday coming up," he announced suddenly.

"Congratulations."

"I didn't want any fuss," he began breezily, "but my wife loves a party. Don't like to disappoint her."

"No," Diana agreed with the beginnings of a smile. "Of course you wouldn't."

"She misses the children, you know. Yes, off they went in every direction," he said in a pained voice, "and not a grandchild between them."

"Ah . . ." Diana said again for lack of anything better.

"A few grandchildren to spoil in her winter years," he continued with a sigh. "But when do children think about their parents' needs, I'd like to know?"

"Well—"

"Anna wants all the children here next weekend," he interrupted. "A family gathering. We'll want Caine to bring you along."

"Thank you, Mr. MacGregor, I—"

"Daniel, girl; after all, you're part of the family now." Back in Hyannis Port, Daniel gave a crafty, secret smile his careless words disguised. "The Mac-Gregors look after their own."

"Yes, I'm sure," she murmured, then laughed. "I'd love to come for your birthday, Daniel."

"Good. That's settled, then. You tell Caine his mother wants him here Friday night. A lawyer, too, hmm? That's handy, aye, that's handy. Friday night, Diana."

"Yes." Baffled again, she stared at Caine's desk. "Good-bye, Daniel."

Diana hung up with the odd feeling she had agreed to something entirely different from a weekend visit to

Hyannis Port. Sitting back in Caine's chair, she thought over the conversation. It seemed, she mused, that Daniel MacGregor was every bit as eccentric as his legend claimed.

I wonder how much Caine's like him, Diana reflected idly. Certainly, Caine had inherited his father's skill in dominating a conversation when he chose. And there was something in the laugh. If she hadn't been thrown off by the way he'd bellowed into the phone, Diana would have recognized the MacGregor patriarch by the faint Scottish burr. And what in the world was all that business about good stock?

Hearing the front door open and close, Diana rose from the desk to walk to the top of the stairs. "Hi."

As he tossed his coat over a hook on the hall rack, Caine glanced up. "Hi."

Recognizing the fatigue in the single syllable, Diana went down to him. "How'd it go?"

He flexed his back. "Three hours with Ginnie Day."

Diana needed no more. Lifting her hands, she began to knead at the tension in his shoulders. "You don't like her," she said as Caine let out a quiet sigh.

"No, I don't." He stretched under Diana's hands. "She's spoiled, selfish and vain. She has all the courtesy of a nasty five-year-old."

"It must have been a very pleasant afternoon," Diana murmured.

Caine chuckled and lifted his hands to her wrists. "I don't have to like her, I just have to defend her. It would be easier if Ginnie herself wasn't the D.A.'s best weapon. There's no way to make a jury see her as a sympathetic victim. Most of the emotion'll be on the prosecution's side, while I'll have to stick with straight law."

"You're going for a bench trial," Diana said as she studied his face.

A hint of a smile played on his mouth as he nodded in agreement. "I'd rather present this kind of case to a judge. When I told Ginnie, she had a temper fit and fired me." Laughing at Diana's outraged expression, Caine cupped her face in his hands, then kissed her. "For about five minutes," he added. "She might be rude, but she's not stupid."

"It sounds to me as though it would have served her right if you'd taken her dismissal at face value and walked out."

"Would you?" he countered.

Her face relaxed into a smile. "No, but I'd have been tempted. Are you through for the day?"

"Yeah." His hand slipped to her waist to gather her closer. "Absolutely."

"Then get your coat," she ordered on an impulse that would have surprised her even weeks before. "I'm going to take you to dinner. Then," she added as she took her own coat from the hook, "I'm going to lure you back to my place."

"Really?"

"Really. Here." Gravely, Diana handed him his coat.

Caine studied her, noting that her eyes were as confident as her words. He touched her hair. "I like your style, counselor."

"MacGregor," Diana returned as she buttoned his coat herself, "you haven't seen anything yet."

Flushed with cold and gripping an icy bottle of champagne, Diana opened the door of her apartment. Dinner had relaxed them, slowly nudging the demands of their work, the people whose lives and problems dominated so many of their hours, to the back of their minds. Now they were just a man and a woman with lives and problems of their own.

"I'll get the glasses," Diana stated, handing the bottle to Caine.

He glanced idly at the label. "I suppose you intend to fuddle my mind with champagne."

Coming back with two tulip glasses, she smiled. "I'm counting on it. Why don't you open that?"

Lifting a brow, Caine tore the foil from the top of the bottle. "I might not be as easily manipulated as you think."

"Oh, no?" Diana set down the glasses, then slid her hands up the front of his suit jacket, slipping it off him. This time, she would test her own strengths and his weaknesses. This time, she wouldn't be led, she would lead. "An open and shut case," she murmured, nibbling lightly on his bottom lip as she loosened the knot of his tie. When she felt his arms come around her, she drew back, keeping her lips inches from his. "How about that champagne?"

"Didn't we drink it already?"

On a low laugh, she caught the end of his tie between her thumb and forefinger. "No." Slowly she slipped the tie off and tossed it aside. She felt a quick thrill at her own action and wondered if he felt it, too. "Why don't you pour it?" she murmured, undoing the first three buttons of his shirt. "I'll put on some music."

As she crossed the room, Diana stepped out of her shoes. She turned the stereo on low, so that the soft, bluesy number was hardly more than a whisper. When she dimmed the lights, Caine glanced over to see her slip off her pine-colored blazer.

"I think," he said quietly as he filled both glasses, "I'm in trouble."

With a laugh that was more of a sigh, Diana walked back to him. "You *are* in trouble." Taking a glass, she sat on the sofa and pulled him down beside her. "Deep trouble," she added, nipping at his ear.

"Maybe I should put myself entirely in your hands." Turning his head, he found her mouth with his, but she allowed him only the briefest taste.

"My thoughts exactly." She touched the rim of her glass to his, then drank. "Have I ever told you," she began while her fingers began to toy with the curls that fell over his ears, "that you fascinate me?"

"No. Do I?" Caine lifted his hand to draw her closer, but Diana caught it in hers.

"Yes." Slowly, she brought his hand to her lips, pressing them against his palm. Tonight she would be all woman, only a woman. "Strong hands." Watching him, she kissed his fingers one by one. "One of the first things I noticed was that they weren't the soft lawyer's hands I'd expected. I wondered how they'd feel on my skin." She laced her fingers with his as she brought the glass to her lips again.

Feeling desire sprint through him, Caine stared at her. She was mesmerizing him. He hadn't known she could, and the feeling left him burning and oddly weak. In the dim light, her eyes were dark and mysterious with that seductively languid look that had stirred him from the first moment. "Diana—"

"Then there was your mouth," she went on, letting her eyes linger on it. "Such a clever mouth." She brushed her lips lightly over his. "The first time you kissed me I couldn't think of anything else. Exciting," she whispered, tilting her head back ever so slightly when he sought to deepen the kiss. "And at times indescribably gentle. I could spend hours and hours doing nothing more than kissing you." But she shifted away to watch him over the rim of her glass as she drank champagne.

"Diana." Caine's voice was low as he cupped his hand around her neck to drag her closer.

Diana kept herself a frustrating distance away with a hand against his chest. More time, she thought greedily. She wanted more of it to explore a power she'd just discovered. "I like your eyes," she murmured. She could feel his need—the tension of his need—in the fingers that pressed into her skin. He had always driven her quickly beyond control each time he touched her. This time, she thought, flushed with power, this time she would drive him, then revel in the consequences. "I like the way they darken when you want me. I can see it." She spread her fingers over his chest. "I love seeing it. You're tense." As she felt his heart thud furiously beneath her palm, her own speeded up to race with it. "You should drink your champagne and relax."

Throbbing, he met the challenge in her eyes. Through sheer force of will, he lightened his grip and fought back the first flood of need. She fully intended to drive him mad, and knowing it Caine determined to regain some of the control. "You know that I want you." Keeping his eyes on hers, he lifted his glass. "You know that I'll have you."

"Perhaps." She smiled again as she shook back her hair. Her scent seemed to drift out from it to wrap around him. The wine bubbled icily over her tongue, adding to the sense of power. "I think of storms when I think of making love to you." Leisurely, she ran a fingertip down his shirtfront, then back up to loosen the rest of the buttons. "That morning on the beach when I first kissed you—that little motel room in the blizzard. Storms and wind. Strange, I never get a picture of anything placid." She ran her hand over his naked chest, slowly, very slowly, moving down.

"If you want me to be gentle," he managed as the soft touch of her fingers tore at his restraint, "this isn't the way."

"Did I say that's what I wanted?" she asked with a low laugh. Watching him, Diana took his mouth again, this time allowing the kiss to linger.

His mind clouded—her taste, that wicked scent. Setting his glass aside, Caine plunged both hands into her hair and dove into the kiss. More, was all he could think. He had to have more and still more. Her mouth had softened seductively under his with a deceptive surrender he would have recognized had his mind been as clear as his need. Her quiet sigh seemed to race through him. With his breathing already labored, Caine reached for the zipper at the back of her dress.

Not yet, not yet, Diana ordered herself as her thoughts began to swim. Passion was lapping at her, as the flames had lapped at the log she had watched in the fire. But she wanted something more tonight. She wanted a few more moments of control, she wanted to prove to herself that she could erase every layer of the polish that lay over the dangerous inner man. She had once feared what would happen if the two of them came together without that safe gloss of sophistication. Now, she craved it. Feeling her dress begin to loosen, she pulled away.

"Diana . . ." Caine began on a half groan, but she evaded him and rose.

"Don't you want any more champagne?" she asked, pouring more into her glass.

In one quick move, Caine stood and grabbed her arm. "You know damn well what I want."

Another thrill of excitement sped into her, reflecting in her eyes even as she kept her voice low. "Yes." Impulsively, she drained her glass, then held it lightly by the stem. "Such a civilized drink. Take me to bed," she invited softly as she stepped closer. "And make love to me."

As the last thread of control snapped, Caine yanked her against him. The glass fell to the rug to roll across the room. "Here," he demanded. "And now." With his mouth crushed on hers, he dragged her to the floor.

His hands seemed to be everywhere at once, seeking, finding, while his mouth stayed fused to hers. Diana gloried in it and, while her body wildly responded, sought to drive him further from reason. Her mouth was aggressive, meeting his with a hot, hungry fury that could only partially show the needs raging inside her. She would feed on his desire even while she stoked it.

She pulled the shirt from his back, and when his mouth freed hers briefly, nipped her teeth lightly into his shoulder. With a half-muffled oath, Caine crushed her roaming mouth with his again.

He peeled the dress from her, quickly, hands rushing to possess the soft, naked skin. Desire was stabbing at him, painful, forcing him to hurry where he would have lingered, driving him to take quickly what he would have savored. He thought he had felt need before, but it had never been like this: unreasonable, unmanageable. A rough urgency took the place of skill when he at last had her naked beneath him.

Her taste filled him, but he hadn't the patience to

relish it. Her soft, rounded curves entranced him, but he hadn't the will to wait. The whispering music seemed to be all bass and drums now—pounding, taunting. And her scent promised no more and no less than the passion of the woman beneath him.

He swore once, with no knowledge of whom, of what he was cursing, then took her with a force that had her gasping out his name. Half-mad, he covered her mouth with his and swallowed the sounds. He drove her, drove himself, until there was only blinding heat and whirling colors. Caine knew nothing else; savagely he wanted nothing else. Caught in the vortex of the storm, they moved like lightning until, shattered, their strength drained. With something like pain, he felt sanity return.

Still, he couldn't move. His breath came in gasps he couldn't control as he buried his face in her hair. He was trembling, he realized with a small sliver of fear. No woman, no passion had ever made him tremble. What was she doing to him? he wondered as he tried to catch his breath. The last thing he clearly remembered was pulling her to the floor. All the rest came back as sensations. They might have lain there for ten minutes or for hours. He couldn't think—even now that the desperation had passed, he still couldn't think.

Had he hurt her? His mood had been close to violent when he had dragged her to the floor. There'd been something about the way she had looked at him when she'd told him to take her to bed. In that moment, he had lost all sense of time and place, and any tenuous claim he'd still held to being civilized.

Dazed, Caine lifted his head to look down at her. Her eyes were open, though those long, heavy lids were nearly closed. Her skin held that flushing glow of passion just spent. Incredibly, he felt fresh desire ripple through him. Dropping his face back into her hair, he took deep, steadying breaths. He needed a minute, he told himself. Good God, he needed a minute or he'd take her like a madman again.

Sighing his name, Diana ran her hands over his back. There'd been something in his eyes just then she'd never expected to see: vulnerability. She didn't feel power now, but wonder—and something else that made her touch gentle and soothing. No, she hadn't expected to see vulnerability, and even as she nestled closer, Diana wasn't certain she wanted to see it. Seeing it in his eyes only forced her to face her own weakness. Slowly, and with uncanny success, he'd scaled the walls of her defenses. And things weren't so simple any longer.

She could feel his heartbeat begin to level. The breath that feathered over her ear grew steadier. When Caine lifted his head again, his eyes weren't giving away any secrets.

"You're a surprising woman, Diana." He kissed her but touched the lips still warm and swollen from his gently.

"Why?" she murmured.

"All that passion, all that . . . fire," he added as his lips continued to nibble at hers. "In a woman who takes such pains to be dignified . . . cool . . . unflappable. You wanted to make me crazy, didn't you?"

She sighed as his mouth began to feast at her throat. Triumph glowed through her. She'd discovered one more part of Diana Blade. "I did make you crazy."

His lips curved into a smile against her skin before he lifted his head again. "We'll have that champagne now before I take you to bed, as you asked." Caine poured more wine into the glass on the table, then offered it to her. "We seem to have lost the other glass—we'll share this one."

Sitting up, Diana drank, letting the champagne pour through her with its icy effervescence. "It tastes even better now," she said with a smile as she passed it back to Caine.

"As you said . . ." He sipped as his eyes answered her smile. "A civilized drink. Diana . . ." Caine lifted his hand to her hair and watched his fingers comb through it. "Stay with me at my place this weekend. We can eat in, watch old movies." The grin touched his eyes again. "Neck on the sofa. We're both going to be under a lot of pressure these next few weeks with the cases coming to trial. It might be the last time for quite a while that we'll have the time to be together like this."

The picture he painted was tempting—and frightening. One more step into intimacy. Yet even as a part of her wanted to back away, she couldn't resist. "I can't think of anything I'd rather . . . Oh!" With a look of comic dismay on her face, Diana paused in the act of reaching for the glass. "Your father."

With a chuckle, Caine took another sip before he handed her the wine. "What does my father have to do with it?"

"He called. I forgot completely." Her eyes laughed at him as she drank. "I believe we've received a royal summons."

"Oh?" Caine traced a fingertip over the slope of her shoulder, enjoying how dark and smooth her skin looked in the dim light.

"For the weekend," Diana elaborated, laughing out loud when his fingertip stopped.

"The weekend?"

"Your father's birthday." Leaning across him, Diana filled the glass again. "He doesn't want a fuss, you know, but your mother—"

"Of course." With a wry smile, Caine shifted so that he could replace his fingertip with his lips. "My quiet, undemanding father would simply treat his birthday as any other day of the year. He'll only go through the noise and fuss and bother of a party for my mother's sake. And naturally, he'll only accept presents because she expects it. If it were up to him, the day would pass without a thought."

Chuckling, Diana struggled to concentrate on his words as he began to lightly caress her. "Well, it was very sweet of him to include me in the invitation; I'm looking forward to it. I enjoyed talking to him, even if the conversation was a bit confusing."

"How?" He carefully traced her ear with his tongue, taking the glass from her as it began to slip through her fingers.

"Mmm. . . . He said something about Justin and I being from good stock. Caine . . ." As he caught the lobe in his teeth, Diana lost track of her own words.

"What else?" he murmured, pleased that her voice was unsteady and her body pliant against his. It wasn't often he could coax her into this kind of surrender. Sweet and complete. This time they would go slowly and he would savor every moment.

"Something—something about it being handy we were both lawyers." Somehow she was cradled in his arms, with his lips roaming her face, his hands roaming her body. And she was helpless.

"I see." And he did. With a sigh that was half-amused, half-exasperated, Caine continued to take her deeper. "Did Rena ever mention to you how she and Justin happened to meet?"

"What?" Drugged, her eyes already closed, her body already melting, she couldn't understand the question or the need for it. "No, no, she didn't. Caine, make love to me."

He wondered how she would react when she learned his father had engineered Rena and Justin's meeting in the hope of their making a match. He wondered how she would react when she learned Daniel MacGregor wasn't above applying a bit of genial pressure to secure what he might feel was a suitable mate for his youngest son. And that she would fit the bill very nicely. He wondered, as his lips toyed with hers, how he felt about the idea himself.

But it wasn't a night for thinking, Caine decided as her arms wound around his neck. It wasn't a night for thinking at all.

Rising, he lifted her and took her to bed.

Chapter Ten

$\mathcal{D}$iana sat behind her desk, staring into the fire that crackled and spat in the hearth. In her hand she held Irene Walker's file. Numb, she stayed perfectly still as a log crumbled quietly in the grate.

She couldn't believe it—even running the conversation over again in her mind, Diana couldn't believe it. Charges dropped, divorce action canceled.

Glancing down, Diana studied the neatly written check that had been left on her desk. Paid in full—thanks, but no thanks. Irene Walker had decided to give her husband another chance.

He's so sorry that he hurt me. Diana could hear Irene's soft, apologetic voice as if her former client were still in the room. *And he promised it would never happen again.*

Never happen again, Diana thought, letting the file folder drop. No therapy, no counseling, but it would never happen again. Irene Walker lived in a dream world, Diana thought grimly, and the next nightmare might leave her with more than a few loose teeth and some bruises.

Damn! After pounding a fist on the folder, Diana sprang up. Damn, we had him cold! All that paperwork, all those hours of careful research for nothing. And sooner or later Irene would be back to go through the whole ugly mess again. Diana stared at the neat manila folder, knowing every word it contained. Yes, she would be back. It was inevitable.

Frustration drove Diana to whirl to the window to glare out at the frost-tipped branches. How could Irene love him after everything he'd done to her? How could she want to go back, take her child back, to that kind of life? It would be like living with an open keg of gunpowder. Dear God, Diana thought on a sigh of disgust, what a pitiful, wasted life.

At the knock on her door, she continued to stare out at naked trees and frosty hedges. "Yes?"

"Bad time?" Caine asked, crossing the threshold but coming no farther into the room.

With her temper heating up, Diana turned. "Irene Walker," she said, moving to the desk to pick up the file. "She just reconciled with her husband."

Caine glanced at the file, then up into the smoldering fury in Diana's eyes. "I see."

"How could she be such a fool!" Diana tossed the folder back down and strode to the fire. "He calls her up, sweet-talks her into seeing him, then, with a few roses for good measure, convinces her he's a new man."

Caine walked to the desk, noting the check. "Maybe he is."

"Are you joking?" Diana demanded, spinning around. "Why should a few weeks' separation make any difference? She's left him before."

"She'd never started divorce proceedings before," he pointed out. "That and the threat of a criminal action might make a man do some serious thinking."

"Oh, he's done some thinking," she agreed bitterly. "No, he didn't want to face a possible jail sentence, he didn't want to lose his wife and child *and* a good portion of his income, but what's he done to deserve clemency? Nothing!" Dragging a hand through her hair, Diana paced the room. "He won't agree to therapy or marriage counseling. She says he doesn't want to make their problems public. *Public,*" she repeated, gesturing broadly. "She burns the meat and he beats her in the backyard in front of the neighbors, but he doesn't want to discuss the problem with a professional. And she . . ." Diana trailed off, dropping into a chair. "She's hopeless. How can she love someone who periodically uses her for a punching bag?"

"Do you think she loves him?" Caine countered. "Do you really believe love has anything to do with it?"

"Why else?"

"Wouldn't it make sense to say she's more afraid of being on her own than she is of risking another beating?" Crouching down in front of her, Caine took Diana's hand. "Diana, love's a strong motivation, but it isn't always the reason for staying with something even when it hurts."

"Maybe not—I don't know." The feeling of helplessness swamped her again. Love. She didn't understand it, for most of her life hadn't had to deal with it. But it seemed love was the one emotion that turned a reasonably intelligent person into a fool. It was a maze, she thought in frustration, full of dead ends, wrong turns and potholes. "She thinks she loves him," Diana said at length. "Because of that she's risking everything."

"We're lawyers," he reminded her, "not psychiatrists. Irene Walker's problem is no longer a legal one."

"I know." On a long breath she squeezed his hand. "But it's so frustrating to know she could've been helped—even he could've been helped, and now—"

"Now you take her folder, file it and forget it." Caine gave her a long, steady look. "You don't have any other choice."

"It's hard."

"Yeah. But it's necessary. We can only advise in a legal frame, Diana. We can only work with the law. Once something goes beyond that, it's out of our hands. It has to be out of our hands," he added.

"Why didn't we choose something simpler?" she murmured. "And something less painful? It looks so basic from the outside—this is right and this is wrong, according to the law. And this is how we might get around it, legally speaking." With a sigh of frustration, she shook her head. "Then suddenly there're people involved and it's not so simple. I wanted to help her. Damn it, Caine, I really wanted to help her."

"You can't help someone unless they're ready for help."

"And Irene Walker isn't ready for help." Diana nodded, but her eyes still smoldered.

How could she explain that she saw the Walker case, her first case out on her own, as her first failure both professionally and personally? Diana had felt that freeing Irene from bondage would somehow have symbolized her own liberation from another kind of domination. Irene's was physical, hers had been emotional, and neither had been healthy.

"I was ready to help her," she said after a long breath. "I needed to help her."

He saw it then, the vulnerability that could creep so unexpectedly into her eyes and bring him twin urges to protect and to run for cover. Caine stayed where he was while a quiet war raged inside him. "You can't keep drawing parallels, Diana."

She closed down instantly. Her emotional withdrawal should have relieved him. He wished it had. "I have to work my own way," she told him flatly.

"We all do," Caine agreed in the same tone. He should have left it at that, but even as he told himself to, he went on trying to reach her. "I defended a kid once—drinking while intoxicated. First offense. I got him off with the minimum. Three months later, he wrapped his car around a telephone pole and killed his passenger." His eyes darkened with the memory but remained steady on hers. "She was seventeen years old."

"Oh, Caine." At a loss, Diana could only reach for his hand.

"We all carry around our baggage, Diana. We can only do the best job we can and hope it's right. When it's wrong, or when one gets away from us, we file it away."

"You're right." The anger seeped out of her as she rose. "I know you're right." Deliberately she took the Walker file and dropped into her desk drawer. "Case closed," she murmured as she shut the drawer.

"Lucy tells me you have two other clients coming in next week."

Making an effort, Diana shook off the depression and looked back at him. "I handled them when I was with Barclay. They must have been satisfied."

Caine grinned at her expression. "Pleased with yourself?"

"Well, after all, they're coming to me, not Barclay, Stevens and Fitz."

Walking over, he lifted his hands to her shoulders. The tension was gone. "You're going to be very busy."

"I certainly hope so." With a smile, Diana slid her hands around his waist. "In order to become the best defense attorney on the East Coast, I require clients."

"It helps," Caine agreed and gave her a quick kiss on the nose. "In the meantime, it's . . . ." He glanced at his watch. "Four forty-seven on Friday evening."

"So late?" Diana smiled ruefully. "I've been brooding for some time."

"Are you finished brooding for the day?"

"Yes, absolutely."

"Then let's go. My father'll carry on for an hour if we're late."

"Don't tell me you're worried about a tongue-lashing?" Diana asked with a laugh as she took her purse from the bottom drawer of her desk.

"You don't know my father," Caine told her, pulling her out the door.

Diana found the trip relaxing and quick. Caine had been right, she decided, in telling her to file and forget the Walker case. And for the weekend, she would slip Chad Rutledge and her other cases to the back of her mind. It was time for the lawyer to ease off so that the woman could breathe.

She could look forward to seeing Justin again, with

none of the doubts and pain she'd taken with her to
Atlantic City. Perhaps this time they would be simply
brother and sister. A family—though not on the same
order as the MacGregor clan.

It was natural to think of them as a clan. Diana had
already seen Caine's close relationship with his sister.
Even if it hadn't been obvious from the way Caine had
spoken of the rest of his family, the phone call from
Daniel clearly showed just how much a family—in
every sense of the word—the MacGregors were. Diana
found herself intrigued, and a bit intimidated, with the
idea. What she knew of family relationships was all
secondhand. That, she mused, meant she knew virtual-
ly nothing at all.

In Boston, Caine MacGregor was a dynamic, successful attorney with a reputation for winning and
women. In Boston, he was her lover, and her associate.
In Hyannis Port, Caine was a son and a brother. Diana
knew very little of that side of him. Would he be
different? she mused. Wouldn't he have to be? In her
aunt's house Diana had always been a different person
following a different set of rules. Logically, she thought
the same would hold true for Caine.

As the car climbed higher, Diana caught a few
glimpses of the Sound, with waves tossing below. For a
moment, she lost herself in it, appreciating the rocks,
froth and energy. But when she looked up again, her
impression of Nantucket Sound faded with a new
image.

The house was gray against the cold winter sky. Huge
and structured like a fortress, it stood with its back to
the water. There was a fairy-tale aura about it, set
apart, built high, standing against a dark, moonless sky

with dozens of windows burning with light. It was ostentatious, a bit foolish and unapologetically pretentious.

"Oh, Caine, it's wonderful!" Diana leaned forward as the Jaguar sped closer. "What a marvelous place to grow up. It's the closest thing to a Scottish castle I've seen outside of a book."

"My father's going to be crazy about you." With a half grin, he glanced at her. "Not everyone has the same impression of it at first glance. My father has a few . . . quirks," he decided after a moment. "He built the house to please himself.

"I can't think of a better reason to build one." She tilted her head so that she could see the top of the tower. There was a flag blowing wildly in the wind. Diana didn't need to see the colors to know it would be a Scottish flag. "You must have loved growing up here."

"Yeah." Caine allowed his gaze to sweep from tower to sea wall. It was odd, he thought, that Diana's reaction brought him both pleasure and relief. Until that moment, he hadn't realized how disappointed he would have been if she'd been politely stunned. "Yeah," he repeated as his lips curved. "I guess we all did. It's huge and the devil to heat. Everything's done on a grand scale, wide, drafty corridors, high ceilings and fireplaces you could roast an ox in. Gothic arches, granite pillars and a wine cellar that's the closest thing to a dungeon I've ever seen. We used to play Spanish Inquisition down there."

"Oh." Diana sent him an appalled look. "What lovely children you must have been."

"I like to think we were inventive."

Laughing, she turned her attention back to the house. "It must be difficult to stay away."

"No, because you know it's always going to be here, and you can come back. There're memories in every room." Caine swung the car around the circular drive and stopped. "Maybe I should warn you that the inside is exactly what you'd expect from the outside."

"Dungeons and all," Diana agreed with a nod as she stepped out. "I wouldn't have it any other way."

"We'll get the bags later." His hand linked with hers, Caine started up the rough granite steps.

On the door was a large brass knocker in the shape of a lion's head. Caine pounded it against the wood as he read the Gaelic inscription over it.

"Royal is my race," he translated with a grin.

"I'm impressed."

"Of course you are." Bending down, he touched his lips to hers, then with a quiet sound of pleasure, he drew her closer. "And so am I," he murmured before he deepened the kiss.

Instinctively, she wrapped her arms around him, pressing her body against the warmth of his as the night wind whipped around them. It was easy, always so easy, to forget everything but the feel and the taste of him. She felt his fingers brush over the nape of her neck as he tangled them in her hair. Her head tilted back, inviting more as her bones began to soften.

"That's one way to ward off the chill."

Diana's head whipped around at the voice. Leaning against the door was a tall, angular man with dark, brooding looks and a full, sculptured mouth that was curved in a smile.

"It's the only way," Caine returned and gave the man a hard, unselfconscious hug. "My brother Alan,"

Caine told Diana as he drew her inside out of the cold. "Diana Blade."

With her hand enveloped in the senator's firm, quick grip, Diana found herself quietly and thoroughly summed up. There was something about that dark, intense look, she thought a bit uncomfortably, that would brush away the nonsense and get right to the core. He was more like Caine than she had imagined, even though there was almost no resemblance between them physically.

"It's good to have you here, Diana." Alan's gaze changed so swiftly from intense to welcoming, she wondered if she had imagined that brief appraisal. "Everyone's in the Throne Room."

At Diana's lifted brow, Caine laughed and drew off her coat. "A family term for one of the drawing rooms. It's a barn." Carelessly, he tossed their coats over the carved lion's head that served as a newel post for the main staircase. "Rena here?"

"She and Justin were already settled in when I got here," Alan answered. Diana watched the silent, subtle look that passed between the brothers.

"Well, I guess that puts me at the top of the list, then."

Alan grinned—a quick, unexpected expression that lightened his features. "Yeah."

Caine swung an arm around Diana's shoulders as they began to walk down the hall. "Bringing Diana should redeem me." He shot his brother another look. "You came alone, I take it."

"I've already had the lecture," Alan returned dryly. "Thirty-five years old and without a wife," he stated in a soft burr remarkably like his father's. "I'm in disgrace."

"Better you than me," Caine murmured.

"Should I know what you two are talking about?" Diana demanded with a puzzled smile.

Caine looked down at her, then up to meet his brother's amused eyes. "You will," he muttered. "Soon enough."

Diana opened her mouth to question, then was interrupted by the sound of a booming voice echoing off the walls. "The boy should come and see his mother more often. Children today are a disgrace. What do they think about the line—their ancestors and the generations to come? Where's the pride in the family name?"

"He's off and running," Caine said under his breath. He paused, his arm still around Diana's shoulders, at the entrance to the drawing room.

To say the room was impressive would have been an understatement. It had the dimensions of a ballroom with one huge, claret-colored rug spreading from wall to wall. At the far end was an enormous stone fireplace piled high with wood and flame. The windows ran from floor to ceiling along one side with stained-glass inserts along the top. The drapes were red and heavy but spread open so that the fire danced in reflection on the many panes.

Furniture was Gothic and oversized to suit the room. A Belter table held an ornate urn and a porcelain casket box. The paintings against the thick, dark paneling were all in fussy gilded frames. Sitting on the stone hearth was a life-size statue of a jackal.

Though there were no less than a dozen chairs and sofas scattered about, the family was grouped in one section around a wide, high-backed chair, carved and curved like a throne and upholstered in the same red as the carpet and drapes. In it sat a barrel of a man, red-bearded, strikingly handsome in a bold, warlike fashion. It was a simple matter for Diana to imagine him with a kilt and dirk rather than the full-cut Italian suit he wore.

There was a woman to his right with fine-boned features and dark, slightly graying hair. As Daniel continued with his complaints, her expression remained serene while her fingers were busy forming a pattern with floss and needle in a cloth held taut on a standing hoop.

To the left, Serena was curled on a curved, over-stuffed lounge, idly watching the colors of the fire reflect in a glass of kirsch. Justin sat beside her, his arm draped carelessly over the back of the lounge, his fingers toying absently with his wife's hair.

They're his court, Diana thought as her lips curved. And they've heard this proclamation hundreds of times before. What a magnificent man, she decided, watching Daniel drain the liquor in his glass before he continued.

"It seems a small thing to ask," Daniel went on, "to have your children pay their respect to their father on his birthday. It might be my last one," he added, shooting a look at his daughter.

"You say that every year," Caine commented before Serena could retort.

"It's his traditional threat," Serena stated as she sprang up to race to Caine. She hugged him fiercely, giving him a hard kiss before turning to hug Diana. "I'm so glad you came," Serena told her, then took both her hands.

Diana was as overwhelmed by the greeting as she was warmed by it. She found the MacGregors' unselfcon-sciously physical shows of affection appealed to her while leaving her uncertain if she were capable of returning them. "I'm glad to be here. You look wonderful."

With a laugh, Serena kissed her again. "I'll pour your drinks. Give me a hand, Alan, you need one, too."

"Diana."

Turning, Diana saw Justin standing beside her. Pleasure and a sudden sense of awkwardness ran through her so that while her eyes lit with the first, her hand reached for his with the second. Justin took it, then lacing his fingers with hers drew Diana to him.

"Will you kiss me, little sister?"

He would ask, Diana thought as the clear green eyes stayed on hers, to give her the choice of backing away. Rising on her toes, she brushed his lips with hers and felt the awkwardness vanish. "Oh, it's good to see you, Justin." On impulse, she wrapped her arms around him and held tight. "It's so good to see you."

Justin kissed the top of her head, returning the embrace as his gaze drifted to Caine's. He felt something—the instinct that tells a person when two people close to him are intimate. The knowledge flashed into his eyes as Caine met his stare without faltering.

Caine read Justin's expression easily and kept silent. He remembered exactly how he'd felt when he had found Serena sharing Justin's suite at the Comanche. Annoyed, uncomfortable, possessive, protective—all the feelings an older brother has when he suddenly discovers his sister's grown up in front of his eyes. Their friendship spanned a decade, but fate had sent them a curve so that each had found himself attracted to the other's sister. Ties of friendship and ties of blood ran strong in both of them.

"Caine." Justin brought Diana to his side, holding her there a moment as he tried to sort out his emotions.

"Well, damn it, are you going to keep the girl in the doorway, or are you going to bring her in?" Daniel demanded, giving an impatient wheeze as he hauled himself out of his chair. "Let me have a look at that sister of yours, Justin. Rena, my glass is empty."

"It's nice to see you, too," Caine drawled as he crossed the room.

"Hah!" Daniel exclaimed as he gave him a stern look. Caine merely grinned at him until the folds on Daniel's wide face shifted with a bellowing laugh. "Disrespectful young pup." He gathered his son to him in a bear hug and gave him three hearty slaps on the back. "You're late, your mother was worried you weren't coming."

"As long as I haven't missed dinner." Caine unfolded himself from his father and went to Anna.

"So this is Diana." Daniel clasped her by both shoulders. "A fine-looking girl," he decided with a quick nod. "You've a bit of your brother in you. Tall, strong," he went on. "Aye, blood will tell."

Diana lifted a brow at the greeting. "Thank you, Daniel. I appreciate you including me in your family weekend."

"Ah, but you're part of the family now, aren't you?" Swinging her around, he faced his wife. "A handsome girl, aye, Anna?"

"Lovely," Anna agreed, then held out her hands. "Don't let him make you feel like a thoroughbred at auction, Diana. It's just a habit of his. Come sit down."

"A thoroughbred at auction?" Daniel blustered. "Now what kind of talk is that?"

"Straight talk," Caine said casually as he sat on the

arm of the sofa beside his mother. "Thanks, Rena." He gave his sister a wink as she passed out drinks.

Daniel harrumphed and settled back into his throne-like chair. "So, we have another lawyer in the family," he began. Caine shot him a long, deadly look, but he continued placidly. "I have great respect for the law, you know, having two sons who passed the bar. Of course, Alan's so busy with politics he doesn't take time for anything else."

"You're top of the list now," Caine muttered under his breath, causing his brother to shrug.

"And you went to Harvard, too," Daniel stated between sips. "Now that's a coincidence for you. Small world, small world." His gaze skimmed briefly over his youngest son. "And now you two are partners."

"We're not partners," Caine and Diana said in unison, then shot each other a rueful look.

"Aren't you, now?" His father's smile, Caine thought, was entirely too bland. "Now I wonder where I got an idea like that? Well . . ." He gave Diana a paternal smile.

"Rena tells me you grew up in Boston, Diana," Anna interrupted tranquilly as she began to embroider again. "Do you know the O'Marra family?"

"My aunt was well acquainted with a Louise O'Marra."

"Yes, Louise, and what was her husband's name . . . Brian. Yes, Brian and Louise O'Marra. Odd people." Anna smiled as she finished another stitch. "They really enjoy playing bridge."

A chuckle escaped Diana before she could muffle it. Glancing up, she caught Anna's quick, knowing wink. "I hate the game myself," Anna went on, stitching again. "Perhaps because I'm so poor at it."

"No," Caine corrected, giving her hair a tug. "You're poor at it because you hate it."

"The O'Marras have three grandchildren, if I'm not mistaken," Daniel put in, then narrowed his gaze as it swept around the room.

"Nice try," Caine murmured to his mother.

"How do you feel about children, Diana?" Daniel leaned back in his chair and fixed his clever eyes on her.

"Children?" She heard a muffled laugh from behind her, which Alan disguised halfheartedly with a fit of coughing. Caine muttered something under his breath that sounded suspiciously like an oath. "Well, I haven't had a great deal of experience with them," she began, sending Caine a puzzled look.

"Where would we be without children?" Daniel demanded, leaning forward again. "To give us that sense of continuity, of responsibility?" As he spoke, he punctuated his words with a thump of his finger on the arm of his chair.

"Your glass is empty," Caine said abruptly and rose. "Keep it up," he said under his breath as he took the glass from his father's hand, "and I'll dilute every bottle of Scotch in the house."

"Well now." Daniel cleared his throat and considered the possibility. "Dinner should be ready soon, shouldn't it, Anna?"

"I think," Serena whispered to Justin, "that we might take a bit of the pressure off our siblings."

"Go ahead." Justin brushed his lips over her cheek. "I'm dying to see his face."

"Speaking of children," Serena said, ignoring the fulminating look Caine shot at her, "I think Dad has a very good point."

"A good point," Daniel repeated, bouncing back to

the topic with gusto. "Of course I have a good point. It's disgraceful, your mother without a single grandchild to spoil."

"Heartbreaking," Serena murmured, sending her mother a wink. "Well, Justin and I have decided to remedy that in about six and a half months."

"And about time," Daniel began, then stopped as his mouth hung open.

"Better late than never," Serena countered. Laughing at his stunned expression, she rose and went to her father. "Nothing to say, MacGregor?"

"You're with child?"

With a smile at his phrasing, she bent to kiss his cheek. "Yes. You'll have your grandchild before the leaves turn in September."

As Diana watched, Daniel's eyes filled. "My little girl," he murmured, then rose to cup her face in his hands. "My little Rena."

"I won't be little for long."

Daniel gathered her close. "Always my little girl."

Diana looked away, moved and strangely unsettled by the scene. She saw Caine, his gaze fixed on his sister, his eyes dark and intense as they were when he worked out a complicated point of law. He's trying to see her as a mother, Diana reflected. He's trying to picture himself as an uncle to her child. Justin's child, she realized with a jolt. Her brother's child. Something stirred in her—that old, buried need for family. Hardly realizing she moved, Diana stood and went to Justin.

"To your child," she said quietly and lifted her glass. "To the health and beauty of your son or daughter, and to our parents, who would have loved it." Justin stood, taking her hand as he murmured something in Comanche. "I don't remember the language," Diana told him.

"Thank you," he translated, "aunt of my children."

"We'll have champagne tonight," Daniel bellowed suddenly, and caught Serena close again. "Another MacGregor's on the way!"

"Blade," Justin and Diana corrected together.

"Aye, Blade." Flushed with good humor, he grabbed Justin in one of his bear hugs. "Good blood," he declared, then hugged Diana for good measure until she was laughing and gasping for breath. "Strong stock."

When he released her, the words played back in Diana's head. A glimmer of a notion flitted through her head, then fixed. Oh, my God, she thought, he was talking about me . . . about me and . . . Stunned, she turned her head so that her eyes met Caine's.

He was watching her, his arm draped around his sister's shoulder. Reading Diana's dazed expression accurately, he gave her a crooked smile and lifted his glass.

He couldn't sleep. Caine didn't have to lie in bed and stare at the ceiling to know he couldn't sleep. Instead he sat in a straddle chair, smoking slowly as he watched the moonlight play on the bare branches outside his window. The house was quiet now, a quiet all the more complete after the noise and laughter at the dinner table.

Strange how right Diana had looked in that enormous shadowy room. Strange, he thought again, how right it had seemed for her to be here, in the home of his childhood. He'd managed—or nearly managed—to rationalize his feelings about her for weeks. He was attracted to her, enjoyed her company, liked to watch her laugh, found pleasure in her passion. It had been true of other women. Perhaps, Caine thought as he studied the tip of his cigarette, it had been true of too many other women.

Why couldn't he stop thinking about her, hour after hour, day after day? Why did he know, before he had even attempted it, that he wouldn't be able to walk away from her? And he wouldn't—by God, he wouldn't—let her walk away from him.

On a sound of annoyance, he crushed out his cigarette and rose. There were times when he couldn't rationalize his feelings. He couldn't quite convince himself he'd just enjoyed helping her along on her road to self-discovery. There were times when he knew— and was terrified—that he was in love with her.

Wanted, needed—those were easy words. Love wasn't—not for Caine. Love meant commitment, one to one. It meant giving and sharing deep intimacies when he'd been very careful never to dip below the surface with any woman . . . until Diana.

For wanting and needing the path was clear, but for loving it took all sorts of unexpected twists and treacherous turns. It sounded like an easy word—an easy word when applied to someone else, he mused. He loved and wasn't sure of his next step.

And how did Diana Blade feel about him? Caine wondered. He stared out the window, his palms resting on the sill. She was a woman who budgeted her affections meticulously. She wanted and needed him, but . . . With a short laugh, Caine turned away to light another cigarette, to prowl restlessly around the room. Love . . . how did a man go about coaxing love from a woman? That was something he'd been very careful to avoid. And somehow, he didn't think love could be *coaxed* from a woman like Diana. It was either there or it wasn't.

Or it was there, he continued thoughtfully, and she wouldn't admit it.

Suddenly, painfully, he needed her—the softness, the heat. She would be asleep in the high, huge four-poster in the next room. Without giving himself a chance to think, Caine crushed out his cigarette and went into the hall.

He knew every inch, every board. Without faltering, he found the door to Diana's room and stepped inside, closing it quietly behind him. There was only moonlight here, pale streams of it slanted over the bed. The fire had been lit but was down to embers that gave neither heat nor light.

She'd snuggled beneath the quilt for warmth. Her slow, quiet breathing barely moved it. Emotions flooded him as he watched her and altered the hunger to an aching tenderness. He knew at once how it would be to see her like this night after night, to know when he woke each morning she would be beside him. And he knew, too, what his life would be like without her. Bending, he brushed his lips over her cheek.

"Diana," he murmured as she sighed in sleep and shifted on the pillow. Whispering her name again, he began to trace kisses over her face, nibbling lightly at her lips until he felt her sleepy response. "I want you, Diana." Pressing his mouth to hers, he let his tongue wake her.

On a sound of pleasure, her response grew more active, then, coming fully awake, she let out a gasp of surprise and scrambled up.

"Caine!" she hissed, aware that her heart was

pounding from a combination of fear and desire. "You scared me to death."

"It didn't feel like fear," he said quietly as he sat on the bed. Taking her shoulders, he drew her closer.

"What are you doing in here—it's the middle of the—" His mouth silenced her sweetly, effectively. Slowly, he slid his hands down, finding to his pleasure that she was warm and soft and naked. "Caine." Her mouth found brief freedom as he tasted the curve of her shoulder. "You can't—your parents' house."

"I can," he corrected, and heard her breath catch as his hands moved lower. "Anywhere. I want you, Diana. I can't sleep for wanting you. Let me show you."

"Caine—" But his mouth was on hers again. There was no protest as he pressed her back against the feather pillow.

Had he ever loved her like this before? Diana wondered dazedly as he moved his lips and hands leisurely over her. Once—once in that first, dreamlike loving. There was no urgency, no hurry. It was as if they'd had years together and were assured of years more. Slowly, he savored the tastes of her mouth, the tastes of her skin, murmuring in approval as he went.

Steeped in him, she could find no will to rush. The blazing passion she had grown used to was banked, smoldering like an easy fire in a comfortable hearth. They moved at the same lazy pace, whispering requests, murmuring in pleasure while they lay flesh to flesh beneath the thick quilt.

She hadn't been aware he had so much tenderness in him—or indeed that she had it in herself. She wanted to please him, and to soothe. Her hands touched gently, as his did, but even gentleness aroused. As the lazy stroking continued, she seemed to become more and more aware of her body—every pore, every pulse. With a long, quiet moan, Diana surrendered to the next phase of passion.

He could hear the change in her breathing, the subtle alteration in the rhythm of her body. Her needs accelerated his own. He was dizzy from the scent of her, mixed with the faintest touch of woodsmoke from the dying fire. The linen sheets, worn smooth and thin through the years, skimmed over his skin as her hands pressed him closer. As her desire deepened, the taste of her seemed to grow darker and sweeter. He kept his mouth light on hers, toying with her tongue, nipping while her fingers dove into his hair.

He slipped into her slowly, aroused by the gasp of surprise that became a moan of need. Though she arched in invitation, he kept the pace easy, murmuring mindless promises against her lips as she shuddered for more. The greater his need, the tighter he clung to control. Hazy waves of passion rippled through him as she crested once, yet he guided her gently up again . . . and again.

Saturated with desire, she murmured his name over and over so that he quieted her with a long, luxurious kiss. He thought he could feel her melt, bone by bone, until her body was limp and he knew her mind was filled with nothing but him. It was then he gave his own needs their freedom.

The red smoldering flame became a blue-white flash that consumed them both.

Chapter Eleven

$\mathcal{I}$t would have taken days to explore every nook and cranny of the house. The more Diana saw of it, the more she wanted to see. She'd spent most of her childhood and adolescent years in proper drawing rooms and parlors, admiring paintings by Reynolds or Gainsborough, Steuben glass and Queen Anne furniture—but nothing had prepared her for the Mac-Gregors' life-style. There were twenty-foot ceilings with arched beams and gargoyles, carved mahogany doors, stone fireplaces with spears crossed over the hearth—even an occasional suit of armor. She might find an ancient blunderbuss and a Favrile compote in the same room. It was a hodgepodge, an Aladdin's cave, at once barbaric and sophisticated. If she chose, she could wind her way down a shadowy corridor lit with gaslight and enjoy a huge tiled swimming pool or steaming Jacuzzi.

As charmed as she was with the house, Diana was equally fascinated by the MacGregors themselves. Whether their environment had grown to fit them or vice versa, she couldn't be certain, but they were an intriguing mixture of the worldly and the primitive. Overlying it all was Daniel's fierce, innate pride in his heritage, his clan and his children.

And she'd been wrong about one thing. Caine was no different here than he was in Boston, than he'd been in Atlantic City. He was exactly who he was, having no need to put on different faces for different people. The security of his childhood, the strong, binding love of his family, had given him that gift. She wondered if he knew what a gift it was.

Because she wanted to think, Diana drifted away alone into what Caine had jokingly referred to as the War Room. Here Daniel kept his collection of weapons —daggers, swords, pistols, ornately carved rifles—and, to her amazement, a small cannon. The fire hadn't been lit, so the room was chilly. Sunbeams filtered through the leaded glass windows to fall in crisscross patterns on the thick planked floor. Diana's heels echoed hollowly as she walked idly from case to case.

So, she thought as she admired an Italian dagger with a jeweled handle, Daniel MacGregor was setting her up. Caine might have warned her—she'd meant to speak to him about it the night before, but they'd had no time alone. Then when he'd come to her room . . .

She couldn't—wouldn't—be pressured by people she hardly knew to make a decision that involved the rest of her life. She'd never thought of marrying Caine. Even as she realized that wasn't quite true, Diana passed over it. She'd never seriously thought of it, she amended. Marriage and children were things she'd never permitted herself to consider. Didn't marriage mean giving up part of yourself to someone else? For so long she had fought to keep that inner part private—so private, she admitted ruefully, that there had been times she herself had forgotten just what Diana Blade was made of.

And marriage meant risk—trusting someone to stay. No, there was only one person she could completely trust and depend on, and that was herself. She'd realized that years ago when she'd known the pain of loss, the fear of desertion. It wasn't going to happen to her again.

Love. No, she wouldn't think of love, Diana told herself as she stared at the empty hearth. She wasn't in love with Caine—she didn't *choose* to be in love with Caine. But something began to pull at her, threatening to cloud the logic with emotions. Frightened, Diana forced it away. No, she wouldn't fall in love, she wouldn't consider marriage. In any case, it was academic. It wasn't Caine who was pressuring her. He'd asked her for nothing, given no promises, demanded none.

It's foolish to worry about it, she reminded herself. I've let his family get to me—that unity, that closeness. It appeals just as much as it frightens.

It tempted her to daydream, and she'd given up fantasies long ago.

"All alone, Diana?"

She turned, smiling, as Justin walked into the room. "I can't get enough of this house," she told him. "It's like something out of the Middle Ages, with unexpected touches of the twentieth century. The MacGregors are fascinating people."

"The first time I walked in here I wondered if Daniel

MacGregor was mad or brilliant." With one of his quick, charming grins, he scanned the room. "I still haven't made up my mind."

"You really love him, don't you?"

Justin lifted a brow at the serious tone of her question. "Yes. He's a man who demands strong emotions. All of them do," he added thoughtfully. "I don't think I fully realized until Serena was kidnapped that I'd made them my family for ten years. I wish you'd had that."

"I had other things." With a shrug, Diana walked to a slightly rusted suit of armor. "I was very self-sufficient."

"Was and are," Justin murmured. "Do you ever think too much?"

She turned back, lifting a brow in almost the identical manner of her brother. "You too, Justin? Have you gotten it into your head to match me up with Caine?"

His eyes remained calm and very cool. "It appears the two of you have managed that all on your own."

"That's my business."

"So it is." Dipping his hands into his pockets, he studied her. She was annoyed and, he suspected, a bit frightened. "I wasn't there for you when you were growing up, Diana. Perhaps it's too late to play big brother now, but I promised to be your friend."

She went to him quickly, pressing her face to his shoulder as she held him. "I'm sorry. It's hard for me—I'm afraid to need you."

"Or anyone?" Justin asked, tilting her face to his. Though she remained silent, the answer was in her eyes. "It's disconcerting to see so much of yourself in another person," he murmured. "Diana, are you in love with Caine?"

"Don't ask me that." Drawing away, she held up her hands as if to ward off the question. "Don't ask me that."

"All right." He hadn't expected to feel concern, or to feel this vague helplessness. "If I asked, would you tell me about the years you lived with Adelaide? Really tell me?"

Diana opened her mouth, then closed it again. "No," she said after a moment. "No, that's over."

"If it was over, you'd tell me about it. Diana," he continued when she would have spoken. "I'm not going to give you advice or tell you what you should do. But I'd like to tell you something about myself. I was in love with Serena, but I didn't tell her. I didn't," he continued with a rueful grin, "tell myself. I'd been in charge of my own life for so long. I'd never loved anyone—you, our parents—that was all too distant. Telling her was one of the hardest things I ever did. There are people love comes gently to. They're not us."

"What about Rena?" Diana wondered. "Was it easy for her?"

"Easier, I think." He smiled then and, sitting on the arm of a chair, lit a cigarette. "She's a great deal like her father—more than any of the others. She'd suffer all sorts of torture before she'd admit it, but when she came to me in Atlantic City, she'd already made up her mind that we'd be together. Daniel's little scheme had worked very well."

"Daniel's scheme?"

Justin blew out a stream of smoke and laughed. "He'd thrown us together, very cleverly, by buying me a ticket for the cruise liner Serena worked on. Of course, he didn't mention to me that she worked there, or to her that he had a friend coming on board. He counted on chemistry—or on fate, as he puts it."

"Fate," Diana murmured, then gave a bewildered laugh. "The old devil."

"To put it mildly." Justin watched her through a mist of smoke. "He knows how to get what he wants. All the MacGregors do. And," he added slowly, "so do you and I—once we acknowledge what it is we want." She shot him a look, but Justin rose and slipped an arm around her shoulders. "Let's go find the clan or Daniel will send search parties."

There was something different about Caine. Diana couldn't quite put her finger on it, but she sensed it. At first, she wondered if perhaps the Virginia Day case was troubling him. He was to go to trial the following week, and Diana knew that he had been pumping his mother for every scrap of information she had on Dr. Francis Day.

On the surface he seemed relaxed enough—laughing with his family, teasing his sister. But there was something going on beneath, an edginess she'd never found in him before. There were times throughout the day that she caught him looking at her in his old direct, dissecting way. It was as if he were seeing her for the first time, as if they hadn't worked and talked together, as if they hadn't been as close as a man and woman could be.

While she felt herself being drawn into the circle of his family, Diana's thoughts of Caine kept her from being completely relaxed. There'd been a change—and if she were honest, she would admit she had sensed it in the way he had made love to her the night before. The road had suddenly developed a new surface. She would navigate cautiously.

"Well now." Mellow, pleased with himself, Daniel sat back in his thronelike chair with his gifts spread out on the floor around him. "A man's compensation for adding another year."

"Of course it has nothing to do with basic greed or the love of opening presents," Serena commented as she crossed her bare feet on the coffee table.

"One of the trials of my life has been disrespectful children," Daniel told Diana with a sigh.

"The curse of parenting," she agreed, knowing him well enough now to play the game.

"The times I've been shouted at, aye, even threatened by my own flesh and blood." Daniel heaved a sigh as he flopped back in his chair.

"I'm getting pretty close to tears," Serena said dryly.

"I can overlook that in your condition." Daniel sent her a stern look. "But don't think I've forgotten how you yelled at me just because I bought that husband of yours a ticket for that boat. Yelled at me," he repeated, turning back to Diana. "And broke half a dozen of my best cigars."

"Cigars?" Anna said mildly.

"Old ones that were just—lying around," he said quickly.

"It must have been difficult, raising three . . . volatile children." Diana felt Caine's fingers squeeze the back of her neck, but she kept her expression bland.

"Ah, I could tell you stories. . . ." Daniel smiled reminiscently and shook his head. "That one," he said, pointing a wide finger at Caine. "Hardly a moment's peace, Anna will tell you." Then he continued before Anna had a chance to. "That one was nothing but mischief when he was a lad, and then there were the females. A regular parade," Daniel announced proudly.

"A parade," Diana repeated. Turning her head, she started to smile at Caine but found him staring at her with that odd light in his eyes.

With their gazes locked, he cupped her face in his hand. "We're both grown up now," he murmured, then covered her mouth in a long, firm kiss.

"Well then," Daniel began with a wide grin as Diana sat silent and flustered.

"You haven't tried the piano yet, have you, Diana?" Anna asked calmly.

"What? I'm sorry?" Out of her depth, Diana turned to see a look of gentle understanding in Anna's eyes.

"The piano," she repeated. "You play, don't you?"

"Yes, I do."

"It's so rarely touched these days. Would you mind playing something, Diana?"

"No, of course not." Relieved, she rose to cross the room to the baby grand.

"You're pressuring the children, Daniel," Anna said quietly.

"Me?" He shot her an incredulous look. "Nonsense, anyone can see that they—"

"Why don't you let them see for themselves first?"

He subsided in a huff as Diana sifted through the sheet music.

She was grateful for the distraction. It was simpler for her to remain outwardly composed when she had something specific to do. The notes came easily to her—a result of years of structured lessons and an affection for music. Music had perhaps been the only one of her accomplishments that had pleased Diana as much as it had pleased her aunt. She used it now as she had often in the past, as a curtain for her private thoughts and private emotions.

What had been in Caine's mind when he had kissed her? Diana wasn't accustomed to, or completely comfortable with, public shows of affection. Certainly not in the boisterous sense the MacGregors were. Yet even with that, she could have accepted a simple kiss. Was it her imagination, or had there been something possessive in the gesture?

Perhaps she was just letting Daniel's not-so-subtle machinations get to her. Those, and Justin's unexpected questions. Why should she feel pressured today when she hadn't felt so yesterday? Last night . . . hadn't it really begun last night?

Lifting her gaze from the keys, she met Caine's eyes. He was silent, brooding, Diana mused as her brows drew together. It wasn't characteristic of him to brood. Nor, she reminded herself, was it characteristic of him to be tense, yet he was. Could something have changed overnight without her being aware of it?

It might have been better if she hadn't come, Diana thought as she felt little fingers of tension probe at the back of her neck. She shouldn't have allowed herself to be charmed by the eccentricities of this family, the closeness, the camaraderie. It might not have been wise to have seen Caine in this kind of setting—away from Boston, the office, her own established apartment. If she wasn't careful, she might find herself forgetting her own goals and the rules she'd set up to accomplish them.

Success was first. It had to be, if she were to justify all the years she had danced to someone else's tune. And success, Diana knew, was a greedy god who demanded constant vigilance. Gaining it, then maintaining it, would require all of her skill and a large chunk of her time.

When she had chosen the law, Diana had made a pact with herself. There would be no personal complications to interfere with her career. She had neither the inclination nor the patience for them. Again her gaze drifted to Caine. The knots of tension tightened.

Hadn't she told herself from the beginning that if she let him get too close, things would drift out of her control? She'd known, yet had somehow convinced herself that she could handle an intimate relationship with him without letting her emotions completely outweigh her logic. Had it been pride that had caused her to accept the challenge? Passion? It hardly mattered, since she had accepted and was now forced to deal with the consequences.

As the music built, her feelings intensified. She could feel them pour through her, hear the crackling snap from the blaze of the fire and sense somehow the varying emotions in play across the room. Why had she let herself get so involved? she wondered in quick panic. She had her life—a streamlined path she'd just begun to follow. There were all those promises to herself to keep, though she could remember, even when she struggled not to, the tenderness Caine had brought to her bed in the dark hours of the night.

Diana let the notes drift into silence, then gripped her hands together, finding they were not quite steady.

"Now that was a pleasure." Daniel gave a windy sigh from his chair. "Is there anything that brings a man more contentment than a beautiful woman and a song?"

Caine reluctantly took his eyes from Diana and gave

his father a long, cool stare. "Did you have plans to survive until your next birthday?" he asked pleasantly.

"Now what kind of talk is that?" Daniel blustered, but then he hesitated.

He'd planted enough seeds for an evening . . . and he knew the value of strategic retreat. "We'll have another bottle of champagne and some more cake," he declared. "Caine, toss another log or two on the fire before you come along."

As the family swept from the room, Serena paused by the piano to squeeze Diana's hand. "He's an old meddler," she murmured, "but he has a good heart."

When the room was quiet, Diana rose and watched as Caine added fresh wood to the already blazing fire. The tension at the back of her head had built to an ache.

"Do you want some more cake?" Caine asked with his back still to her.

"No. No, not really." Diana linked her hands together and wished they were back in Boston. Would she be more certain of her moves there?

"Another drink?" Now this is a ridiculously polite conversation, Caine thought in disgust as he turned to her.

"Yes, all right." Moistening her lips, Diana searched for some safe topic. "Did you get the information you wanted on the Day case from your mother?"

"Just a corroboration on Francis Day's character." Caine shrugged as he poured from decanter to glass. "It was nothing that I didn't already have, but my mother has a way of getting to the heart of a matter without all the fuss. He interned under her at Boston General. Still, it's nothing I can use in litigation." As he handed Diana her drink, Caine brushed at her bangs in a habitual gesture. When she stepped back, he narrowed his eyes but said nothing.

"It always helps to get an objective viewpoint before you go to trial."

"Am I on trial, Diana?"

Her eyes came swiftly to his. "I don't know what you mean."

"You're hedging." Taking a step closer, he circled the back of her neck, then lowered his lips to hers. He felt the tension beneath his fingers, felt her initial resistance to the kiss. As he drew back, Caine lifted an ironic brow. "Yes, it seems I am. But I can't make my plea until I'm sure of the charges."

"Don't be ridiculous." Quickly annoyed, Diana lifted her drink and swallowed.

"Don't be evasive," Caine countered. "I thought we'd gotten past that point in our relationship."

"Stop pushing me, Caine."

He took a long hard look at the drink in his hand but didn't taste it. "In what way?"

"I don't know—every way." She dragged a hand through her hair as she walked away. "Let's just drop it, I don't want to fight with you."

"Is that what we're doing?" With a nod, he drank, then set down his glass. "Well, if it is, let's do it right. You get the first shot."

"I don't *want* the first shot." Abruptly furious, she whirled back to him. "I'm not going to stand in your parents' drawing room and snipe at you."

"But you would if we were somewhere else."

"Yes—I don't know. Caine, leave me alone!"

"The hell I will." And the very calmness of his tone

warned her of his mood. "Let's hear it, Diana. I want to know why you're pulling away from me."

"I'm not pulling away, you're imagining things." She took a quick, nervous sip of her drink and turned away again. When his hand touched her shoulder, she jerked, then cursed herself.

"Not pulling away," Caine murmured, trying to ignore the slash of hurt. "What's your term for it?"

"Look, it's late—I'm tired." Diana fumbled for the excuse, knowing it was a weak one. "Caine . . ." With a frustrated sigh, she moved away from him again. "Please, don't pressure me now."

"Is that what you think I'm doing, Diana? Pressuring you?"

"Yes, damn it! You, your family, Justin—all in your own separate ways." Setting down her glass, she leaned her palms against a table. She was overreacting but for once couldn't summon the logic to clear her mind. "Caine, can't we just leave this alone?"

"No, I don't think so." He would have gone to her, but somehow the distance she had put between them stopped him. He felt awkward, and close to furious with her for making him so. And he hurt—that was something he would think about later. "It's not my intention to pressure you, Diana," he said in a low, precise voice that had her digging her teeth into her lower lip. "But there are things that I think should be said now."

"Why?" she demanded as she spun back around. "Why this sudden urgency? There weren't any complications when we were in Boston."

"What kind of complications are there now?"

"Don't cross-examine me, Caine."

"You have an objection to that question?"

"Oh, you make me furious when you act like this." Seething, she dug her hands into the pocket of her skirt and whirled around the room. "I've felt like I've been under a microscope off and on since I walked through the front door. You might have told me I was top of your father's list as the proper mate for his second son."

"My father has absolutely nothing to do with you and me, Diana. I'd apologize for his lack of subtlety, but I don't feel responsible for it."

"I don't want your apology," she fumed. "But it would have been more comfortable if I'd been prepared. Damn it, I like him—and the rest of your family. It's impossible not to, but I don't like the quiet looks of speculation and the unasked questions."

"What would you like me to do about it?"

"I don't know. Nothing," she said as she moved to stand in front of the roaring fire. "But I don't have to like it."

"Did it ever occur to you that I might not particularly care for it myself?" Simmering with anger, Caine swirled his drink and stared at her back. "Did it ever occur to you that I might not care for the interference in my life, no matter how well intentioned?"

"They're your family," she tossed back over her shoulder. "You're bound to be more accustomed to it than I. I spent twenty years trying to live up to my aunt's plans for me. I didn't get this far to follow someone else's."

"The hell with your aunt!" Caine exploded. "And with everyone else that isn't you and me. What do you want, Diana? Why don't you just spell it out?"

"I don't know what I want!" she shouted, shocking herself with the admission. "I knew yesterday, and now . . . Damn it, Caine, I can't deal with this. I can't deal with having my private life poked into—not by your father, my brother, anyone. It's my life, and I'll make my own decisions."

"You can't deal with it," he murmured, then gave a short laugh before he drained his glass. "Then deal with this. I'm in love with you."

Diana stared at him in utter shock, in utter silence. She wondered if her heart had simply stopped, and she didn't move a muscle as a log snapped loudly and sparks sprayed against the screen at her back.

They watched each other, both pale, their eyes dark with what seemed more like anger than any other emotion. How had it come to this? she wondered. And what in God's name would they do about it?

"Well, you don't seem thrilled to hear it." Furious with himself for having made the statement so baldly, Caine reached for the decanter. With studied calm, he poured a brandy. How could he have known that silence could bring this kind of pain? As he listened to the brandy splash against the glass, he wondered why he had waited more than thirty years to say those words to a woman to find only emptiness. "Would you like the statement stricken from the record, counselor?"

"Don't." Diana squeezed her eyes shut for a moment. "I don't know what to say to you—or how to handle this. It's easier for you. There've been other women—"

"Other women?" he exploded. He wasn't pale anymore, but his eyes were even darker, more furious than she'd ever seen them. Instinctively, Diana stepped back as he walked toward her. "How can you say that to me now? What do I have to do to make up for a past that happened before I even met you? And why the hell should I?" He gripped her by the shoulders, fingers digging into flesh. "Damn it, Diana, I said I love you. I *love* you."

His mouth came down on hers in anger and frustration, as if by that alone he could wipe out the hurt she brought him, the doubts he brought her. Something built inside her, threatening to burst. Diana dragged herself away with a cry of alarm.

"You frighten me." Her eyes swam with sudden tears as they faced each other again, their breathing unsteady. "I said that you didn't, but it was always a lie. From the very beginning—" She choked back a sob and pushed her hair away from her face with both hands. "You're what I've always avoided. I can't risk it, don't you understand? All of my life someone's played carrot and stick with me. Do this, fit into this mold and you'll have security, you'll have normalcy. I've just found my own mold, I won't fit someone else's expectations now!"

"I'm not asking you to fit anything," he tossed back. "I've never asked you to be anyone but yourself."

Perhaps it was the truth of that which frightened her more than anything else. She dragged a hand through her hair as the last lingering fear broke through. "How do I know you'll stay? How do I know, if I let myself love you, that one day there wouldn't be someone else, something else, and you'd just walk away? I can handle being alone now, I know how. But I can't—I *won't* be left again."

Caine struggled against fury, against the sense of his

own impotence. "I've asked you more than once to trust me. It's not me that frightens you, Diana. It's ghosts, and your own self-doubt."

She swallowed, winning the battle with tears. "You don't understand. You've never lost anything."

"So you intend to go through your life never taking a chance because you might lose?" His eyes hardened as they swept her face. "I never took you for a coward."

"I *choose* the chances I take," she countered furiously. "*I* choose. I won't put myself in a position to be hurt, I won't take chances on my career—"

"Why do you automatically assume I'll hurt you? And what in God's name does your career have to do with my loving you? I have the same profession, the same demands. Who's asking you to make a choice between love and the law?"

"Did you have to chop down a tree, Caine? We're halfway through the cake and champagne, and . . ." Serena trailed off as she reached the center of the room. The waves of tension and hurt poured over her so that she stared in awkward silence from Caine to Diana. "I'm sorry," she said, knowing of no gracious way to cover up the intrusion. "I'll tell everyone you're busy."

"No, please." Diana met the banked fury in Caine's eyes before turning to his sister. "Just tell them I'm a bit tired. I'm going to go up now." Quickly, without looking back, she walked from the room.

Caine watched her in silence, then turned to retrieve his snifter of brandy from the sideboard.

"Oh, Caine, I'm so sorry. It seems I couldn't have picked a worse time to barge in."

"It doesn't matter." He drained the remaining liquor, then poured more. "We'd said all we had to say."

"Caine . . ." Serena went to him, distressed by the controlled voice and stony expression. "Do you need a sympathetic ear, or solitude?"

"I need a drink," he answered, taking both the snifter and decanter to a chair. "I need quite a few of them."

"You're in love with Diana?"

"Right the first time," he said, and toasted her.

Ignoring the sarcasm, Serena sat beside him. "And you'd like to murder her."

"Right again."

"It's easy to be right when you've been through it. I don't know what went on in here tonight, but—"

"I told her, in the midst of a nasty little argument, that I was in love with her." He brought the snifter to his lips again and swallowed deeply. "It seems my timing—and my delivery—were a bit off."

"I'm going to do something I despise," Serena said with a sigh.

"Which is?"

"Give advice."

"That's my territory, Rena. Save it."

"Shut up." Firmly, she took the snifter from his hand and set it down. "Give her some room, and some time. You're not an easy man to love in the best of circumstances. I should know."

"I appreciate the testimonial."

"Caine, a lot of things have changed in Diana's life very quickly. She's the kind of woman who needs to make her decisions a step at a time—at least she thinks she is."

He gave a quiet laugh as he leaned back in the chair. "You were always an excellent judge of character, Rena. You'd have made a hell of a lawyer."

"It comes in handy in my line of work, too." Reaching out, she took his hand. "Don't press her, Caine. There are storms inside Diana. Let her battle them out."

"I might have pressed her too far already." On a long breath, he shut his eyes. "Oh, God, I hurt."

Serena wanted to comfort and forced herself not to. "Love has to hurt, it's rule number one. Go to bed," she ordered briskly. "You'll have a better idea what to do in the morning."

Caine opened his eyes again. "It's a hell of a thing that I should be sitting here taking advice from the kid sister who sharpened her left jab on me."

"I'm a comfortable matron now," Serena said majestically as she patted her stomach.

"Hah!" Caine retorted in an accurate imitation of their father.

"Go to bed," Serena advised. "Before I take it into my head to see if that jab's still effective." Rising, she tugged him to his feet.

"You always were a bossy little busybody," Caine told her as they walked toward the doorway. "I'm still crazy about you."

"Yeah." Serena grinned up at him. "Me too."

Chapter Twelve

Diana sat in the empty courtroom, numb and nauseated. The hands she folded together on her briefcase were ice cold and nerveless. She knew she had to pull herself together—go out and get in her car, drive home. Somehow she knew if she stood up at that moment, her legs would buckle. She sat as still as a stone and waited for the feeling to pass.

Logic told her she was being a fool. She should feel wonderful—she should celebrate. She'd won.

Chad Rutledge was free, exonerated. Beth Howard's father would face perjury charges. And so would Beth, Diana added silently as she stared at the empty witness chair. It was unlikely the girl would be convicted, not when a dozen witnesses had seen so clearly that it had been fear that had caused her to lie about the rape. Not when a dozen witnesses had watched how pitifully she had fallen apart under examination.

Not, Diana thought as a small pain rippled through her, when a dozen witnesses had watched Diana Blade, Attorney at Law, rip her to shreds.

Diana could hear the echo of her own voice in the now silent courtroom—cold, accusing, merciless. She could see the pale, fragile face of Beth Howard as it crumbled—and the tears, the near hysterical confession. She could hear Chad's loud, furious demands that Beth be left alone. Then there had been chaos in the courtroom as Chad had been restrained and Beth had wept out the entire story.

When the courtroom had been cleared, Diana had remained to deal with her victory and the cost of it in human terms.

She had never felt more alone or more lost than at that moment. She wanted to weep but sat dry-eyed. She was a professional, and tears had no place. Caine; oh, God, she needed Caine. Diana closed her eyes as the numbness faded into pain.

She had no right to need him or to use him as a lifeline when she felt she was sinking. Though two weeks had passed, she could still see the look in his eyes as they had faced each other in his parents' drawing room.

Hurt. She had hurt him, and now they treated each other like strangers. Each time Diana tried to tell herself it was for the best, she remembered that look in his eyes and the flood of feeling that had risen in her only to be forced back in panic.

Love. She couldn't afford to love him, couldn't afford the risk. It would be best if she found another office, perhaps left Boston altogether. *Running away?* a small voice asked her. With a sigh, Diana stared down at her hands. Yes, that's what she had in mind. If she ran fast enough, she might be able to escape Caine. But she wasn't going to be able to escape herself. And if she were honest, she would admit it was herself she was running from.

When had she started to love him? Perhaps it had been when he had shown her such gentleness and understanding after her first meeting with Justin. Or perhaps it had been on that snowy beach when he'd made her laugh, then made her ache with need. She'd known it was happening but had pretended otherwise. Every time her emotions had begun to take over, she had closed them off. Afraid.

She looked around the empty courtroom again, then slowly rose to her feet. It was twilight when she stepped outside. In the west, the sky was clumped with clouds that glowed with bronzes and pinks. The lengthening of days was the only sign of spring, as the wind was as sharp as a knife and the dark, leafless trees shimmered under a thin coat of ice. Diana saw Chad hunched in his coat, sitting near the bottom of the courthouse steps. She hesitated, not certain she was strong enough for a confrontation, then, squaring her shoulders, she walked down the remaining steps.

"Chad."

He looked up, staring into her face for a long five seconds before he rose. "I've been waiting for you."

"I can see that." With a nonchalance she wasn't feeling, Diana flipped up the collar of her coat against the wind. "You should have waited inside."

"I needed the air." He kept his hands in his pockets, his shoulders rounded against the cold as he watched her. "They wouldn't let me see Beth."

"I'm sorry." Carefully, she kept all emotion and all weariness out of her voice. I hurt, too, she thought in despair. For you, for myself. Must I always have the answers? "I'll arrange for you to see her tomorrow."

"You don't look so good."

Diana gave him a thin smile. "Thanks." As she turned he caught at her arm.

"Ms. Blade . . ." Awkwardly, Chad dropped his hand and stuffed it back in his pocket. "I gave you a hard time in there—I guess I've given you a hard time all along."

"It comes with the territory, Chad. Don't worry about it."

"Watching Beth . . ." He swore softly, then turned away to stare at the traffic. "I couldn't stand watching her cry in there. I hated you for making her cry like that. When I came out here to wait, I had a lot of things I was going to say to you."

Diana gripped her briefcase tighter and braced herself. "Go ahead, say them now."

He gave a shaky laugh and turned back to her. "I had some time to think. I guess I don't do enough of that." He took out a cigarette, cupping his hands around the match as he lit it. Diana saw that his hands were steady. "I've got something different to say to you now, Ms. Blade." Chad blew out smoke on a long breath before he met her eyes. "You saved my life, and I think maybe you saved Beth's, too. I want to thank you."

Unable to speak, Diana stared at the hand he held out to her. After a moment, she accepted it, then found hers clasped hard. "All I could think about in there was that you were hurting her. I couldn't see past that. Sitting out here, I started thinking about that cell, and what it would be like to be in one for the next twenty years. You don't know how good it is to sit outside and know nobody's going to come along and lock you back in a cage."

When his voice trembled, Chad swallowed but kept his hand tight on hers. "I'd have done that for her, and I guess, after a while, I'd have hated her. And she . . . she'd have lived with that lie crawling around inside of her. Beth wouldn't have made it. I know that."

"It'll be over for her soon." Diana lifted her free hand to cover their joined ones. Objective? she thought. Only a robot could be cool and objective when someone looked at them like this. He needed to give his gratitude, but he was also asking for comfort. "No court's going to punish Beth for being terrified."

"If they—if she has to go to court, will you help her?"

"Yes. If she wants me to. And you'll be there for her."

"Yeah. I'm going to marry her right away. The hell with money, we'll figure something out." His hand relaxed as he smiled for the first time. "I was always thinking I had to prove something, you know? To Beth, to myself, to the whole damn world. Funny, it doesn't seem so important anymore to prove that I can make it all by myself."

Diana gave him an odd look and shook her head. "No," she said slowly. "I suppose only fools think that way."

"It won't be so easy with Beth finishing school." He grinned now, as though the challenge appealed to him. "But we'll be together, and that's what counts."

"Yes. Chad . . ." She dropped her hand to her side. "Is it worth it? The risk, the pain?"

He tilted back his head and drew in the cold evening

air. "It's worth anything. Everything." With a wide, brilliant smile he looked back at her. "You'll come to the wedding, Ms. Blade?"

"Yes." She smiled back at him, then gently kissed his cheek. "Yes, I'll come to your wedding, Chad. Now go home, you'll see your girl tomorrow."

Diana walked to her car, realizing the sickness had left her stomach. The dull threat of a headache at her temple had vanished. They were so young, she thought as she joined the long stream of traffic, with a dozen strikes against them. Yet that look of shining hope in Chad's eyes made her believe. They'd face the odds together, and if there was any justice, they'd make it.

And what about you? Diana asked herself. Are you determined to be a fool, or are you going to face the odds? Just how much Blade blood, gambler's blood, was there in her? Perhaps, like Chad, she had been flirting with spending her life in a cell. There was a certain safety there to compensate for the lack of freedom.

Words began to flit through her head—Justin's voice telling her that love came gently to some people, but not to them. Caine furiously telling her that he loved her, demanding that she trust him. She could hear her own voice, edged with nerves, telling him she wouldn't risk being left alone. What was she now, Diana asked herself, if not alone? Alone and aching with love and needs, but letting those old fears—the ghosts, Caine had called them—rule her life. In doing so, she was breaking the most important promise she had ever made to herself. To be Diana Blade.

She'd intended to go home but now found herself pulling up in the drive beside the office. Instinct? she wondered, seeing that Caine's car was parked there.

Her nerves began to jump again. What would she say to him? It might be best to go home, wait until she could think clearly and plan. Even as this went through her mind, Diana stepped from the car.

She could see the light in the window of his office. He's been working too hard, she thought. The Day case. The trial should be nearly over by now. Diana knew more of its progress from the press reports than from Caine. Had they spoken a dozen words to each other in the last two weeks? she wondered. What would she say to him now?

The first floor was dark and silent. She could hear the quiet creak of the door as she shut it behind her. Glancing up the stairs, she slipped out of her coat. Her timing was probably very poor, she thought, and caught her bottom lip between her teeth as she again considered going home. She walked up the stairs.

Caine's office door was open. Diana could hear the whispers from the fire as she moved toward it. Hesitating at the doorway, she studied Caine while he sat behind his desk. His head was bent over a stack of papers. His jacket and tie had been tossed in a heap over the back of a chair so that he wore the black vest unbuttoned and his shirt open at the throat. In the ashtray a cigarette he hadn't quite put out smoldered. As she watched, he dragged a hand through his hair, then reached, without looking up, for his coffee cup. She studied him, as she hadn't permitted herself to do since that night in Hyannis Port.

God, he looks tired, she thought with a jolt. As if he hasn't slept properly in days. Could the case be going so badly? Suddenly, he swore softly under his breath and ran his hand over his face.

Swamped with concern, Diana stepped forward. "Caine?"

His head jerked up. For an instant he stared at her with eyes that were dark and unguarded. She felt his need as a tangible thing, then, just as quickly, it was gone.

"Diana," he returned coolly. "I didn't expect you back tonight."

Maybe she had been mistaken. It might only have been surprise she had seen in his eyes, her own emotions she had felt. She searched her mind for all the things she wanted to say. "Chad Rutledge was acquitted," was all that came out.

"Congratulations." He leaned back and studied her with apparent dispassion. Was she more beautiful than she'd been yesterday? he wondered as the ache crept into him. Was he going to go mad seeing her day after day, loving her and not being loved in return?

"It was ugly," she said after a moment. "I'm not particularly proud of the way I treated Beth Howard on the stand."

Caine balled his hand into a fist, then flexed it. Her vulnerability would always tear at him. "Do you want a drink?"

"No, I—yes," she decided. "Yes, I'll get it." Moving to a cabinet across the room, Diana found a decanter and poured without having any idea what the liquor was. This wasn't happening the way it should, she told herself. All the words she wanted to say to him stuck in her throat. Self-doubts; hadn't he told her she was plagued with them? As usual, he'd been accurate. Now, she simply didn't know if she could find the right phrasing, the right tone, to tell him she wanted to do what he'd asked of her almost from the beginning. To trust.

Moistening her lips, she tried to break some of the tension hovering in the air. "Is the Day case giving you problems?"

"No, not really. It's nearly over." He sipped at his coffee and found it cold and bitter. It suited his mood. "The prosecution didn't have as tight a case as I'd imagined. I put Ginnie on the stand today. She was hard as nails, unsympathetic and perfectly believable. He couldn't shake her testimony an inch in cross-examination."

"Then you're feeling confident about the verdict?"

"Virginia Day will be acquitted," he said flatly. "But she won't get justice." At Diana's puzzled look, he pushed his coffee aside and rose. "Legally, she'll be free, but the public will look at her as a spoiled, rich woman who murdered her husband and got away with it. I can keep her out of jail, but I can't vindicate her."

"A lawyer I admire once told me a defense counsel has to keep his objectivity."

Caine shot her a look, then shrugged. "What the hell did he know?"

Diana set down her glass and walked to him. "Why don't you let me buy you a drink and some dinner?"

He needed to touch her. Caine could feel his fingertips tingle with the need to stroke the softness of her skin. Rejection. The thought of facing it again had him slipping on his armor. "No." He moved back behind his desk. "I've got a lot to catch up on tonight."

"All right. I'll see what's in the refrigerator downstairs."

"No."

The single sharp word stopped her. The pain registered, pushing her back a step. Turning, she stared at the fire until she was certain her voice wouldn't tremble. "You'd like me to go away, wouldn't you?"

"I told you, I'm busy."

"I could wait." Unable to keep her hands still, she toyed with the handle of the brass fireplace poker. "We could have a late supper at my apartment."

He stared at her, the slim, straight figure in jade-green wool. She was offering him the opportunity to go back to the way things had been, the way it had always been for him with women before. Fun, games, no complications. Nothing had ever seemed so empty. With a sigh, Caine looked down at his hands. How many times in the last two weeks had he thought about her—about the way things had been between them? He'd considered begging; it wasn't a matter of pride. Once, in the early hours of the morning, he'd considered going to her apartment and using force for lack of anything better. Every possible angle from reason to abduction had gone through his mind, and every one had been discarded. He'd had to remind himself that love couldn't be forced or coaxed or pleaded out of a woman like Diana.

He wanted her, needed to lose himself in that mindless passion they could bring each other. He could almost taste her from where he stood, that not quite sweet, not quite sharp flavor of her mouth when it heated. It would have been simple once, but it would never be simple again.

"I appreciate the offer," he said curtly. "I'm not interested."

She shut her eyes at that, surprised again at how

much pain words could bring. "I hurt you badly," she murmured. "I don't know if there's any way to make up for it."

He gave a quick, hard laugh. "I can do without the sympathy, Diana."

Distressed by his tone, she turned around. "Caine, that's not what—"

"Drop it."

"Caine, please—"

"Damn it, Diana, let it alone!" Struggling for control, he lifted his coffee again. She saw his knuckles go white on the handle. "Go home," he ordered. "I've got work to do."

"I have things I want to say to you."

"Doesn't it occur to you that I don't want to hear them? I stripped my soul for you," he tossed out before he could stop himself. "Made a fool of myself. I've already heard your reasons why you can't give me what I want. I don't need to hear it all over again. I don't think I can take it."

"Stop making this impossible for me!" she shouted at him.

"I don't give a damn about you at the moment." Enraged, he grabbed her arm and yanked her against him.

Before he could stop himself, his mouth was on hers, savagely, brutally. The hell with love, he told himself. If this was all she wanted from him, then it was all he would give. He let the needs and frustration take him, oblivious to her response or protest until she was limp and trembling. On a wave of self-disgust, he shoved her away. Love, he realized helplessly, could not be ignored.

"Get out of here, Diana. Leave me alone."

Shaken, she gripped the back of a chair. "No, not until I've finished."

"All right. You stay, I'll go."

But she was at the door ahead of him, slamming it shut and leaning back against it. "Sit down, shut up and listen to me."

For a moment, she thought he'd simply yank her aside, throttle her for good measure. There was murder in his eyes as he glared down at her. Then he hooked his thumbs in his front pockets. "Okay, say your piece."

"Sit down," she repeated.

"Don't press your luck."

Her chin jerked up at the soft threat. "All right, we'll stand. I'm not going to apologize for the things I said two weeks ago. I meant them. My career is important to me—vital, because it's something I've done for myself. And trusting someone, trusting them with my emotions is the most difficult thing in the world for me. No one can make me do it, it's my own choice."

"Fine. Now get out of my way."

"I'm not finished!" She swallowed, then heard herself say, "I think it's time we were partners."

"Partners?" The fury in his eyes was replaced by blank astonishment. "Good God, you're standing there —now, after everything I've said to you—giving me a *business* proposition?"

"This has nothing to do with business," she shot back. "I want you to marry me."

She watched as Caine's eyes narrowed, sharpened, until she could read nothing in them at all. "What did you say?"

"I'm asking you to marry me." Diana kept her eyes level and wondered why her legs didn't buckle.

Brows drawn together, he stood where he was. "You're proposing to me?" he asked carefully.

She felt the color warm her cheeks but wasn't certain if it was embarrassment or annoyance. "Yes, I thought it was perfectly clear."

He laughed, quietly at first, then with more feeling. Running his hands over his face, Caine turned and walked to the window. Diana watched his reaction with a mixture of anger and anxiety. "I'll be damned," he murmured.

"I don't think it's funny." Diana crossed her arms over her chest and felt like an idiot.

"I don't know. . . ." Caine continued to stare out the window as he tried to sort out his thoughts. After all the pain of the last two weeks, she suddenly appears on his doorstep and asks him to marry her. "Somehow it appeals to my humor."

"I'll just leave you alone to enjoy your little joke, then." She fumbled with the knob, but even as she jerked the door open, Caine was there, slamming it shut again.

"Diana—"

"Get away," she demanded as she attempted to shove him aside.

"Wait a minute." Taking her shoulders, he pressed her back against the door. "Are we always going to be at cross purposes?" he wondered. His eyes weren't laughing at her but were deadly serious and a bit wary. "I'd like to know why you asked me to marry you."

Diana glared at him a moment, then swallowed her pride. "Because I knew, after the things I had said to you, that you wouldn't ask me. I wasn't even sure you'd forgive me."

He shook his head, and his fingers tightened demandingly on her shoulders. "Don't be ridiculous, it's not a matter of forgiveness."

"Caine . . ." She wanted to touch him but kept her hands at her sides, not certain she could accept that kind of unquestioning clemency. "I hurt you."

"Yes. By God, you did."

"I'm sorry," she whispered, but it wasn't pity he saw in her eyes. The first wave of relief washed over him.

"You haven't answered my question, Diana." He kept his hands firm on her shoulders, his eyes direct on hers. "Why do you want me to marry you?"

"I suppose I need a promise," she began, feeling the flutter of fear again. "I think when people just live together, it's too easy to walk away, and—"

"No." He shook his head again. "That's not what I want, and you know it. Why, Diana? Say it."

She swallowed as the slivers of fear grew to panic. "I—" Faltering, she closed her eyes.

"Say it," he demanded again.

Her lashes fluttered up so that she met his eyes levelly. Once the words were said, she knew there'd be no backing away. For her, they would be the complete commitment. He knew it as well, she realized—and needed it. Why had she been so foolish as to think she was the only one with fears?

"I love you," she whispered, then let out a long, shuddering breath. With it went the fear. "Oh, God, Caine, I love you." She fell into his arms, clinging, and felt the release bubble up in laughter. "I love you," she said again. "How many times would you like to hear it?"

"I'll let you know in a minute," he murmured as his lips found hers. With a groan of pleasure, of relief, of joy, he drew her closer. "Again," he demanded against her mouth. "Tell me again."

She laughed and tugged him down until they lay on the rug. "I love you. If I'd known how good it would feel to say it, I would have told you before. Caine . . .." Framing his face with her hands, Diana looked down at him with her eyes suddenly serious. "Being with you, belonging to you, is worth everything. I've known—I *have* known, but it seemed safer to pretend I could live without you."

Taking her hand, he pressed his lips to the palm. "I still can't give you guarantees, Diana. I can only love you."

"I don't want guarantees." She drew him down so that her cheek rested against his. "Not anymore. I'm going to gamble on you, MacGregor." Slowly, she ran her hands up his back. "And I'm going to win."

Caine slipped the jacket of her suit off her shoulders as his lips toyed with hers. "It's a night of firsts," he decided. "My first proposal . . ." He began loosening the buttons of her blouse. "The first time I manage to drag those three little words out of you . . ." His lips followed the trail of his fingers. "And the first time I make love with you in my office."

Diana sighed as she stripped his shirt from him. "There's a minor point of order, counselor."

"Hmm?"

"You haven't answered my proposal yet."

"Aren't you supposed to give me time to think it over?" He caught the lobe of her ear between his teeth.

"No."

"In that case, I accept." He lifted his head as a gleam

of amusement lit his eyes. "Do we intend to add to the MacGregor line?"

With her lids half-closed, she gave him a lazy smile. "Absolutely. I come from very good stock."

Laughing, he pressed his lips against her throat. "Diana, you've made my father a very happy man."

The Silhouette Cameo Tote Bag Now available for just $6.99

Handsomely designed in blue and bright pink, its stylish good looks make the Cameo Tote Bag an attractive accessory. The Cameo Tote Bag is big and roomy (13″ square), with reinforced handles and a snap-shut top. You can buy the Cameo Tote Bag for $6.99, plus $1.50 for postage and handling.

Send your name and address with check or money order for $6.99 (plus $1.50 postage and handling), a total of $8.49 to:

Silhouette Books
120 Brighton Road
P.O. Box 5084
Clifton, NJ 07015-5084
ATTN: Tote Bag

SIL-T-1

The Silhouette Cameo Tote Bag can be purchased pre-paid only. No charges will be accepted. Please allow 4 to 6 weeks for delivery.

Arizona and N.Y. State Residents Please Add Sales Tax

Offer not available in Canada.

READERS' COMMENTS ON SILHOUETTE SPECIAL EDITIONS:

"I just finished reading the first six Silhouette Special Edition Books and I had to take the opportunity to write you and tell you how much I enjoyed them. I enjoyed all the authors in this series. Best wishes on your Silhouette Special Editions line and many thanks."

—B.H.*, Jackson, OH

"The Special Editions are really special and I enjoyed them very much! I am looking forward to next month's books."

—R.M.W.*, Melbourne, FL

"I've just finished reading four of your first six Special Editions and I enjoyed them very much. I like the more sensual detail and longer stories. I will look forward each month to your new Special Editions."

—L.S.*, Visalia, CA

"Silhouette Special Editions are — 1.) Superb! 2.) Great! 3.) Delicious! 4.) Fantastic! . . . Did I leave anything out? These are books that an adult woman can read . . . I love them!"

—H.C.*, Monterey Park, CA

*names available on request